SOMETHING RECKLESS

SOMETHING RECKLESS

NEW YORK TIMES BESTSELLING AUTHOR

LEXI RYAN

DEDICATION

Dedicated to the NWBs—Sawyer Bennett, Lauren Blakely, Violet Duke, Jessie Evans, Melody Grace, Monica Murphy, and Kendall Ryan. You make me laugh, you hold my hand, and you make me better. I love and am grateful for every one of you ladies.

NOTE FROM THE AUTHOR

First, THANK YOU SO MUCH for buying *Something Reckless*. Whether you read the other books set in New Hope or if this is your first book by me, I hope you love this one as much as I loved writing it. This story was supposed to be this light and fluffy escape, but—as always—it turned out to be so much more. I hope you'll enjoy the twists and turns of Liz and Sam's story as much as I did.

I included *Something Wild* for your convenience. Feel free to skip past it if you already enjoyed it as a free download. Or read it again if you need a refresher course on Sam's skills in the shower. That's up to you!

Liz and Sam's journey concludes in *Something Real*, available in March 2015.

Thank you again for reading. I am so grateful for you!

Love,

Lexi

SOMETHING WILD

NEW YORK TIMES BESTSELLING AUTHOR

LEXI RYAN

CHAPTER ONE

Sam

Liz: *My undersexed phone would like to invite your undersexed phone to exchange some inappropriate text messages we'll regret when we're sober.*

WHEN I LOOK UP from the message, I catch Lizzy Thompson watching me from her table not five feet from mine. Another woman might blush. *Liz* winks.

She's in red heels and one of those short, tight dresses that's scientifically engineered to make a man's jaw drop. Her legs are crossed and on full display from where she's propped on a stool.

I lift an eyebrow, questioning, and she shrugs.

Brady's is buzzing with activity tonight. The seats at the bar are crowded with men trying to escape their women for the night, and men trying to find a woman to take home are surrounding the pool tables. I'm somewhere in between, at a table with a beer and a few empty shot glasses. I'm not in the mood to socialize, but going home and being left alone with my thoughts sounds even worse.

Last week, I'd been complaining that Will's phone was getting more action than mine, and Liz asked for my number. I *thought* she was joking. Apparently not.

At the time, I would have been all over some dirty sexting with the leggy blonde who's starred in more than a few of my fantasies. At the time, I had no idea how badly one person could fuck over my world.

But that was last week. Tonight, I'm a different man. I'm changed. Hell, I'm broken.

I can't tell Liz that. I can't tell anyone. Because telling would lead to questions I don't care to answer.

Her lips pull into a subtle pout, and I sigh and type a reply.

Sam: *While my undersexed phone would enjoy that, my undersexed brain worries it would put ideas in your head.*

I watch her as I wait for my message to go through. She reads it and smirks for a beat before her fingers fly across the screen. Thirty seconds later, my phone buzzes again.

>**Liz:** *Oh, the ideas are already there. What's wrong? Your little guy not UP for the task?*

That almost makes me smile. *Almost.* I didn't think I could smile tonight, but Liz is the most likely candidate to make that happen. She's one hundred percent no-nonsense. Sure, maybe half the shit she says is for shock value, but it's usually what everyone else is thinking. I've always liked that about her.

>**Sam:** *Sorry to say, I don't have a LITTLE guy. But my dick is up for anything you've got. It's the next morning that would be a problem. I'm not your type, Rowdy.*

>**Liz:** *Really? What's my type?*

>**Sam:** *You need a good guy. A long-term guy. One who does dates and romance and emotional strings.*

>**Liz:** *And what kind of guy are you?*

>**Sam:** *I'm just an asshole who wants to tie you up, make you come, and walk away.*

I make sure I'm watching when that one goes through, but she doesn't blanch. Instead, her lips part—fucking beautiful lips, pink and full and perfect. I kissed those lips before, tasted them. It was all I could do to end it there, but I've remembered that kiss and thought about a repeat performance a hell of a lot more than once.

She lifts her gaze to mine. Nothing on her face says she's insulted by my text. Her chest rises and falls and her cheeks flush pink.

No one can tell me I lead women on to get sex. I've never needed to. I take women to bed without any promises and make damn sure they don't regret it. I don't do commitment or forever, and I don't hide it.

Her eyes darken, and her tongue darts out to wet her lips.

Fuck. Me.

Standing, I throw some money on the table to cover my tab. I have to get out of here before I take her up on her offer. Demons are clawing their way into my easy life, and using her to escape them would only hurt us both.

Liz

"I could have gone the rest of my life without seeing that."

I tear my gaze off my drink and look up to see Della Bradshaw sliding onto the stool across from me. "Seeing what?"

"You were eye-fucking my brother." She shudders. "Not exactly what I had in mind when I asked you to figure out what's wrong with him."

"He's hot, Del. All the girls think so. I'm just the only one honest enough to tell you."

She gags and rolls her eyes. "Well, whatever. Did he tell you what's going on?"

Della's boyfriend, Connor, says Sam's struggling with something, but Sam won't tell his family what it is. Della asked me to figure it out. Seemed like an obscure request to me—doesn't everyone have a secret? But I could tell she was worried about him, so I agreed to launch a little investigation. "Not yet, but have patience in my process."

"I'm starting to think your *process* might involve things I don't want to think about."

"Are you worried I'll break your brother's heart?"

She snorts. "Try the other way around. Don't say I didn't warn you. I saw the way you were looking at him."

"Consider me warned."

She hoists her purse onto her shoulder and hops off the stool. "Connor's waiting for me."

"Tell him I'm sorry I don't know anything yet."

She waves away my apology. "He doesn't know I asked you. I plan on taking *all* the credit when you figure it out."

I arch a brow. "And what do I get?"

"You get to make *fuck me* eyes at my big brother without me vomiting all over you."

"Oh, gee, I'll try to contain my excitement."

5

SOMETHING RECKLESS

"See you at the wedding tomorrow night?"

"Of course. There's an open bar to look forward to." I grin mischievously. "And your brother in a suit."

She shakes her head. "You're playing with fire, Lizzy."

"Tell Connor I said hi," I call as she leaves.

I can tell them that Sam's having romantic troubles. Everything about his face tonight says someone broke his heart. But I don't think that's specific enough to be of any help, nor does it make any sense. As far as I know, he hasn't been seeing anyone seriously—and it's hard to keep a relationship secret in a place as small as New Hope.

I might have ulterior motives for helping dig a little into Sam's life. I'm pretty sure there's an unspoken rule for teenage girls that requires them to crush on their friends' older brothers. For me, that was Della's brother Sam—right up until he rejected me.

I still can't believe he walked out the door tonight, disregarding my blatant invitation. I'm in shock, but I can't be offended. Not when I caught the way his eyes raked over me on his way out. And not when his last text message is making my imagination run wild.

I'm just an asshole who wants to tie you up, make you come, and walk away.

CHAPTER TWO

Liz

"Don't do it."

I take my very full glass of red wine from the bartender and frown at Connor Everett. "Do what? Don't drink this wine? Or don't get so trashed that my wine goggles get me laid tonight?"

"Don't try to seduce information out of Sam Bradshaw." He leans against the bar and scans the reception. Connor's cute, long, and lean, big hands and kind eyes. Some might even call him handsome, but long ago I gave up on trying to get my brain to see him as something I find more sexually appealing than a

Care Bear.

Apparently he finds what he's looking for—or whom—because he stops scanning the crowd and swallows hard. "You'll only get hurt."

I follow his gaze to see Sam sitting at a table with his family. "A little pain is okay, as long as it's consensual."

Connor gives me a look. "I've got this under control, okay? Cancel any of your plans to help me out by letting Sam under that skirt." His gaze skims over me and he grins. "Looking hot tonight, by the way."

I smack his arm. "You're with Della now and not allowed to say those things to me."

He winces and rubs his arm. "Even if it's true?"

I roll my eyes. "Have you *met* Della?"

"Good point," he mutters. "Stay away from Sam."

"What are you, his keeper?"

"He needs one, but no. Della admitted she asked you to help." He dips his head and locks eyes with me. "I'm telling you now that I don't want you to."

"Are you *jealous,* Con?" I singsong. My smile falls away when something flashes in his eyes. "No. You're with *Della* now."

He looks away, guilt all over the hard angles of his face. "I know. And this isn't about jealousy. It's about me trying to take care of a friend. Della shouldn't have pulled you into this, but that's my fault for telling her anything to begin with."

"Well, I'm already *in* it, so you might as well tell me what's going on."

His jaw hardens.

"Okay," I say. "I'll just tell Sam you're poking around and see if he knows why."

Connor whips his head around. "Don't."

"Then tell me."

"I'm going to kill Della," he grumbles.

I take a long swallow of my wine, waiting.

"Last week, he withdrew a large sum of money from his account, and his father's concerned Sam might be involved with something bad."

"Like what?"

Connor shrugs. "Gambling? Hookers? Hell, this is Sam we're talking about. It could be anything."

I swallow the rest of my wine and settle the glass on the bar.

Sam's at his table by the dance floor, nodding as his father tells him something. I think Connor's right to be worried. There's something different about Sam tonight. He's distant. Distracted. Again, he seems . . . heartbroken.

Could it be that Sam—a notorious player—has allowed someone close enough to his heart to break it? Or is my loneliness making me see things that aren't there?

That doesn't explain the money, though.

"So we have a deal?" Connor asks. "You'll forget that Della told you anything?"

"Sure." I nod to the bartender, who refills my glass. God bless him and enablers everywhere.

Connor's shoulders sag. "Good. I know it's none of my business who you sleep with, but you can do better than a player like Sam."

"I didn't say anything about not sleeping with him."
I take another swallow of liquid courage as Connor
grimaces. "Oh, stop acting like I'm some vestal virgin
who needs protecting."

"Connor!" Della calls. "There you are! Come dance
with me!"

I shoo him away. "Go have fun."

I wait until Sam's family has evacuated their table,
then make my way over to him. He's sitting back in his
seat, legs spread wide, rolling a bottle of beer between
his hands as he watches the drunken wedding guests go
"to the left" then "to the right." My own table cleared
out earlier, but I said I wanted to stay and dance a little.
In truth, I just wanted Sam.

I turn my chair to face the dance floor, like his, and
sit. He looks over at me, and his gaze snags on my
crossed legs—at the spot where the hem of my skirt
meets my bare thighs.

Sam's always been a good-looking guy, but tonight,
in his suit and tie, his face smooth, his eyes smoky,
there's something about him that makes my mouth
water. Or maybe it's that my lady parts are on high alert
since our texts yesterday.

"Hey," he says, then turns his gaze back to the dance
floor. His eyes might be there, but his mind isn't. He's
somewhere else tonight. How sexy is a man with a
broken heart?

Is there a ladylike way to say, *"Hey, you seem a
little down. Want me to ride you until you can't
remember her name?"*

I've known Sam since we were kids. He's a few

years older than me and he moved away while he completed his undergrad. When I was in high school, I crashed one of his parties and tried to find my way into his bed. He was a junior at Notre Dame with a reputation for being a player. I was a senior in high school, dumb enough to admit I was still in possession of my V-card.

But even bad boys have a code of honor, and that night, Sam followed the code to the letter.

"Wanna talk about it?" I ask.

He swings his gaze around to meet mine, and the intensity of the feeling in his eyes almost pushes me away. That's what it's supposed to do—shut people out, make them back off. This isn't the happy-go-lucky Sam I've always known.

"About what?" he asks, the dare in his eyes.

"The girl who broke your heart."

He lifts a brow. "Is that what the gossip mill is saying? That my heart is broken?"

No. That's what every inch of your face is saying. "That's the rumor," I lie. There's no rumor, only my suspicion.

He releases a noncommittal huff then really looks me in the eye for the first time all night. "Do you think I'm the kind of guy who gets his heart broken, Rowdy?"

"*Liz,*" I correct him, surprising myself. I've never minded the nickname he gave me when I was fifteen. And I've never minded *Lizzy,* either. But tonight, I want Sam to call me something else. Something more mature. "And there's nothing wrong with getting your

11

heart broken. It just means you're human."

Something flashes in his eyes—hurt or defiance, or maybe both.

"Do you want to dance, *Liz*?" He emphasizes my name, and I like how it sounds on his lips—slow and sensual, like a lazy morning spent naked in bed.

I follow him to the dance floor, completely aware that he hasn't taken my hand or given me so much as a smile. When he pulls my body against his, it doesn't matter. This is what I've been waiting for since last night. Maybe for four years. The feel of his hard chest, his hands on my back, so warm I can feel their heat through the thin fabric of my dress. It's almost as if his heat is marking me.

"Let me help you forget her." When he stiffens, I pull back to see his reaction. Surprise only shows in his eyes for a split second before he covers it with a smile. His crooked grin says, *I know what you want and I'm going to give it to you.* Even knowing he's using it to hide something, his smile sends a little shimmy through my insides that settles as a thrumming pulse between my legs.

"Hey, Rowdy," he whispers against my mouth. "You're not still a virgin, are you?"

I hesitate at the question, then tug at his tie to bring his body closer as we move. "What if I was? Would it be so terrible, being my first? Isn't there some old-fashioned part of you that would enjoy that, Bradshaw?"

His smile vanishes, and that gives me a small amount of satisfaction, but aside from that, I can hardly make out his expression in the flickering candlelight. "I said I don't do strings."

"I'm no innocent." Not since that weekend I surprised him at Notre Dame. Sam may have turned me down, but I didn't spend the night alone. "And I never offered strings."

"Are you sure? Because while I don't do strings, I do enjoy . . . restraints." He brushes a thumb over my bottom lip.

My breath catches and my pulse picks up speed. "If you're trying to scare me off with talk of bondage, it's not going to work. I'm not a little girl anymore, Sam."

His gaze dips to my cleavage and rests there for a moment. "I can see that."

"And I can take anything you can dish out."

"Have you ever sucked dick with your hands tied behind your back? Ever been on your knees and let a man guide your mouth just where he wants it?"

My pulse triples at his words, and my girlie bits go wild. They're pathetic, really, but who can blame them? They've waited four years for this, and I've made them suffer through some seriously subpar male attention in the meantime. "You talk a big game." I tuck my hips to rub against him. My sober, intellectual self would be offended by the idea of Sam seducing me with talk of a blowjob. But I'm not sober, and if he's trying to turn me on, it's working.

"It's not just talk," he says, his voice low, promise in his eyes.

Yes, even bad boys have a code of honor, and tonight I plan to find a loophole in that code.

SOMETHING RECKLESS

* * *

Sam

Liz leans her head on my shoulder, and the smell of her shampoo fills my nose—something flowery and feminine. Damn, she smells good. And she feels good in my arms.

I didn't want to come to the wedding tonight, and I was attempting to bail out when Dad gave me that *look*. That "You will not disappoint me or this family" look. I barely know the bride, but her parents are friends with my parents, and, being a Bradshaw, I'm expected to keep up appearances at all costs. Smile when you're supposed to smile, show up when you're supposed to show up and, above all, don't fuck up.

If my father only knew . . .

On the other side of the dance floor, my dad catches my eye and nods toward Sabrina, who's talking to my mom. Dad's told me more than once that I need to dance with her tonight. "Shit," I mutter.

"What?" Liz asks, following my gaze to the redhead across the room. "Who's she? She looks familiar."

"Her name's Sabrina."

"Fancy," Liz says. "Let me guess, she's not the kind of girl who has a nickname like *Rowdy*?"

Not at all. "She's a friend of the family, and the governor's daughter."

She draws in her breath. "That's why she looks familiar. Wow. They could be sisters. She looks so much like her mom."

"Dad would like me to woo and wed her to make sure he gets Governor Guy's endorsement when he runs for the position."

"Your dad wants to be governor?"

"He's been laying the groundwork for years. He'll run at the end of Guy's second term."

"So you should probably go dance with her," she says.

I let my hand drift to her ass, and when I squeeze, her big blue eyes get bigger. "Probably," I admit. "But I'd rather dance with you."

Ever since Asia surprised me at my house on Thursday night and dropped the bomb of all bombs, it's been as if the world was trying to eat me alive. Right here, though, with Liz in my arms and her sweet perfume filling my head, I feel . . . safe. Bigger. Like I can face my demons and come out stronger. Maybe it's because she's petite or because she's always been my little sister's friend, but the way Liz looks at me makes me feel like a fucking gladiator.

"Don't worry about it." She shrugs. "I understand family stuff. Truly."

I join my hands at the small of her back and pull her closer. "I'm not done with you."

Sighing, she leans her head against my chest. "Best news I've heard all night."

"You'll be around when I'm done humoring my father and his dreams of arranged marriages?"

As she laughs, her teeth sink into her lower lip. She traces invisible patterns on my dress shirt, in no hurry to leave my arms, thank Christ.

"I used to work here when I was in high school," she says out of nowhere. "I helped serve at wedding receptions and Christmas parties."

"I bet you rocked the uniform."

She grins. "You know it. Nothing as sexy as a girl in a bow tie."

"You could pull it off. In fact, I'm picturing you in a bow tie right now."

She pulls back to look at me. "Odd fantasy."

"I didn't say you were wearing anything *else*."

She lowers her voice a fraction. "There's a small conference room outside of the ballroom and to the right. Meet me there after your dance."

Then she steps out of my arms and walks away, and I'm left watching the way her ass swings in her skirt and wondering just what she plans to do in that conference room.

Liz is sweet. I've had to remind myself of that fact since she was fifteen and staying over with Della. I'd come home long after everyone else went to sleep and find her lounging in the family room in a sleep shirt with no bra underneath. I'd find her watching me when she didn't think I noticed. A couple of years later, I was at Notre Dame, and she showed up at a house party looking for trouble. She got drunk and threw herself at me, and I turned her away. Because she was seventeen and I was twenty. Because she was drunk and I was sober. Because she was a virgin and I had experiences most grown men only get to dream about.

Now the rules have changed. She's not seventeen anymore. And she's waiting for me in the conference room.

My imagination doesn't get far before my father is standing in front of me with the governor's daughter, his politician face firmly in place.

"Samuel, you remember Sabrina."

"Of course." Offering my hand, I go through the motions of the introduction and even dance with her, but my mind is on Liz, and I'm counting down the seconds until I can sneak out of here to meet her.

CHAPTER THREE

Liz
Four Years Before . . .

THERE'S A PARTY of epic proportions rumbling in Sam Bradshaw's basement.

The room is packed—everyone dancing and talking at once. Everyone drunk. There's a long wooden bar along the far wall where three girls in short shorts and heels are standing, dirty-dancing and grinding on each other. I'm so out of my depth.

I told my mom I was visiting a prospective college and drove to Notre Dame to see him at the house he rents with friends. This isn't what I expected. I should've dragged Hanna or Maggie along. But I left them at home because I didn't want them to stop me from what I'd planned—namely, seducing Sam and losing my virginity.

I've been searching for Sam in the crowd for half an hour, and with every minute that I don't find him, the excitement that fueled my drive north leaks out of me. What if he's back in New Hope for the weekend? Hell, what if he has a girlfriend?

I drain the rest of my drink—my third since I arrived, and whoever's mixing them is making them strong.

"Hey, beautiful. Come dance."

The request comes from a tall, dark-haired guy. Not over-the-top gorgeous but okay. Attractive on most scales, though only average to a girl who grew up with the Samuel Bradshaws of the world.

As I nod, the room does a little spin and shifts off-kilter, like an awkward toddler ballerina. Something in my mind warns me to *slow down*, but I ignore it and head to the dance floor with Mr. Tall, Dark, and Average.

The back corner of the basement is cast in shadows and the booming music makes my ears ache, but alcohol buzzes through my blood and dancing feels good.

I relax into my movements, lose myself in the bass and the crowd. Time falls away as I lose more and more of my inhibitions with the help of the alcohol.

The guy works his hands up my shirt, and I don't even care. Maybe I should. But I came here looking for

Sam, and I'm disappointed. I want to prove I'm mature enough to come to a party like this and have a good time, so I let the guy touch my stomach, let him slide his fingers farther north.

Just as his hand closes over my breast, he's yanked off me. "What the fuck do you think you're doing?"

Sam.

As if someone jumped on the accelerator to my heart, my pulse speeds into high gear. I bite back a smile at the aggravation in his voice, stupidly happy he's jealous.

Too late, I realize his angry words aren't intended for the guy feeling me up. They're intended for *me*.

"Is she yours?" my dancing partner asks.

I scowl. "Are you kidding me? I don't *belong* to anyone."

"She's not *mine*," Sam says. "She's seventeen."

The guy's eyes go wide and he throws up his hands and backs away, muttering something about jailbait.

Sam made me a pariah at this party. Fantastic.

I spin on Sam. "What was *that*?"

He arches a brow. "You smell like a liquor bottle. How much have you had to drink?"

"I didn't come here looking for a new daddy, so stop trying to protect me."

"Someone needs to," he mutters. "What do you think you're doing here?"

I push past him. The crowd swallows me as I work my way to the other side of the basement, straight to the bar. The girls have vacated the smooth wooden surface, and now it's as if waiting for me.

"Want some help up?" A blond guy grins at me, as if seeing me dance on the bar would make his night.

"Yes, please." I give him my hand and flash a look over my shoulder to make sure Sam isn't here to boss me around and tell everyone I'm a child.

The second I climb on the bar, I'm hyperaware of my short skirt. Guys gather beneath me, no doubt to a great view of my purple silk panties, but I make the best of it and dance to the music, running my hands over my stomach and hips as I find the beat.

There are catcalls, and part of me likes it—the attention, feeling important, even if it was for something as trivial as my body. When you feel stupid all the time, it's nice to be appreciated for *something*. Anything. It doesn't take long for another girl to climb up to join me. We dance together, much to the delight of the guys watching.

"Body shots!" one of the guys in the crowd calls. Then others join in to an increasingly insistent chant of, "Bo-dy shots! Bo-dy shots!"

The next thing I know, the girl shoves a shot glass in her cleavage. "Be gentle," she croons so the guys in the crowd can hear.

I know what they want—what they expect—and before I can think too much, I duck my head and wrap my lips around the glass. The guys howl their approval, and I come up with it slowly, shooting it back without the help of my hands.

"My turn!" the girl says, lifting another shot in the air. She turns to the crowd. "Where should she put it?"

"Between her legs!" someone answers. A chair is

hoisted next to me on the bar. It doesn't quite fit, and I have to balance it on three legs as I position the shot between my thighs.

As quickly as I wonder what I've gotten myself into, I remember Sam saying someone needs to watch out for me, and I pull my skirt a little higher.

My partner in crime giggles as she lowers onto her knees. "I'm not really into girls," she whispers, "but you *are* pretty hot."

Then she licks my inner thigh, and it shocks me so much that I lose my balance. Both the chair and I fall off the bar and into the crowd. Someone catches me, but I hit several people and drinks on my way down. It seems like there's beer everywhere, including streaming down my shirt and covering my legs. Gasping at the cold, I pull the wet fabric of my shirt off my skin.

"Shit," someone says. "Are you hurt?"

Turning toward the voice, I find myself looking into the face of Sam Bradshaw, his eyes on my soaking wet shirt. "I'm okay."

"You're covered in beer." His gaze roams over me one more time before he lifts it to my face. "You really are rowdy, you know that?"

Even though I'm covered in goose bumps, his closeness makes me feel warm. I probably smell worse than I look, but I have Sam's attention. Finally.

He grabs my hand and pulls me away from the guy who caught me. "Come on, Rowdy. Let's get you out of here." His smile's so gentle, so comforting, I want to curl into it. Then he walks away and I have to think really hard to remember that I'm supposed to be following him.

I let him lead the way up the stairs, my eyes on his back the whole time.

He opens a door on the landing and nods inside. "In here."

My drunken heart skitters and stumbles at the sound of his voice and the idea of following him into his room. I follow him inside and close the door.

Sam took me to his bedroom.

My stomach's a mess of nerves—fear, anxiety, and excitement, all wrapped in my crush on him. I pull off my beer-soaked shirt and drop it to the floor as Sam looks in his closet.

My head spins, and some of the happiness that comes from drinking too fast begins to fade, replaced with a faint sense of shame. I was trying to loosen up, to fit in, to find the courage to approach him, and I became another reckless drunk girl.

When he turns back to me, T-shirt in hand, my face is hot with shame. His eyes widen for a moment as he takes me in, then he averts his gaze. "Put this on," he says, offering the T-shirt.

"Sam," I whisper. I step forward, lift onto my toes, and press my mouth against his.

He freezes for a minute, then slowly—so flipping slowly—he brings his hands to my hair and kisses me back. This isn't how I imagined it would happen. He doesn't deepen the kiss or draw my body against his. He doesn't push me back on the bed and climb on top of me. He just kisses me back. Softly. Briefly. Then he pulls away and traces my jaw with his thumb. "What was that for?" His voice is low. Husky.

"The usual reasons a girl kisses a boy."

I want him to talk again. Want to have that voice against my ear. I want to feel the heat of his chest against my body and have his hands all over me.

My eyes are so heavy with intoxication and exhaustion, I let them close. I feel the shirt slide over my head. I don't want him to be *dressing* me, but the shirt's soft and warm and smells like Sam, so I push my arms through the sleeves.

When I open my eyes, he's pulling down the covers on his neatly made bed.

"Climb in," he says. I obey, too tired to question him, and he draws the blankets over me. I don't want to sleep, but the next thing I know, he's waking me up. "Drink this and swallow these." He hands me a couple of pills and a glass of water.

"What is it?"

He shakes his head. "*Now* you're going to start showing some sense? Ibuprofen. I'm trying to save you from a killer hangover—no promises, but this should at least keep it manageable."

"Thanks," I mumble.

Brushing the hair off my face, he presses the softest, sweetest kiss to my forehead. And as I close my eyes and surrender to sleep, I feel the distinct sensation of falling.

When I open my eyes again, it's dark, save for a thick swath of streetlight cutting across the room from the gap in the curtains. Sam's asleep in a chair by the door, hands folded in his lap, half his face in the light, half in darkness.

I blink at the clock. Four a.m.

"Sam," I whisper. Something flutters in my belly at the thought of him sleeping there all night, protecting me while I was too drunk to protect myself. I climb out of bed and walk across the room. "Sam?"

His eyes open and he straightens. "Are you okay?"

I nod. "I'm fine. You don't have to sleep in the chair."

"Don't worry about it."

"I'd rather you sleep with me." In an attempt to be bold and sultry, I straddle his lap and press a kiss to his neck. "I really like you."

He winces. *Cue the mortification.* He isn't just being a gentleman. He doesn't *want* to share his bed with me.

"I thought . . ." I bite my bottom lip. "I thought you liked me too." *Stupid alcohol.*

"I do like you, Liz." He gives me a careful smile— the kind you give a child before you break the news that Santa isn't real. "But you're my friend."

"What better way to lose my virginity?" *Oh my God, why am I still talking?*

His breath draws in with a hiss, then he shakes his head. "You're my friend," he repeats, ticking the reasons off on his fingers. "You're drunk."

"Not anymore," I promise.

"And you're a virgin."

SOMETHING RECKLESS

✳ ✳ ✳

Present Day...

The memory fills me with old mortification. There's a reason I haven't pursued Sam in the last four years. I don't want to be the desperate girl who threw herself at him. I don't want to remember how his rejection made me feel.

Sneaking into this room seemed like a great idea when I was on the dance floor with him, his hard body pressed into mine, but alone in the quiet conference room, I'm pretty sure this could be the most reckless thing I've ever done.

What if someone catches us in here? Hell, what if he doesn't come? What if he *does*? I've thrown myself at Sam before, and it didn't end well. He has no idea how hard I took his rejection, or the decisions I made after I left his room that night.

I should leave. I should . . .

The door clicks and then Sam steps inside, his eyes raking over me.

"Hey," I whisper. "You came."

He closes the door behind himself, turns the lock, then stalks toward me.

Thank you! the girlie bits shout. *Stupid brain upstairs was about to ruin everything!*

"Are you sure you want to do this?" His voice is a low rumble that I swear I can feel right between my legs.

Hell yes, I want to do this.

But I also don't. Because Sam's no longer some unrequited crush. He's a friend. And if this goes to hell, it'll make my life exponentially more awkward.

"We need rules," I say quickly.

He takes another step closer. And another. Until I'm looking at his chest, smelling his aftershave. He tilts my chin up with his index finger then traces my lips with his thumb. "Hold that thought?"

I nod, nearly breathless at nothing but the touch of his thumb skimming my lips.

"I need to do this first." He cups my jaw in his big hand and brushes his lips over mine. My lips part in surprise at the gesture that's almost . . . *sweet.* He deepens the kiss, slanting his mouth over mine and sliding his tongue inside.

He tastes like beer, and I want to get drunk on this kiss—to overindulge until I can't see straight, to imbibe until sobriety is a distant memory.

This is how kisses should be. I love the way his hand slides into my hair as he samples my lips, love how his kiss manages to be simultaneously gentle and demanding. It's the kind of kiss that makes your toes curl, the kind worth remembering in five years when you're lonely and bored and wondering if kissing had ever been so sweet.

When he pulls back, his eyes are hooded, darker. Sexy as sin. "Now, what were you saying?"

I have no idea. "Ru . . . rules?" I manage.

"Ah, yes. Well, I've never done well with rules, but

tell me yours and I'll see what I can do."

I take a breath and try to figure out a rule that isn't just *Kiss me like that every time*, or *Please don't make me fall for you.*

"You keep looking at me like that," he warns, "and I'm going to kiss you again, and we may never get to discuss these rules of yours."

Right. "We can't tell anyone," I say. Cally and my sisters will try to make more of this than the one-night stand I know it to be.

His expression shifts and becomes unreadable. "Okay. What else?"

"This doesn't change anything between us. We're friends." Something in my chest objects to that rule. It feels like a betrayal. But I want to say it before he does. I have to.

"Sex changes *everything*, Liz. That's half the fun."

"It doesn't have to. I want us to still be friends after tonight."

"Oh, we can be friends." His breath ruffles my hair as he skims his fingertips down my bare arms, sending delicious shivers through my body that land low in my belly and turn my insides to goo. "But it'll be different."

"How so?"

"We won't be able to look at each other without remembering what it was like. And if I have my way—" He dips his head to my ear and tugs the lobe between his teeth. A shudder rocks through me. "—every time you look at me, your panties will go damp as you remember what I did to you."

"Oh." I can't begin to form a more intelligent response, not while his lips are running along the side of my neck. His hands move to my hips and his fingers massage delicious circles there.

"And I have my own rules."

I blink up at him. His honey eyes have gone dark and intense. "What are they?"

"No expectations beyond tonight. If you give me tonight, I'm going to touch you and taste you and fuck you until your legs shake."

I swallow. Because dear God, I want that.

"And then I'm going to walk away."

"Understood. What else?"

"You tell me to stop if it's too much for you or if you don't feel completely safe. We can always slow down or stop."

My lips part as questions fill my mind. Namely, what on earth does he plan to do with me that might make me feel unsafe or make me want to stop? But instead of asking, I say, "I trust you."

He takes a fistful of my dress and tugs it up to my waist, then he lifts me onto the conference table and steps between my legs. "We don't have much time," he whispers. "They're going to be looking for us. But I can't go back out there until I feel you."

Then his hand is between my legs and he's rubbing my clit through my panties. From our talk alone, I'm already wet and swollen, and my back arches at his touch. My hips lift off the table, pushing into his hand.

"I love that you're already wet for me." He tugs my hips to the edge of the table, and I have to balance by propping myself up on my hands behind me. He steps back to peel off my panties. Then he spreads my legs and looks at me.

For a second, I feel ridiculous and want to cover myself. I must look absurd, sitting on this table with my dress bunched around my waist, the most private part of me bare, exposed to him.

Then I look at him and I stop worrying. I stop thinking. His eyes are locked on that intimate flesh between my legs, his nostrils flaring as his breathing goes shallow.

I know that men like to look, and that's not what surprises me about this moment. What surprises me is the intensity in his gaze. What surprises me is that watching him look at me could turn me on so much. That watching him look at me could intensify this ache, make the need I feel so powerful it could swallow me.

Staying where he is, he softly pinches my clit with two fingers, and I close my eyes and bite back a moan. I want him closer. I want the weight of his body on top of mine.

"Open your eyes," he commands. When I obey, he says, "Look at how beautiful you are."

CHAPTER FOUR

Sam

SHE LIKES IT when I tell her what to do.

Her eyes follow my hand, and she watches as I circle her clit then slide one finger inside her.

She gasps at the contact, and hell, so do I. I don't intend to do more than tease her in this room—not with my family on the other side of those doors. But she's so fucking tight all I want to do is drop my pants and drive into her, hold her hips and fuck her right here on this table. She'd let me. Beg me, even. I see it in her eyes.

When you spend four years wanting something, you don't rush in. I'm going to take my time with her tonight, and this—right here and now in this room—

this is just the warmup.

Her breasts thrust forward as she arches her back. I keep my hand between her legs and step closer. With my free hand, I tug down her dress and expose one lace-covered breast.

"You're beautiful. I can't wait to undress you, to see all of you." I suck at her nipple through the lace, and her pussy clenches tight around my fingers.

I love a woman with sensitive breasts. I pull back and tease her with my tongue, circling her nipple before drawing it into my mouth again, all the while pumping my fingers in and out of her.

She squeezes me. Tighter and tighter, and I know she's close to coming. I need her to come before I go back out there. Once she left my arms on the dance floor, I felt like I was drowning again, looking at my father and knowing what he'd say if he knew how badly I've fucked up.

She moans, and the sound washes away some of the chaos in my mind. I need more.

"So fucking beautiful." My lips brush her ear as I speak. I want to taste her there. Everywhere. "I've always liked to look at you. Always loved the way you're comfortable in your own skin, the way you own a room the minute you walk into it. But you're even more beautiful when you're about to come."

I circle her clit with my thumb. Someone knocks on the door.

She startles in my arms, but I hold her still.

"Stay with me." She's so close, and I want to feel her come on my hand, around my fingers.

"Samuel?" My father's voice. "Did I see you go in there?"

"Come for me," I say into her ear as he knocks again.

Then I kiss her hard, swallowing her moans as her body contracts and she squeezes around my fingers.

Liz

Sam ignores his father's voice and cups me for a few more breaths, allowing me to come down from my orgasm before he pulls away.

"Didn't you say you saw him go in here?" his father asks someone.

Sam puts his finger to his lips, telling me I should be quiet. The door clicks at the lock as someone turns the knob.

"Call him," another female says. I recognize the voice as belonging to Della. Despite our jokes at the bar last night, I don't think she'd be thrilled to find me indecent with her brother. "Here. I'll do it."

Sam grabs his phone from his pocket just as it starts to ring. He silences it, but not before they hear the distinct ring tone.

This would be hilarious if it weren't mortifying.

His father clears his throat. "Come on, Della. He's clearly . . . busy."

Della snorts. "God, leave it to Sam."

We listen to the sounds coming from the other side of the door. After a minute or two passes, we both relax and Sam chuckles.

Standing, I smooth my dress down then smack his shoulder. "I can't believe we almost got caught."

Sam grins and grabs me by the hips, pulling my body against his so I can feel the evidence of his erection. "I think you liked it."

"Liked what?"

That cocky grin again. That *I know what gets you off better than you do* grin. Hell, he might. "You liked almost getting caught," he says.

"I didn't!"

"Nothing shameful there, Rowdy. There's nothing wrong with a harmless exhibitionist fantasy or two."

I roll my eyes and scan the floor. "Where's my underwear?"

Sam shrugs and points over his shoulder as he backs toward the door. "I'd better get back out there."

"Give me my underwear back," I grind out between my teeth.

He smirks. "Not a chance." The lock clicks as he releases it, and then he's gone, leaving me alone, red-faced, panty-less, and *holy shit,* so not done with him.

I'm not going to play his game. Hell, I'm not sure what kind of game has a girl going to a wedding reception without panties.

Sam Bradshaw's kind of game, the slutty angel on my shoulder purrs. But I only go commando in public on my own terms, not because some cocky bastard steals my panties.

Okay, and maybe I'm too embarrassed to go back out there. Maybe I don't want his dad to look at me and *know* I was the one holed up in the conference room with his son.

I sneak out a few minutes after Sam and make a beeline for the exit.

I've just reached the door when Connor calls my name from behind me. "Wait up a minute."

So close.

"I don't want a lecture," I warn him.

"Tell me you're not driving and I'll have no reason to lecture you."

Turning, I see that he has no clue I was with Sam. I shake my head. I drove here, but I'm still too buzzed to drive home. I'll leave my car in the lot and walk the half-dozen blocks to the house I rent with my twin sister. "I'm walking. I live close," I say.

Connor shoves his hands in his pockets and nods. "Just making sure. Do you want me to walk you?"

"I'm okay, but thanks." Something tugs in my chest—that old regret that I couldn't want a nice guy like Connor. That night Sam turned me down at Notre Dame, it was Connor who found me sitting on the porch. He'd been cleaning up from the party and shooing the stragglers out the door. He was that guy. The one who made sure everyone had a ride home, the one who got the worst of the mess cleaned up so the house didn't smell like the bottom of a beer keg come morning.

We talked on that porch under the moonlight for a

long time before he even acknowledged that I'd been crying when he found me. As I walk home through the crisp autumn air, the memory consumes my thoughts.

* * *

Four Years Before . . .

"So, who's the asshole who broke your heart?" Connor asks me.

"The asshole is trying to be a nice guy," I say. We've been sitting on the back deck of the house for half an hour, making casual chitchat about nothing. Me, trying to shake the sick weight of rejection, Connor pretending I hadn't been crying when he found me. "I'm just a stupid girl who thought being with me might be more appealing than being a good guy."

"I see. So, he has a girlfriend?"

I shake my head. "I'm friends with his little sister. And since he sees *her* as a little girl . . ."

He drew in a sharp breath. "Ouch."

I'm covered in goose bumps, but I'm grateful for his company. Before Connor found me out here, I was feeling sorry for myself, wishing I were one of my sisters—anyone but myself. All my life, I've been the fun one, the wild one. The stupid one. No one takes me seriously. I wanted Sam to be the exception. "I think my age is just an excuse," I say. "A good one, I guess, but even good excuses are just excuses."

"You're gorgeous, Liz. If this guy doesn't see that, he's blind. Hell, the thirty minutes sitting here with you have been the best of my day."

"Thanks," I whisper. But looks have never been my problem. My insecurities are about what's on the inside.

Connor and I talk more. Laugh a little. He's good at making me laugh, and I like that he doesn't seem to take himself too seriously.

"Tell me what would fix this night for you," he says.

I look up to Sam's window. The light's on and I see him standing there, looking down on us. When I turn back to Connor, I say, "Kiss me?" I know it's wrong to ask for this just to make Sam jealous, but I can't help it. I'm hurt and embarrassed, and I want Sam to see that I'm worth wanting.

Connor smiles slowly and releases an exaggerated sigh. "If I have to." He winks, then slips one of those big hands around my neck and slowly lowers his mouth to mine.

The kiss isn't long or especially heated, but it's nice. When he pulls away, he leans forward, settling his elbows back on his knees. "If you ever want me to kiss you when he isn't watching, give me a call."

Guilt stabs my gut. "I'm sorry."

He shrugs. "Tonight, I got to kiss the most beautiful girl at the party. Don't apologize. Whatever your reasons, it was still the highlight of my day."

The back door squeaks open and thumps closed again. "Come inside, Liz. It's late. Nothing good happens at this hour." Sam shifts his gaze to Connor as if to support his point.

"I'm good. Connor and I are just going to hang out for a while."

"She's seventeen," Sam tells Connor, a warning in his voice.

Connor nods. "Noted."

The door rattles as it slams behind Sam, and I look at my hands, embarrassed.

"Seventeen?" Connor says.

"Afraid so. Not for long, though."

Then he kisses me again. His lips warm my cold skin, but the heat doesn't spread any further. He isn't Sam and he doesn't light me on fire, but it's a nice kiss.

When he pulls back, I frown at him.

"What's that look for?" he asks.

"I guess I thought you'd run the other way when you found out how young I am."

He smiles. "Being with you is *way* more appealing than being the good guy."

CHAPTER
FIVE

Liz

KₙₒcₖᵢₙG. Someone's knocking at my front door.
Thank you, sweet baby Jesus.

I texted Sam as soon as I got home. One sentence.
Seven words. An invitation.

I have the house to myself tonight.

I've sat here for nearly half an hour, waiting, staring
at my too-silent phone and wondering if I'd be better
off drawing myself a bath and sinking into it with a
dirty book and a large glass of wine.

Grinning, I peek through the peephole and see Sam on the stoop. The top buttons of his dress shirt are undone and his tie is loose around his neck. In one hand, he's holding a bottle of wine.

As casually as I can, I open the door to greet him, but deep down inside, I'm like an ill-trained dog that wants to jump on him, lick his face, and hump his leg.

"Hey," I say softly, leaning against the doorjamb.

His gaze skims over me, and my nerve endings fire to life in the wake of his appraisal. "You left."

"You stole my underwear."

His lips quirk into a grin. "Yes, I suppose I did."

"Listen, there's no shame in wearing women's panties. Gender identity is really fluid these days, and if you prefer lace to cotton under your trousers, who am I to judge?"

He cocks a brow, apparently unfazed by my attempts to emasculate him. "Are you going to invite me in, Rowdy?"

Stepping back, I swallow and motion inside the house. "Come on in." He offers the bottle of wine, and I take it. "Thanks. I'll go get a couple of glasses."

"Just"—I'm two steps toward the kitchen when he grabs my wrist and spins me around—"stop for a minute."

"Wha—"

His mouth crushes against mine. With one hand, he grabs me by the waist and pulls me closer, while the other wraps around the side of my neck. The hand at my neck makes me feel so small—fragile, as if I'm something he wants to protect. The hand at my waist makes me feel powerful—as if I'm something he wants to possess.

And PC or not, I want to be possessed by Samuel Bradshaw. I want to taste his kind of pleasure, to be bound and at his mercy. It's not just what he's told me. I've heard the rumors, the whispers. I don't know that I've ever craved something like that before, and with any other man, I probably wouldn't.

When he breaks the kiss, our breathing is unsteady, louder, as if the air in the room grew heavier while our mouths touched and now it's harder to breathe.

"I'll go pour the wine," I say. I turn toward the kitchen before I can lose myself in his eyes. His steps sound behind me, but I focus on finding two wine glasses and the corkscrew, and try to think of a safe subject. It's not like I've never had a booty call before, but this is awkward. Because it's Sam? Or because I need to prove to myself that I can have the one thing I've denied wanting for four years?

"Did you end up dancing with the governor's daughter?" I ask.

"I did."

"What do you think?" I pour the wine, watching the deep red liquid fill the glass. "Wife material? Think you'll let her have your babies?" When I allow myself to turn, I nearly drop the glasses. He's removed his tie and is wrapping it around his fist. Why didn't I realize what nice hands he has? They're big and strong, and . . . capable.

Something flickers in his eyes and is gone again in a breath before his gaze darkens. "I'm not interested in marrying anyone. My father will come to terms with that." Again, I think, *Heartbroken, Sam is heartbroken*, but as far as I know he wasn't even seeing anyone, and I'm not sure where I'm getting that idea. Maybe it's wishful thinking. Maybe I just want him to be the kind of guy who gives his heart to be broken. Maybe I want to be the one to put it back together again.

Sam

"Think you'll let her have your babies?" Tonight, her innocent question is salt in a fresh wound. I'm not the kind of man women see as the father of their children.

Shit. A few days ago, my biggest problem was trying to figure out how I was going to tell my parents—my conservative, model-citizen, bank-owning parents, with political aspirations—that I fucked up, and that my life was now inextricably tied to a woman I wasn't even sure I liked.

I was scared out of my mind, but I pulled her into my arms—this woman I hardly know and might not even like—and stroked her hair and promised it would be okay. I'd take care of her. I'd make this right. I held her and turned my problem over and over in my head like a puzzle that needed solving. As soon as she told me, I acted. I got her out of her shitty apartment and into a nice little condo, and gave her a nest egg to hold her over until she could find a new job. But I still hadn't figured out how to tell my parents that this soon-to-be-ex-stripper was the one I'd be bringing home for family dinners.

Two days ago, she took that problem right out of my hands when she showed up at my place and told me it was over. She said it was for the best. And when I asked her to reconsider, she called me a selfish bastard. And maybe I am. Because I'd do anything to get her to change her mind.

"Hey." Liz snaps me back to the present. She's still holding a glass of wine in her hand as she lifts it, brushing her knuckles across my cheek. "Tell me what's wrong."

I wrap my fingers around her wine glass and, without taking it from her hand, bring it to my lips. My breathing slows. Something releases inside me at the feel of her fingers under mine, and the softness in her eyes. The taste of the wine slows my racing heart.

After three long swallows, I take the glass from her hand and put it on the counter. "I need you naked and wet."

SOMETHING RECKLESS

Liz

Naked and wet. Yes, please.

God, I love the way his eyes continually rake over me, as if he's trying to make sure I haven't gone anywhere and at the same time he wants to take me all in, memorize me.

"Shower with me?" he asks.

I blink and nod to the hallway.

After a few steps in that direction, he turns back to me. "You coming?"

To the shower. My stomach somersaults with nerves and anticipation. This is really going to happen.

I follow him, conscious of the ache between my legs with every step. Maybe I should stop this before it goes any further. He's made it clear how he feels about romance, about forever, and I can tell he's only here to distract himself from something else—probably from some*one* else.

But I can't focus on that when there's something more captivating keeping my attention. Namely, the sight of a Sam Bradshaw stripping in the middle of my bathroom. He's turned on the shower, and the sound of the water hitting the tiles fills my ears as he sheds his dress shirt and tugs his undershirt off over his head.

Lord have mercy, this man's body is just insane.

His chest and shoulders are broad and sculpted, his waist narrow. A trail of light brown hair draws a path over his belly before disappearing under the waistband of his pants. I want to follow it with my fingers, then my mouth. I want to see if that muscled torso is as hot as it makes me feel.

When he turns and catches me watching him, he smirks. "Like what you see?"

"You should be shirtless more often. As in, as often as possible." I shake away my awe. Before tonight, I had only a vague idea of what might be under his clothes. Now that I'm up close and personal with his hard body . . . I want more.

I reach for the button on his pants, and he stops me.

"Not yet," he says. Then with a single sweep of his hand down my back, he's unzipped my dress and it's falling to the floor, pooling around my feet. My breasts are swollen, their peaks tight with need under the dark lace of my bra. "Jesus, Liz. You take my breath. You always have."

That makes something flutter in my belly. Something stronger than lust and more dangerous. Something that pushes me closer to this edge I'm clinging to so precariously. I can't fall. Not for Sam.

I reach back to release my bra, and he grabs my hands and stops me. His eyes flash to mine. "I want to do it. Don't get used to your hands being free. They won't be for long."

As he steps forward, my hands instinctively go to his chest, desperate to feel him while I can. He releases the clasp then slides his hands under the straps and over each shoulder, letting it fall to the floor. Then he shifts his hands so they're cupping my ass. He bows his head, his lips hovering just above mine. "How do you want it? Soft? Hard? Slow or fast?"

"Yes," I whisper. "All of it."

SOMETHING RECKLESS

I feel like a starved woman being served for the first time in months, like I need all I can get from Sam. I'm not inexperienced, but the men I've given myself to didn't make me feel the way he does—the way he's made me feel since I was a young, awkward teenager trying to impress my friend's older brother. My fantasies of Sam set the standard, and no man has ever measured up.

Until now.

One of the hands cupping me finds the seam of my ass, following the path down over my most sensitive, private parts until he reaches the wet, hot, aching center of me. I arch my back, urging his circling fingers inside.

"I want to taste you here."

"Just fuck me," I beg. "I want you."

He groans. "Not yet. First, I want you bound and writhing while I fuck you with my fingers and tongue."

I drop my hand between our bodies and push his pants and briefs from his hips in one desperate movement. I wrap my fingers around his cock and stroke him. He's long and hard, thick in a way that might scare me if I weren't desperate to take everything he has to offer.

I moan, willing him to make good on his promise, willing him to slide his fingers into me. I've never felt so empty. So needing to be filled.

But before I get what I'm looking for, he steps away. "Not so fast, Rowdy." He grasps my hands at the wrists and wraps them with his tie, binding them securely with expert efficiency. My lips part in surprise and he ducks his head, forcing me to meet his gaze. "Remember the rules. You tell me if it's too much."

"I trust you." But I can't speak the lie without squeezing my eyes shut. I trust him with my body, but I'm scared for my heart.

Slowly, he turns me toward the mirror and stands behind me, his front to my back. He kisses the side of my neck. Sucks. Works his way down with the same delicious torture that fills my body with heat and need and a want so intense it's an ache. "Open your eyes, beautiful. I'm going to touch every inch of you, and then I'm going to taste you." His big hand presses between my shoulder blades, and I follow the unspoken command and lean over from my hips, arching my back. It would be so easy for him to slide into me right now. His cock is practically nestled between my legs. One shift of his hips, and he'll be where I want him.

I watch our reflection fog up in the mirror as he runs his fingers down my spine.

"Would you watch?" he asks. "If I fucked you here, in front of the mirror? Would you watch me take you?"

Balancing myself with my bound wrists against the vanity, I arch my back harder and grind into him. "Yes."

He leans forward and presses an open mouth to the small of my back then sucks hard enough to draw the skin between his teeth. "Soon."

CHAPTER SIX

Sam

"YOU LOOK SO fucking sexy right now."

"How so?" Liz is breathless, bent at the waist, ass against my dick, wriggling in a way that's more instinctive than calculated, but still likely to make me lose my mind.

"I can't decide what would be sexier—you like this or on your knees with my dick in your mouth. Do you have any idea how many times I've imagined you with your hands bound?"

Slowly, I run my hands over her skin, down her back, over her hips, over her stomach, and up to her breasts. She understands my unspoken command and stays still as I touch her. Leaning forward, I mold my body against hers and trail kisses across her shoulders as I cup her breasts.

I want to watch her eyes grow hot in the mirror, but the shower has gone hot and the room is filling with steam. I draw her up and press my mouth to hers. She loops her bound hands over my head and presses her body closer to mine, and I need to take a minute and register that this isn't just a fantasy.

Liz is real. So real. And tonight she's mine.

I lead her into the shower and take a minute to watch the hot water wash over her skin. Unable to resist, I duck out from under her arms and catch a rivulet with my mouth as it rolls off the tight bud of her nipple. Her breasts are the perfect size. Not very large, but enough to fill my mouth and hands. I draw her nipple between my teeth, and she gasps.

Her hands go to my hair, and I'm tempted to change my plans, to let her keep her hands free, pulling on my hair as she fucks my face. As appealing as that sounds, I remember the look in her eyes when I told her I wanted her bound as I tasted her. Carefully lifting her hands over her head, I hook the tie onto the showerhead.

The position keeps her face just behind the spray, and when she lifts her eyes to mine, there's so much heat and lust there it nearly stops my heart.

"I've wanted you for a long time. But you were off-limits." The confession makes me feel oddly vulnerable, but I love the way she reacts. Her lips part and she draws in a surprised little gasp of air.

"I've been legal for a long time."

"But Max claimed you first."

"Claimed me? I was never his. He didn't own me."

I merely arch a brow. "But he wanted you, and the feeling wasn't one-sided."

She shakes her head. "I don't want to talk about Max right now."

"Good." I cup her face in my hands and press my mouth to hers. I know she's here for the wicked and dirty things I whispered in her ear at the wedding, but I want more than that. I kiss her hard, rubbing my tongue against hers as my hands find her hips and squeeze her ass. When we're both breathless and our hips are rolling of their own volition, I start down her body, kissing and sucking my way from her neck to her breasts. She rocks into my mouth, and I scrape my teeth over her nipple. Her cry echoes in the shower stall, and I move to the plump curve of her breast, sucking her hard into my mouth—marking her.

By the time I get to her navel, I'm on my knees, right where I planned to be. I run soft kisses across her stomach. Lower. Inching closer to her bare, swollen sex.

I trace my finger down the center of her sex, and the whimper that slips from her lips sends blood rushing to my cock.

As I graze my teeth over each hipbone, I lift her legs one at a time and position them on my shoulders. She gasps, but I squeeze her ass and hold her close, her pussy nestled against my face. Then, slowly, I taste her. I start with her clit, licking it before sucking the swollen flesh between my lips. She cries out and her ass flexes, her thighs tightening around my head. I suck a little harder, and she rocks toward my face, but then catches herself and stills.

I pull away and look up at her through the water. She's so fucking beautiful from this position. Arms tied above her head, breasts thrust out, and—sexiest of all—her gaze locked on every move I'm making between her thighs.

"Don't hold back," I command. "I want you to ride the pleasure. Fuck my face until it feels so good, I get to taste you as you come." I punctuate my command with my tongue at her entrance, sliding into her, tasting her, filling her. And she obeys. As I kiss and explore every inch of her, her hips rock. I find the sensitive spot at the top of her inner thigh, and gently nip her flesh. And through every second of it, I hold her tight, squeezing her ass and pressing her closer to my mouth, like her pleasure is salvation and I'm a lost and broken soul.

When she comes, it's spectacular. She comes with her whole body, all of her muscles clenching and squeezing until everything releases and she's whimpering in the aftermath, and I feel like a fucking god.

Slowly, I lower her feet to the floor, one at a time, and stand to release her arms. I'm surprised to find my own legs shaking—not from exertion but weak with need. When I untie her wrists, she takes my face in her hands and kisses me as hard as I kissed her earlier.

"I love that you're not afraid to taste yourself on me," I whisper against her lips, the water pouring down my back.

She smiles. "Anyone ever tell you how good you are at that?"

"At what?"

The pink in her cheeks deepens a little. *"That."*

I grunt. "I never would have guessed you'd be shy about saying the words."

She drops her gaze to her body. "I'm feeling a little naked and exposed here, that's all."

"Hmm. Well, I hope you're not counting on changing that anytime soon."

Something flashes in her eyes, and the only promise I make is in my grin. I turn off the shower and grab the towels to dry us off.

* * *

Liz

He dries me slowly, and almost everywhere the towel touches, he follows with his mouth. When he reaches my wrists, I'm surprised to have him release them. As hungry as I've been to touch him, I'm almost disappointed to be freed. I didn't want that part of the fantasy to end.

The second I relax my arms, my shoulders scream in protest. I didn't realize how sore they were from being pinned back until he released them.

"You okay?" He wraps the towel around me and rubs my shoulders with strong, sure fingers, and the tension releases. His mouth follows his fingers as he trails soft kisses across my shoulders.

"I'm fine." I force a smile, but it's hard to act carefree when something inside you is melting. I wasn't prepared for melting. For falling. I invited him here for hot, dirty sex. He made his terms clear, didn't he? I won't be that girl who up and changes the rules. "Come on, let me show you to my bedroom."

His eyes flash in approval as I take his hand, leading him down the short hallway to my room.

Sam looks around slowly, then cocks a brow at me. "It's . . . pink."

I grin, kick the door closed, and drop my towel. "I like pink."

He skims his gaze over me, his mouth hitching up into a lopsided smile. "It suits you." He nods to the bed. "Lie down."

"Bossy."

"You have no idea."

Grinning, I climb on top of my comforter—also pink—and prop myself on my elbows. "Why are you still wearing that towel? The only thing you should have on is a condom."

He rakes his gaze over me—assessing, approving. Even the way he looks at me turns me on. He climbs into bed beside me and props himself up on one elbow. "Don't rush me, woman." The command and the roughness in his tone steal my breath. "You're going to need to roll to your stomach if you want me to make those shoulders feel better."

"It's fine," I protest, but he just shakes his head and

nudges me onto my stomach.

The second his fingers start working magic on my shoulders, I'm glad he insisted. The muscles are sore from being held so long in such an awkward position, and the tension melts away at his touch.

I'm practically falling asleep by the time his touches turn to kisses and he rolls me over.

* * *

Sam

When Liz looks at me, her gaze is heavy but happy. "Are you going to make me beg you, Sam Bradshaw?"

"Beg?"

"Not that our shower didn't leave me . . . satisfied, but . . ." She takes her lower lip between her teeth in a way that's both cute and really fucking hot.

She shifts under me, then wraps her legs around my waist, bringing my dick to rest against her slick folds.

I groan. *Condom. Get a fucking condom.* Everything about this moment is an invitation—the way she's looking at me, the heat in her eyes. I've never been so tempted to slide into a woman without protection. It's not an option—now more than ever—but fuck, if it's not tempting at this moment.

"Liz," someone bellows.

We both stiffen.

"Lizzy?" It's a guy, and he's right outside her door.

A drunk, belligerent man, in her house, at her bedroom door. My body tenses, shifting gears, ready to fight.

Liz seems to sense the change in me, and she wraps her hand around my wrist. "Relax. It's just Connor."

"Connor? As in, my sister's boyfriend? That Connor?"

"As in your *friend* Connor. I think he's drunk." She's already climbing out of bed, not worried about explaining to me why the hell Connor is showing up drunk at her bedroom door in the middle of the night. "I'm going to check on him."

She starts opening drawers and pulling out clothes. So she can go see *Connor*.

I don't want Connor to see her like this—freshly showered, her cheeks still flushed from coming. Or maybe I do. Maybe I want to make sure he knows. She's here with me. *Mine*.

My jealousy is so irrational it catches me off guard.

I take her hand, stopping her from pulling on her pants, then I latch my mouth onto her neck. She moans as I kiss and suck, then cries out as I bite down.

I pull back, satisfied when I see I've marked her. Good.

"Liz? I need you." He's practically whimpering.

"I'm coming," she calls. "Just a minute."

Fucking Connor. I'm not letting her go out there without me.

Suddenly, I remember that none of my clothes made it to the bedroom with us.

Liz bites back a grin, apparently realizing my conundrum. "You're not going out there anyway, so don't worry about it." Giggles lace her words.

"The hell I'm not. He's drunk."

"Sam?" Connor says on the other side of the door. "Is that you, man? Oh, shit. Did your sister send you here? I told her to stay out of it."

I don't know what he's talking about, but I shoot Liz a pointed look. "I'm going with you."

"Want to borrow some panties? How do you feel about pink?" This time, she lets the giggle free.

I snatch the towel off the floor where it landed earlier. "I'll go get my clothes."

I sneak out the door before she can protest, and pull it shut tight behind me. Connor's sitting in the hall, eyes half closed, and I don't bother explaining myself before I cross to the bathroom to pull on my pants and undershirt.

When I get back to Lizzy's room, she's dressed. If you can call it that. She's in a worn-out Sinclair tee and nothing else, as far as I can tell.

I skim my gaze over her down to where the shirt ends at mid-thigh. I love the way it looks on her—stretched across her breasts, her nipples poking at the fabric, and the way it shows off her long, flawless legs. I *don't* love the idea of her greeting another man in nothing but that. Especially Connor.

I open the nearest dresser drawer, grab a pair of thick flannel pants, and shove them in her hands. "If you're going out there, would you please wear these too?"

She smirks. "Are you jealous?"

Raking my gaze over her again, I shake my head. "Don't mistake my selfishness for jealousy. I don't want to share."

I wait for her to put on the pants—not that it helps much. How does she make a T-shirt and flannel pants look so goddamn indecent? For a minute, I contemplate ordering her to stay in the bedroom, but I know that wouldn't go over well, so I head to the hall to find Connor.

This guy was one of my best friends through college. We got thrown together as roommates freshman year, and our friendship formed from there. I've never been as close to him as I am to Max and Will, but we were cool.

Until he started dating my little sister.

Connor's passed out in the hall, his head slumped to the side as if he's trying to use his own shoulder as a pillow.

Liz pads over to him and places her hand on his back. "Con, wake up."

He blinks at her then rolls over and awkwardly pushes himself to his feet. "What are you doing here?" he asks Liz, dragging his eyes down to her breasts. Can I punch him in the face for looking at her the way any man would?

"This is my house," she says patiently. She slides her arm under his. "Let's get you to the couch."

I grab the other arm and help him onto his feet to hobble to the couch. She turns to me. "Would you mind getting him a glass of water?"

Reluctantly, I turn to the kitchen to fetch the water and remind myself that Connor didn't know I'd be here tonight. But somehow that only makes me feel worse, not better.

I spot a bottle of ibuprofen on the counter and take it and the glass of water back to the living room.

Connor and Liz are nestled together on the couch. He's stretched out across it, resting his head against Lizzy's shoulder. Cozy as shit. She's laughing about something. I don't like how comfortable they are together, and I know Della wouldn't like it either.

"Connor was just telling me about the time you went roller-skating in college." She giggles again and her eyes dance with amusement as she brings them to mine. "Is it true you got asked to the Snowball Dance by eight different junior high girls?"

Yeah, I'm gonna punch him in the face. Any minute now. I grunt instead of answering and hold up the water and the pills. "Sit up, idiot."

Liz frowns. "Empathy is not your forte, Sam."

"He's the one who got himself in this position."

Connor scrambles to sitting, putting his hands on Liz way more than necessary in the process, and I shove the glass at him. Water sloshes onto his lap, and he jumps.

I step back and cross my arms. "What brings you here tonight?"

"I needed a place to crash," he mutters. "I locked myself out of my apartment, and Della's pissed at me so she wouldn't bring the spare key."

A glance at the clock above his head confirms that it's after three in the morning. "Where were you tonight that you just realized you locked yourself out at this hour?"

Liz gapes at me. "Sam," she hisses. "Aren't you

supposed to be more supportive? Bros before hos and all that?"

"That *ho* you're talking about is my sister."

She turns to Connor, giving me her back. "You deserve better than her, Con."

"Watch it," I warn.

"I know she's your sister," Liz says, "and I know her better than most. I grew up with Della, remember? But she stomps all over Connor."

My jaw tightens. I don't want to talk about this, because talking about it is going to make me think more than I want to about why Liz is so bent on defending him and why he'd come here, of all places, when he needed a place to crash. "I'm sure you're not as innocent as this one thinks," I tell Connor, "and in the morning, I expect you to apologize to Della."

Liz rolls her eyes. "He just went to the strip club with his friends after he left the reception. It's *not* a big deal."

My face heats with a rush of anger, and Connor winces. Clearly, he wasn't intending to share that part with me. "You're lucky I don't make you sleep in the street," I mutter.

I can't face him anymore, so I head back to the bedroom, slamming the door behind me.

I can hear them talking, but I can't go back out there.

CHAPTER
SEVEN

Liz

THE ROOM IS DARK when I return. Connor's tucked in on the couch, and I've done all I can for him tonight, but he'll have one hell of a hangover tomorrow—from the booze and the aching heart. Sam doesn't understand how much Connor loves Della, how hard he tries to please her.

I can't make out anything in the darkness, so I click on the bedside lamp and find Sam in my bed, still dressed in his undershirt and dress pants. His hands are folded behind his head, his feet crossed at the ankles.

"I'm sorry you didn't like what I had to say about your sister," I say as I sit on the side of the bed.

He grunts. "We both know that's not an apology."

"I'm sorry I spoke poorly of your sister in front of you. That put you in an awkward position."

"He's lucky I didn't cut his dick off when I found out he was sleeping with her," he says.

"It's not like he used her for sex and walked away. They're a couple, and he loves her, even if their relationship is a little . . . dysfunctional."

"There's a code. Seducing my little sister was totally unacceptable."

"Della's my friend, but so is Connor. She's a grown woman, and he's a good guy. Seriously, if your sister was going to give it up to anyone, Connor's a good choice."

His jaw tightens, and when he raises his gaze to meet mine, I freeze. *You said too much, Liz.* But why should I care? It's not like Sam wanted me, and Connor was . . . the sweetest guy I ever met. Maybe he still is.

"Why would you say that?" he asks softly.

"Because it's true." I shrug. "When you turned me down all those years ago, I was crushed. Connor cheered me up."

"I fucking bet he did."

"What's that supposed to mean?"

"It means I know he's wanted you since he met you at that party that night, and he was supposed to stay away from you."

"Wait. What? You were telling your friends to stay away from me?"

"Just Connor. I didn't like the way he looked at you."

"You mean you didn't like that he looked at me like

I was a woman when you still wanted to see me as a child."

"Sue me for being a decent guy."

"You rejected me, and Connor was the one who talked me through it. Who's the decent guy?"

"Did you sleep with him? Did you let him take care of your little virginity problem?"

"I—" I lift my palms. "Why are we talking about this? It was over four years ago."

Some emotion I don't recognize flashes in his eyes.

"I wanted *you,* Sam. Not some stand-in. *You.* And you broke my heart." As soon as the words are out of my mouth, I wish I could take them back. I've just made myself too vulnerable to him. More vulnerable than I was when my hands were bound and I was at his mercy.

"I broke your heart?"

"Don't worry about Della. Connor will take care of her."

"You didn't answer my question. You said I broke your heart."

You don't want me to answer your question. I stand and stare at my light pink wall. I should have kept my mouth shut. "I was young. Foolish. It's not like I've been hung up on you all this time or something." *Much.* Hell, who am I kidding? It's very much like that.

"Rowdy." The mattress shifts as he moves to sit next to me. "I told you I don't do emotional strings."

"And I told you that's not what I'm looking for."

He shakes his head. "I never wanted to hurt you." He stalks toward me, and I stand frozen, waiting for him to decide what happens next.

The frustration in his eyes turns to heat then lust, and then something more dangerous. I stand still until he cups my face in his hands and lowers his mouth to mine.

Everything after that happens in a desperate rush. We shed our clothes, throwing them to the floor until we're skin to skin. Sam presses me against the wall and hitches one of my legs around his hip.

"Condom," I whisper.

"Done."

I have no idea when during the frenzy of kissing and undressing he pulled on a condom, but I don't care. His cock is between my legs, poised at my entrance, and I want him. Need him.

Almost in one fluid motion, he pulls up my other leg and drives into me. He's big—almost too big—and my body tightens in protest, but when he tries to withdraw, tries to give me a moment to adjust, I claw at his back to hold him close. And then he thrusts, in and out, and I have to bite back a cry every time he sinks deep.

"Don't do that," he says in my ear. "Don't hold back."

"But Connor—"

"Let him hear. I want him to know that you're mine."

I love that. *You're mine.*

"For tonight," he says. "Just for tonight."

I squeeze my eyes shut, denying the hurt that wants to flood me at those words. And before I can think about it too much, before I can dwell on any disappointment or hurt I feel, he's sliding a hand between our bodies and finding my clit, stroking as he pounds into me.

Behind his back, I lock my feet at the ankles and loop my arms around his neck, holding on tight as he leads me up to more and more pleasure.

Suddenly, he spins me around and settles my ass on the bed. In a smooth motion, he's changed our positions, moving my legs so my ankles are resting on his shoulders and his cock slides even deeper.

When he drives into me from this new position, his eyes locked on where our bodies are joined, I do cry out, and he groans his approval and pumps harder.

"I needed my hands free," he murmurs. His fingertips graze my breasts and he pinches my nipple. "I needed to touch you."

I watch him, trying to memorize how dark his eyes are as he fucks me, the way they roam over me again and again, as if every part of me is fighting for his attention and he can't decide where to give it.

But then his eyes drop between my legs and stop roaming altogether. He focuses on watching our bodies come together through thrust after thrust.

His thumb strokes my clit, and my back arches off the bed. He pumps into me again. Again. All the while, stroking that sensitive piece of me until it's almost too much.

"Tonight, you're mine," he whispers again.

And it's those words and the intensity in his eyes that pushes me over the edge and has my body contracting in orgasm.

He turns his head and places a tender kiss on the arch of my foot. Then he thrusts again, the head of his cock swelling inside me. His jaw tightens and he comes too, hand wrapped around my ankle.

After he goes to the bathroom to clean up, I curl into my bed and remind my heart that it wasn't invited to this party.

I don't normally do this. I'm not the kind of girl who tries to mentally rewrite every hookup into a happily-ever-after. My mind understands that sometimes I just need sex for the sake of sex. But this is Sam, and my brain has never been very good at showing up where he's involved.

He'll want to leave. Maybe he'll take Connor with him out of some misguided protective instinct, but I don't expect him to sleep over. So when he comes back into the room and slides into bed with me, when he pulls me into his arms so my back is against his chest and his arms are wrapped around me, I'm waiting for the goodbye. The *thanks for the good time, see ya around.*

Instead, he kisses me just below my earlobe and says, "Sleep well, Rowdy," and settles his head into the pillow as if he intends to sleep with me in his arms.

SOMETHING RECKLESS

Sam

I know better than to stay, but I can't make myself go. I tell myself it's because Connor is sleeping in her living room, and I don't trust him not to try something with her, but that's a bunch of bullshit. The truth is, I love the way she feels in my arms and the way her hair smells, and I don't want to leave.

I never intended to take her so roughly tonight. I can't believe I fucked her against the wall. But my attraction to Liz has always been something that skates on that line between want and need. I don't mind want. Want is a thing you can control. Want you can deny. But I hope to never *need* a woman the way I felt like I needed her tonight. Need makes me weak. Desperate. Completely under her power.

It's not that I expected her to still be a virgin. Hell no. She's a damn fine grown woman with a healthy sexual appetite and confidence to boot. I didn't think she waited all this time for me, but the idea that Connor was her first . . .

My arms tighten around her instinctively. I don't like this jealousy I feel, but I can't deny it either. I fucking hate that she gave him her virginity. I guess part of me was waiting for her to come back to my room after she turned eighteen. I was cocky enough to believe it was *me* she wanted, not just anyone.

Fuck Connor.

I swear he's wanted what's mine since the day I met him. He was fascinated by my family—the size of it, the way we all seemed to sincerely love each other. Part of me was happy to give him a place there. I brought him home on holidays when his parents couldn't be bothered to scrape together the money to fly him back to California; I got him the internship working for my father as he laid the groundwork for his political campaign; and I introduced him to Della, his now girlfriend, despite my mother's objections over them living together before they're married.

Part of me has always known Connor's a better fit in my own life than I am. My father loves him, my mother thinks he's a prince, and he loves my big family when it's always made me feel claustrophobic. It's like he's taken the parts of my life that I denied—the job with my father . . . *Liz.*

I bury my nose in her hair, and she sighs in her sleep, a soft, sweet sound. "He can't have you," I say. "You're mine." I try to mentally add *for tonight*, but it feels like a lie. I want more than tonight. I don't want to miss another night falling asleep to the smell of her hair just because I'm scared I might be more like my father than Connor will ever be.

Because even if I think Liz belongs with me, not him, I know he's the better guy.

I know why he was at the strip club tonight, and he'll let Della believe the worst just to protect her from the truth—to protect me. Connor's a better hero than I'll ever be, but he can't have Liz.

"Mine." Then I close my eyes.

SOMETHING RECKLESS

* * *

I wake up to the sound of someone knocking softly on the bedroom door, and for a minute I'm disoriented and expect to find myself in my own bed.

"Liz?" Connor calls from the other side.

Liz shifts in my arms, and I climb out of bed. "She's sleeping," I say through a crack in the door.

Connor's eyes widen and he blinks at me. "Oh. I didn't know . . ."

I arch a brow. "Let her sleep, okay? I'll be out in a minute." I shut the door on his startled face, then pull on my clothes. And, yeah, I just broke one of her rules. Maybe even intentionally. I know Connor's with Della now, but I also know how he's always looked at Liz.

When I return to the hallway, Connor is waiting with a mug of coffee in each hand. He shoves one at me.

"So, you and Liz?"

My jaw tightens without my permission. When it comes to Liz, I have no poker face. "None of your business."

He nods and sips his coffee, then he meets my eyes and his body stiffens. "Don't hurt her again."

"Again?"

"She had it bad for you . . . back in the day."

"And you stepped right in to take advantage of that, didn't you?"

Connor pulls back as if I've struck him.

Fuck. I shouldn't have said anything. For one, it's

not my business. For another, I don't want Connor knowing how I feel about his history with Liz.

"She told you about that?" he asks.

"She was seventeen," I say, sidestepping his question.

Connor looks away. *He* knows it was a dick move. "Don't tell Della," he says. "She doesn't know, and it would change things between her and Liz."

"I won't tell." My shoulders sag, some of the fight draining out of me. It's a relief just to know that he cares how Della would feel. "You were at the club last night snooping into my business, weren't you?

Connor drags a hand through his hair and nods. "Your dad saw the money gone from your account. He asked me to look into it, and someone said they'd seen you spending time with one of the girls there."

Fuck. I drop my gaze to the floor, doing my best to calm the surge of anger I feel at the thought of Asia. Oddly, my anger isn't as hot or volatile as it was yesterday. A night with Liz was like a balm to my soul. "Tell my father there's nothing going on that's a danger to his precious campaign, so he can relax."

"You know, I'm not the enemy."

I sigh. He's not. As much as I hated Liz defending Connor last night, she was right. He is the best kind of good guy, even if it sometimes feels like he stole my life. "I'm sorry I was shitty with you last night. I didn't like you coming here. Didn't like the idea of you just showing up at her bedroom door in the middle of the night."

"We're friends. Liz is honestly one of the best

people I know."

Yeah, that's the problem. "Think about it from Della's point of view before you come running here next time."

"Say what you mean, Bradshaw."

I roll back my shoulders. "I mean, you still have a *thing* for Liz. It was all over your face when you two were cuddled on the couch last night."

"Is this about me, or is it about you?"

"If Della knew you'd come here, she'd be pissed."

He grimaces. "Yeah, I guess. Are you two . . .?" He nods to Lizzy's bedroom door. "Are you going to be spending time together?"

"Are you asking me if I'm going to make an honest woman out of her?"

He grunts. "You should. I don't like the idea of you using her as an escape from your problems and then sneaking out of her bed like she's one of your random hookups."

"Don't."

He must see the warning in my eyes, because he shows both palms in surrender. "I'll get out of the way. You sure you don't have something going on you need to talk about?"

"I'm sure."

He nods and heads toward the front of the house.

I sneak into her room one more time before I leave. She's on her stomach, her head turned to the side, those crazy blond curls fanned out around her head. If it weren't for the way she was drooling on the pillow, I might think she positioned herself like that trying to look irresistible.

But Liz doesn't *try* to look irresistible. She just is. Smoothing a few locks off her face, I kiss her forehead. Because even with everything hanging over my head right now, even with Connor's guest appearance, last night was amazing.

For maybe the first time ever, I'm thinking about . . . *something more.*

CHAPTER EIGHT

Liz

"GOOD AFTERNOON, Miss Thompson," Mr. Bradshaw, Sam's father, says when he sees me walk through the bank doors on Monday. "How can we help you today?"
"Is Sam available?"

"He's in the back office. Could I help you with something?"

"Um, no. I just needed to discuss something with Sam. Thanks."

My stomach does a wild, fluttery flip-flop as I make my way to Sam.

When I step into the office, my first thought is that I

have the wrong place, because the man behind the desk doesn't look like the Sam I know. His face is covered in hard lines and tension, a study of stress and anger.

"It looks like you're doing actual work in here," I say, going for light. "Careful, someone might see you and ruin your reputation."

His head lifts slowly, and as his eyes settle on me, it's gratifying to see some of that tension leave his face, some of the anger leave his eyes.

But that doesn't change what I see there. He's working through something heavy. I have no idea what it is, but I know exactly how to help him.

He rakes his gaze over me slowly, taking in my button-up blouse, unbuttoned past my collarbone, my fitted black skirt, and my four-inch red heels. It was an outfit I chose very deliberately. It's sexy, but not so overtly that it's obvious I dressed for him—though I did.

I tug my lip between my teeth. I want more than his gaze on me. More than his hands, even. I want the weight of his body pressing into mine, the feel of his mouth on my skin. His eyes lift to mine, and tension fills in the air between us—the good kind of tension, the kind with snapping teeth and tongues and promise.

I reach for the door and shut it behind me. Sam lifts an amused brow, more of that anger melting away. It's good to see the man I know back in that face. This other guy, the stranger, he scares me a little.

"Why are you here, Rowdy?"

Swallowing, I walk to behind his desk and go to the window that overlooks the side of the parking lot and the river beyond. I feel him move behind me as I pull the blinds shut. His fingers brush my neck, moving aside the few strands that have escaped the twist. My eyes float closed at the contact.

He steps closer. "You didn't answer my question," he whispers against my ear.

I turn to face him, but he's too close, and even in my heels I'm staring at his chin. I crane my neck to meet his eyes. I wonder if he can tell that I'm practically trembling with nerves. With need. "I'm here to collect on your promise."

"What promise?"

"The promise you made me at the wedding. The ideas you put in my head. You did not follow through on all the dirty things you whispered in my ear."

He groans, low and guttural, and some of my nerves flitter away.

I grab his tie in my fist and tug him down an inch, two. "Don't assume I'm like other girls," I whisper against his lips.

"Oh, I know you're not like other girls. That was never the question." His lips are so close I can practically feel them brushing over mine as he speaks.

I want his kiss badly. Too much. So much that I step around him and away from the temptation to take it, because I don't want to kiss him. I want *him* to kiss *me*. The distinction normally wouldn't matter to me, but it's different with Sam. Everything's different with Sam.

Sinking back into his chair, he rests his elbows on his knees and drags a hand through his hair. "I'm going through some fucked-up shit right now."

"And I'm here to distract you." I push the papers on his desk aside and hoist myself up to sit in their place. Sam's eyes immediately seek out the exposed thigh where my skirt is riding up, but I have something so much better for him to see. Leaning back on my hands, I part my legs, watching with satisfaction as his gaze follows my skirt higher up my thighs.

His eyes meet mine, as hot as I feel. "You came to my bank without panties?"

I shrug. "I don't know. Why don't you check?"

He stands, gaze flicking to the door, then back to me. "The bank's closed, but we're not alone." He touches my knee, and my eyes practically roll back in my head from the pleasure of his skin connecting with mine. His hand inches north so slowly; the swirling ache of want low in my belly causes me real pain.

I'm already wet. I feel it between my legs, gathering for him. For this. When his thumb meets the slick juncture of my thighs, his breath draws in with a hiss.

My eyes float closed and my hips lift of their own volition, pushing closer to his fingers, his touch. When he dips his head down to my ear, his fingers dance across the swollen flesh between my legs—teasing, promising, but not delivering. It's all I can do not to grab his wrist and cup his hand firmly against me.

"You know how fucking delicious you look?" he whispers. "All I want to do is shove your skirt up, spread your legs, and bury my face between your thighs. I want to tease you with my lips and tongue until you beg me to let you come."

I gasp—at his words, at the buzz of the pressure of

his thumb against my clit.

"Could you handle it, Liz?"

"Why do you think I'm here?" I'm so proud of myself for constructing that sentence, so I try for another. "As far as I can tell, Sam Bradshaw, you're all talk."

"I'm asking if you could let me touch you here"—he runs two fingertips down the length of me—"and not make a sound."

My lips part, but I can't think of a damn thing to say that would leave me with any dignity.

His honey-brown eyes flash hot, and he slides a finger into me. "Jesus, you're hot."

I reach down and draw my skirt higher up my hips, and his hand stills between my legs. He shifts his stance slightly to the left, his gaze darting to some spot behind my head.

"Liz." He leans his head against mine and says, "We can't."

"What?"

"Not here." His gaze darts to that spot behind my head again. "Cameras."

Two emotions zip through me simultaneously—horror at what I'd have done with Sam right here without thinking of those cameras, and an erotic thrill at the thought of having it recorded.

Slowly, he removes his hand from between my legs and smoothes down my skirt.

My cheeks burn with the shame of rejection. I lift my chin an inch. "Wouldn't have thought a little video tape would slow down a man like you."

His chuckle is low and pained. "Normally, it wouldn't. But since a woman who used to change my diapers sits at the desk by the video monitors, I think it's best I practice a little restraint this time around." He gives an apologetic smile and rubs his thumb across my cheek in a movement that's almost tender.

I nod, that ugly feeling of rejection still hanging over me as I slide off the desk I'd hoped he'd fuck me silly on. I follow him out of his office and to the parking lot.

We stand by my car for a minute—the awkward aura of *hookup interruptus* around us.

I shift, my too-high heels pinching my toes. "Well, that didn't go as I planned."

Again, that low, deep chuckle. Can you be touched by a sound? Because his laugh seems to stroke me in all the right places. "I didn't think you were the type, Liz."

"What's that supposed to mean?"

He rubs the back of his neck. "You're a nice girl."

I snort—loudly—breaking the tension. "God, Sam, can I give you a hint? When a girl shows up at your office without panties, the last thing she wants you thinking is that she's a nice girl. I'm not nice." *I'm horny.* But I don't say that, because I have a little dignity left. "I'm as dirty as the last trollop you took to bed." Or I could be. With a little practice and the right teacher.

He lifts a brow. "I'm pretty sure the last woman I took to bed wouldn't appreciate you calling her a trollop."

SOMETHING RECKLESS

* * *

Sam

Ever since I left my office tonight, my hands have been itching to pick up the phone and call Liz. I want to do more than call her. I want to have her in my bed, naked, bound, and moaning.

Her invitation to take her on my desk was almost more than I could resist. But I'm a Bradshaw, and we're trained very carefully to be mindful of things like cameras. That doesn't mean I can't invite her over tonight, though.

But by the time I walk in my front door, my plans change. Because Asia is waiting for me in my living room, and she says the only words powerful enough to keep me away from Liz.

"I'll keep the baby."

CHAPTER NINE

Liz

I FIND MYSELF in Sam's driveway, jacked up on lust and optimism. I have no idea how our night together left him feeling. I'm not even sure what this is *I'm* feeling. But I know I don't want to walk away, and I know things would have gone further in his office if it weren't for those pesky security cameras.

There's more to him than a hard body and a dirty mouth, and I feel like I just got a peek at it. I want to know more, to explore him like I explored the woods by the river as a child. I want to get him to open up to me when he doesn't open to anyone else. And I'm going to tell him so.

Only I don't make it out of the car before I see him through the picture window at the front of his house. It's dark and all the lights are on, framing and illuminating the two people on the other side of the glass like a scene on a screen for everyone to see.

He has his arms wrapped around a woman—a beautiful woman in a tiny black dress and sky-high heels. My heart stutters in my chest and I can't remember how to breathe, and when I try, it hurts. It actually hurts to pull oxygen into my lungs while watching him hold her.

I force the air in, and suffer the sharp pain of my lungs expanding against the jagged tear in my heart. Any hope I had that she's a sister or cousin, or that there's some completely reasonable explanation for him touching her, flees. He brings his hands to her face and lowers his mouth to hers—gently, softly. It's a kiss filled with all that tenderness I yearn for, the affection men just don't feel for me.

I'm frozen, the jagged edge of my heart sawing at the soft tissue of my slowly expanding and deflating lungs. I can't take my eyes off him—I can't unsee this side of Sam I just came to believe was there and hoped to resurface for myself. When he breaks the kiss, he lifts his head and looks right at me. There's so much on his face that he'd typically hide behind his ever-present cocky grin, but I see it now. Hurt. Regret. *Terror.*

For a moment, I think he can see me, but then he looks away and I remember I'm concealed by darkness while they're visible to anyone who might happen by.

And he doesn't care.

That snags on a piece of my heart and it breaks off, tumbling to the pit of my aching stomach. He didn't want anyone to know about us this weekend, but he obviously feels differently about whoever she is.

"Stupid, stupid, stupid," I whisper to no one. Why do we call ourselves names when we're alone? Does confessing the worst about ourselves to the darkness make our flaws easier to bear? Or is it because we fear only the darkness is willing to take us as we are—imperfect, incomplete, and so desperate to be accepted?

Sam wraps his arms around her shoulders and gestures outside, and when he gives her that smile—not the cocky grin, but the sweet, vulnerable boy smile—I finally find the strength to put the key in the ignition and drive away.

One night. I promised him I could play by his rules. He worried I'd want more. He was right, and I'll never let him know.

* * *

I'm a girly girl and proud of it. I wear heels and makeup and do my hair and nails. I don't like getting sweaty and I love romantic books and movies and the color pink. When Hanna and I got this house together to live in while we finished at Sinclair, the first thing I did was paint my bedroom a very pale shade of pink. I loved it. It was just pink enough to be girly without looking like it should be a baby girl's nursery. But when I walked in from going to Sam's last night, the color made me sick to my stomach. Don't ask me how the color pink makes me think about having my hands tied behind my back and my mouth on Sam, but it does. I can't live with it anymore.

"Are you okay?" Hanna asks from my bedroom doorway. Maybe she's asking because I've been on a tear all morning, and now all the bedroom furniture is pushed to the middle of my room, draped in pink sheets, and the walls are almost completely repainted.

Beige. It's a terrible color and a terrible way to feel, but I've chosen to surround myself with it. *Beige.* Stupid beige.

I force a smile, because Hanna's sensitive, and I don't want her worrying about me. "I'm fine. Ever feel like you just need a change?"

The wrinkle between her brows tells me she's not buying my fake peppiness, but she knows when not to push it. "Sam's here and asking for you. What's that about?"

My stomach protests at the thought of Sam waiting for me at the front of the house—fear and hurt and hope all take hold of my heart and engage in a three-way game of tug-of-war. Part of me wants to imagine he's here because he has feelings for me, but it's more likely that he wants to make sure I don't tell Miss Little Black Dress about our night together.

He never struck me as the kind of guy who would cheat.

I wipe my hands on my pink sheets turned paint rags

and climb down the ladder. "Does he need a cup of sugar?"

She lifts a brow but doesn't argue with my suggestion. "I'll be here when you want to talk about it."

"Talk about what?" My smile is so plastic you could make Barbies with it. I push past her and find my way to the living room, where Sam is standing, looking out the window with his hands shoved into his pockets.

He's in a simple white T-shirt and jeans, but he's so gorgeous it hurts to look at him. Sometimes it's nice to want things you can't have, and sometimes the want is so deep that it's a flame tearing through your heart.

"Hey, Sam!" I call, keeping my Barbie smile in place.

He turns, and I wait for his eyes to skim over me in my too-short cut-offs and tank, but they don't. In fact, he's looking at me, but I can tell he's not seeing me at all. "Can we talk?"

"Sure! Let me slip on some shoes." I don't want to leave with him, but I'm so ashamed of the position I've put myself in, the heartbreak I brought on myself, that I don't want Hanna to witness this conversation either.

I slip on my flip-flops and grab my hoodie from the hook by the door, then lead him outside. We walk for a bit without talking, just breathing in the cool, late-autumn air and trying to figure out where we fit with each other now. Or at least, that's what I'm doing.

"I know we said it was just one night," he begins.

I can't handle hearing more, so I butt in before he can speak again. "No strings, no attachments, no expectations. You're not here because you've changed your mind on me, are you?"

He stops walking and blinks at me. "I . . ." He shakes his head then swallows, his Adam's apple bobbing. "A friend gave me some news this morning, and I wondered if I could take you out. Talk to you about it."

His tongue down her throat sure made it seem like she was more than a friend. "I'm kind of busy." My heart trips on the tangle of emotions in my chest, but I'm determined to get through this with my pride intact. I've been rejected by Sam before. I can't handle being rejected again. "No expectations, Sam. But that has to go both ways. I don't want this to be all awkward now."

He cocks his head, studying me. "You're special, Rowdy. Sometimes I get the feeling you don't actually know that."

Don't do this. Don't say nice things that make me want to love you. "I'm just a girl who needed a good lay. Thanks for that."

He flinches. Sam Bradshaw actually *flinches* at my rough words. Inside, I'm flinching too. "I don't even know what to make of you."

I shrug. "Do you really need to know?" *Oh, fuck.* Tears burn the back of my throat and I can't let them out. Not here while he can see. "Can you do me a favor? Don't tell anyone about our little . . . indiscretion? I'd like to keep it our secret. I don't want people getting the wrong idea about me."

"Who would I tell?"

One more time with the plastic smile. *This is it*, I

promise myself. *Just one more minute smiling, and you're out of here.* "It was sweet of you to come by, but you don't need to worry about me."

I give a little wave, turn, and walk away, and I feel his eyes on me with every step.

"Rowdy," he calls when I'm nearly to the door. I turn to face him but don't trust myself to talk. He jogs to the porch and a takes a deep breath. "Her name's Asia. I thought it was over, but things might get . . . serious."

"Why are you telling me this?"

"I . . ." He shrugs. "I wanted you to hear it from me first."

"Good night, Sam."

When I get back into the house, Hanna's on the couch, her legs curled under her, her laptop perched on the coffee table. "Is Sam okay?"

"Yeah, he's fine. He just wanted to talk to me about Max." Hanna's whole body flinches at the mention of her unrequited love, and I hate myself a little more than usual for bringing up his name. "Nothing like that," I say. "Just trying to get me to join the gym to support Max. *As if*, right?"

Hanna's eyes go a little hazy, and I know I've thrown her off the trail of my troubles for a couple of minutes.

"I'm going to go finish painting."

Back in my room, a four-by-four patch of pink wall stares at me. Suddenly, I regret everything—pretending I was okay with Sam, painting my room, going to his house last night . . . the whole damn weekend.

I rush to the bathroom and turn on the shower, wiping the tears from my face as fast as they fall. I'm not sure what makes me grab my phone, but I text Connor.

Her name's Asia. That's all I know.

Then I climb into the shower, lean against the wall, and let the hot spray wash away my foolish hopes and all my naïve beliefs that I might be something special to him.

EPILOGUE

Sam
Two Years Later...

HER DATE is at least fifteen years older than her and could probably find steady work as a stunt double for Smokey the Bear.

Not that I care. I definitely don't care who Liz Thompson is sleeping with.

She laughs at something Smokey says and then excuses herself and heads to the restroom, her tight ass swinging with every step.

"You're staring," Max says.

I bring my attention back to my table and find William and Max both studying me. Max is smirking. *Asshole.* "I'm not staring at anything."

"You were definitely staring," Will says. "And before you were staring at *her,* you were giving her date the I'm-going-to-hang-you-by-your-balls-over-a-pit-of-vipers look."

"Don't give him a hard time," Max says. "That's a completely normal reaction to have when you catch someone out with your wife . . . but wait. She's not your wife, is she? Or your girlfriend even? Huh."

Will smirks. "Can't tell by the way he's looking at her."

I lean back in the booth. "You're both assholes."

"You could just ask her out," Max suggests.

"I'll pass," I say, but the words come out as a growl, revealing too much. I clear my throat. "Excuse me."

I head back toward the bathrooms with a half-cocked plan to corner her and make her talk to me. But about what? We haven't talked since last summer—out of respect for my sister Della, I've kept my distance. The last thing my pregnant sister needs is to see her big brother making nice with the woman who nearly tore her world apart.

When I reach the back hallway, I spot Liz and my steps slow. Smokey the Bear must have snuck back here to meet her when I wasn't looking. He's shoving his tongue down her throat and feeling her up. *Jesus.* Couldn't they at least go somewhere private?

Smokey goes in for another kiss, and Liz turns her head to the side. "Sorry," she says. "I don't have sex on the first date. Ever."

I grunt and watch for a minute, wondering if he's going to buy the shit she's shoveling.

"Want me to take it slow, baby?" her date asks. "I can take it slow. With me, you'll want it to last all night."

"Listen, Ha—"

"If you'd excuse me," I say, interrupting. I can't stomach much more of this.

Liz narrows those pretty blue eyes at me and lifts her chin. "Did you need something?"

"Restroom." I point behind her.

She blushes prettily. Everything Liz does is pretty. The way she drinks a beer is pretty, the way she nuzzles her pillow in her sleep, the way she kisses her way down my stomach before . . .

Fuck that. I skim my eyes over her date. If that's what Liz wants, she can have it. There's no reason for me to stand in her way. I attempt a smile. "You two kids have fun."

I push into the bathroom and let the water run hot in the sink as I stare at myself in the mirror. "You don't need her, Bradshaw," I mutter at my reflection, and my stomach knots at the words. I may not need her, but I want her—a *want* that's so intoxicating, so potent, it masquerades as *need.* I want her. I miss her. But none of that matters because I can't forgive her.

SOMETHING RECKLESS

NEW YORK TIMES BESTSELLING AUTHOR

LEXI RYAN

CHAPTER
ONE

Liz

Riverrat69: *I'm jealous of your date tomorrow.*

Tink24: *Why? I thought you didn't like dating.*

Riverrat69: *I'm jealous of what he gets to do to you. Or maybe I'm just thinking of what I'd do to you if I were your date.*

Tink24: *Do tell . . .*

Riverrat69: *I'd start by making sure you wore a*

skirt. With nothing underneath.

Tink24: *Maybe that could be arranged . . .*

Riverrat69: *I'd take you somewhere with really good wine, and I'd have you sit next to me in the booth so I could watch you enjoy your food and your wine, and so it would be easier to slide my hand under your skirt. Have you ever gotten off in the middle of a crowded room?*

Tink24: *Can't say that I have . . . Not sure that I could . . .*

Riverrat69: *Don't worry. I'd get you there. My touch would be light at first, warming you up while you sipped your wine. Then I'd slide a finger inside of you and whisper in your ear. The waiter would come over, and you'd have to order. I think it would turn you on—knowing I was touching you like that and we could so easily get caught.*

Tink24: *It might. If you played it right.*

Riverrat69: *Oh, I'd play it right. Soon, I'd add a second finger and feel you squeeze around me. Are you a screamer? Because the key to getting off in public is not letting anyone else know what's happening under the table. Could you be quiet while I fucked you with my fingers?*

Tink24: *I think I could manage, but what about you in all of this?*

Riverrat69: *This is just the foreplay, baby. If you're wet, I'm good.*

Tink24: *I would be . . . I am.*

Riverrat69: *It'd be after the restaurant. After I got you off right there in public, after I watched pleasure wash over your face as you came, then it would be my turn.*

Tink24: *Would you take me home? Tie me up?*

Riverrat69: *Maybe we'd go to your place but I'd bring everything I needed to tie you to the bed. Would you like that?*

Tink24: *I want that.*

Riverrat69: *Since this is all just a fantasy and we both know you'll be with some other idiot tomorrow night, would you do me a favor?*

Tink24: *What's that?*

Riverrat69: *Put your hand in your panties.*

Tink24: *Who said I'm wearing panties?*

SOMETHING RECKLESS

Riverrat69: *You're going to be the death of me.*

REREADING LAST NIGHT'S CONVERSATION has me shifting uncomfortably in bed. One hell of a way to start my day, but I went to sleep thinking about him, dreamed about him, woke with him on my mind.

I close my eyes and picture everything he described. I imagine Sam next to me in the restaurant. Sam whispering dirty words in my ear while he fingers me under the table.

I press my head into the pillow and whimper. Sam would do those things. And as much as I question my ability to orgasm in a public place, I know Sam could do it. He'd have me coming on his hand before dessert came. And after . . .

Rolling over, I bury my face in the pillow. It doesn't matter what would happen next. Like River said, everything he described is just a fantasy. And this idea in my head that my anonymous online friend—who likes to talk dirty to me, who wants to tie me up—the idea that he is Sam, that Sam is River, that's probably just a fantasy too. Albeit a long-running one.

And if it is Sam, the idea that he could forgive me enough to want to do those things with me again? That's definitely a fantasy.

Sam

I plunge my hands into her hair and open my mouth against her breast, drawing her nipple between my teeth—a little rough, just like she likes it. She's blindfolded and her hands are stretched above her head, tied with my ropes to the second floor banister. She's completely at my mercy, a fact that arouses us both.

I'm working my way down her body, kissing, tasting, licking every inch of skin along the way. Liz moans my name. I don't stop. Instead, I suck at the tender flesh over her hipbone and slide my hand between her legs, where she's hot and slick and ready for me.

"Sam!" she screams this time. "Sam! Sam!" Then again and again until my name becomes more of a piercing screech than a word.

Groaning, I roll over and smack the snooze button on my alarm clock with more force than necessary. I'm not interested in examining why I'm dreaming about Liz Thompson when I don't even talk to her anymore. The dreams are frequent and increasingly frustrating, and my cock doesn't give two shits that I shouldn't want her, so I take my dick in my fist, close my eyes, and imagine Liz tied up like she was in my dream.

I tighten my grip and imagine cradling her ass in my hands as I drive into her so hard the walls rattle. I can practically hear the breathy little noises she makes when I'm touching her. And though my hand is a piss-poor substitute for being inside her body, the fantasy makes jacking off more satisfying than usual and has

SOMETHING RECKLESS

me coming hard and fast before the alarm sounds again.

CHAPTER TWO

Liz

ONCE UPON A TIME, I believed there was nothing I loved more in this world than a dirty-talking man—the scratch of his beard against my neck between quiet suggestions in my ear, the low rumble of his voice, the heady intoxication of knowing where the night was going, knowing he wanted the same things I did.

But I was wrong. Because while a lot of men can talk dirty, I can count on one hand the number of men I've met who can do it well. In my dating escapades of the last eight months, I've learned there are two kinds of dirty talkers in this world: the ones who use language like foreplay and make my knees turn to putty, and the ones who talk dirty by channeling bad rap lyrics.

"I wanna put it in you, baby," my date says.

His name is Harry. And he is—hairy, I mean. He's the kind of guy who wears his polo shirt unbuttoned so thick tufts of wiry chest hair stick out. I'm not opposed to chest hair, but I am in favor of grooming and trimming where appropriate. If that's the condition of the stuff on his chest, can you imagine what's happening under his briefs?

"You want me to put it in you, don't you?" He sounds so sure of himself.

No, hairy Harry, I don't want *it* anywhere near me. But I don't say that. He's between the ages of twenty-three and thirty-four (or so says his profile), has a steady job, loves his family, and is looking for someone to settle down with, preferably in New Hope. These are all the qualities I'm looking for in a man, and I'm supposed to be giving him a chance. I *want* to give him a chance.

Hot bodies and stellar bedroom skills have always been my priorities when choosing what men to date—which probably explains why I'm twenty-four and haven't had a single romantic relationship that lasted longer than three months.

"Hmm," I reply, dodging a second beer-flavored kiss. "Sorry, I don't have sex on the first date. Ever." *Anymore* would be more accurate than *ever*, but I don't think God cares about lying when it's done to avoid regrettable sex.

We're in the back hallway at Brady's. I met Harry here for a drink, and he cornered me after I finished in the ladies' room, which was an expert seduction move on his part because nothing says "sexy" like the smell of urine and stale beer.

His breath is hot and sticky against my neck, his hand inching up my shirt. I grab his wrist to stop him, and decide to give a mental count to ten before pushing him off me. He seemed nice online. Maybe nerves are the reason behind tonight's metamorphosis into a douchecanoe.

"You want me to take it slow, baby? I can take it slow. With me, you'll want it to last all night."

Yeah, I doubt that. "Listen, Ha—"

"If you'd excuse me?" a deep voice asks.

I push Harry back so I can see over his shoulder and find myself looking at Sam Bradshaw. Sam *God-Between-the-Sheets* Bradshaw. Sam *Knows-What-I-Look-Like-Naked* Bradshaw.

The look on Sam's face says he has witnessed more of my private time with Harry than even *I* wanted to witness. I'm not sure *mortification* is a strong enough word for what I'm feeling right now.

I lift my chin. "Did you need something?"

Sam points behind me. "Restroom."

"Oh. Right."

Sam gives Harry a once-over then looks at me, smirking a little. "You two kids have fun."

Now there's a man who knows how to talk dirty. Sam pushes through the swinging door into the restroom. He's all broad shoulders and swagger. And there's not a tuft of chest hair in sight.

Harry clears his throat. "You know him?"

Biblically. "He's an old friend."

He nods toward the back exit. "Wanna bounce, baby?"

I'm trying, I really am, to keep an open mind about men who don't look like Sam Bradshaw—men who don't *turn me on* like Sam Bradshaw—but a thirty-something white dude with a gut shouldn't try to talk like the frat guys down the road at Sinclair University.

"I'll take you back to my place," he continues. "Show you what I have to offer." He winks at me—to make sure I'm picking up on the double entendre, I guess.

I shift uncomfortably. "Sorry, Harry, but I meant it when I said I don't have sex on the first date."

Of course Sam would choose that moment to appear again. Sam, for whom I've put out on two different occasions and with whom I've gone on a grand total of zero dates. He grunts softly, flashes a knowing grin, then heads toward the barroom and leaves me alone with horny, hairy Harry.

"We don't have to have intercourse. I'll show you a real man can give you pleasure without crossing that line."

"It's just that . . ."

"Tell me what you want, baby."

I know what Harry means, but my eyes are on Sam's retreating form and I can't stop thinking that what I *want* is a second chance. With Sam. "Nothing. I'm just tired."

"Next time, then." He pulls me forward and presses a wet kiss on my mouth, sucking both of my lips

102

between his. I'm not sure if he's trying to kiss me or eat me. *Yuck.* "Night, sugar."

I mumble a good night and watch him exit through the back door, simultaneously relieved and defeated when I'm alone again.

What am I supposed to do with myself now?

I could go home to my empty house and warm up a TV dinner, but that would be a lonely reminder of why I'm driven to dating guys like horrible Harry. I could surprise my twin, Hanna, at her house and visit my gorgeous little nieces, but then I'd have to watch my soon-to-be brother-in-law drool over my twin. Nate's adoration would remind me why guys like Harry will never seem good enough. Or I could spend some quality time on the job websites, continuing my seemingly endless search for a new job.

Drinking it is.

I head to the bar and wave down Brady, the owner of this dive my friends and I love so much.

"That guy? Really?" Brady says.

I shrug. Brady's seen me meet a lot of guys for drinks in the last few months, not many of them more than once. "He looked good on paper."

He pours me a shot and hands it to me across the bar. "If you're going to start going for the older men, I'd like to take a number."

I grin, then shoot back the tequila, welcoming the warmth it sends humming into my chest. "He claims to be thirty-four. And anyway, I don't think I could keep up with you." I return the shot glass to his wrinkled, age-spotted hand.

SOMETHING RECKLESS

Chuckling, he refills the glass. "Not many girls can." Then, more seriously, "Still no prospects?"

I shake my head. "It's possible I'll be single forever."

"Maybe not," he says.

His eyes shift to the other side of the bar, and I follow his gaze to the booth where Sam is sitting with his best friends, William Bailey and Max Hallowell. Will and Max are laughing about something, but Sam's eyes are on me. He holds my gaze for a moment before turning back to his friends, and my heart stutters out its disappointment.

"Sam and I wouldn't be a good match," I tell Brady as I straighten in my seat. Like any barkeep worth his salt, Brady knows more about my love-life woes than my best friends do—mostly because my best friends are so busy with their perfect love lives that I don't want to bore them with my hopeless one.

"Why would you say that?"

Because he can't forgive me for one drunken night of poor judgment. "He's the consummate playboy," I say instead. "Fun when I was younger, but not the kind of man who wants to settle down and make babies." The thought of making babies with Sam sends my pulse into a tizzy. Now *that* would be fun. Le sigh.

"I think you're underestimating him," Brady says.

I shrug. "Call it women's intuition." Or *once bitten, twice shy.* I know the score with Sam. I learned it the hard way the first time we hooked up. By the time I decided I needed second helpings, I knew what to expect. Or, better yet, what not to expect.

"I call it foolish," Brady says with a shake of his head. "You keep fishing for men in that barrel of losers called the internet and act shocked every time you reel in a dud."

I take my second shot, grimacing a little less this time. "There are plenty of men who do online dating who aren't losers."

He huffs. "You haven't brought any of them *here*." With that, he heads to the other end of the bar to wait on a new customer. I'm left staring at my empty shot glass and contemplating my equally empty life.

No job. No boyfriend. No prospects.

My phone dings in my purse—not just any notification ding, but the special tone assigned to the Something Real chat application. The sound makes my lips curl into a smile and my stomach flutter in anticipation. It shouldn't, but it does. There's only one person who contacts me using that app, and the idea of a new message from him always brings a smile to my lips.

Riverrat69: *How'd the date go?*

Tink24: *Let's put it this way—my sister's Rottweiler's kisses do more for me. I'm officially striking out with this dating thing.*

Ever since my sisters and best friends started finding their true loves, I've been determined to take my own dating life more seriously. I've always been more interested in the hottest guy in the room than the most stable one, but those days are over. After my Super Summer Screw-Up, I decided it was time to step up my game, and started using online dating sites, but the traditional online dating route has gotten me nowhere. Brady's right about that, and tonight's date with Harry the Horrible is evidence enough.

While I haven't given up on the ForeverLove.coms of the world, I decided to roll the dice and gave a new service a shot. Something Real is the hot new dating website for New Hopers. Some web developer put the program together and has it in beta testing for people in and around the New Hope area. What makes Something Real unique is that it doesn't allow its users to share pictures or even names until they hit certain relationship benchmarks. That's how I met Riverrat69, my anonymous friend and current obsession.

Something Real is all about the kind of commitment I'm looking for—people who want babies and forever and old-age handholding. Only, River wasn't on there looking for love. He's someone who had an opportunity to invest in the program. He wanted to try it out and explore the user experience before ponying up the cash the developer needs to take the site to the next level.

River doesn't want any of the things I do, and he's been clear about that from the start. But we hit it off anyway.

Over the last two months, we've gotten into the habit of sending each other messages throughout the day, and I anticipate each one like an addict waiting for her next hit. I like him, but after all this time, as far as I can tell, the only thing he wants from me is to tie me up and make me come.

Not so different from what Sam Bradshaw once said he wanted from me.

My phone vibrates in my hand as his next message comes through.

Riverrat69: *You can do better than that guy anyway.*

How does he know? I sink my teeth into my lower lip. Is that just a generic thing someone says, or does he know whom I was with tonight? I glance over my shoulder back to the table where Sam is sitting. Max is on the phone and William is gone, and Sam has his phone is in his hand, and he's typing something. My heart shimmies in tandem with my girl parts, and I tell both to calm the eff down.

Sam lifts his head and his eyes lock with mine. When my phone buzzes in my hand again, I jump.

Riverrat69: *I have a confession.*

Tink24: *What's that?*

Riverrat69: *I can't stop looking at that last picture.*

I close my eyes and try to imagine my faceless friend looking at the picture I sent him before work this morning. After rereading last night's texts left me hot and bothered, sending a picture of my hip was the best outlet for my sexual frustration.

SOMETHING RECKLESS

From the beginning, we seemed to have an unspoken agreement that we'd keep it anonymous, but I've sent him pictures. My bare legs stretched out in bed from the knees down, my toes after a pedicure, my ass in a new pair of black panties—pieces to an erotic puzzle I desperately want him to solve.

Tink24: *I'll confess, I hoped you'd have that problem.*

Riverrat69: *I can't talk right now, but message me when you climb in bed tonight.*

Suddenly, climbing into bed alone again sounds better than it has in weeks. I reread his message. *Can't talk right now.*

Snapping my head up again, I see Sam sitting with his phone under his hand. I was so absorbed in River's messages I forgot to watch to see if Sam was typing before each new one.

I don't know if my online friend lives in New Hope, but I know he lives in the area and that he went to New Hope High School. I know he has a big family and that he's in finance, like Sam. I know he's been burned by love and doesn't want commitment.

I know he dirty-talks like a pro and wants to tie me up—and so began my suspicions that the anonymous stranger I've been talking to isn't a stranger at all. Every clue points to Sam Bradshaw, God's gift to women everywhere. The suspicions started early in our exchanges, but I disregarded them as wishful thinking.

However, every clue pointed to him, and for as long as we've been swapping dirty messages, I've been picturing Sam.

I force myself to turn away from him. My only problem now is that I can't decide if River is really Sam or if I just want him to be.

Okay, that's not my only problem. If River really is Sam, that presents a whole new list of problems. On the top of that list? Since my Super Summer Screw-Up, Sam hates me.

When I look over again and see he's left, relief washes over me. Because I'm a coward, and I'm not ready to admit to myself how much I want Sam to be the man I've been talking to online.

Sam

"Hello there, Mr. Bradshaw."

The sound of that voice makes me go cold, but I refuse to let my body tense.

Asia Franks is sitting in the glow of my front porch light. Her dark hair is cut in short little wisps that lie close to her scalp and give full attention to her big blue eyes. She's wearing a skimpy skirt not at all appropriate for the weather, and a cigarette hangs from her fingertips.

With the exception of the occasional cigar with my

friends, I've never been a smoker. But the sight of her alone is enough to make me want to steal the cigarette and smoke it down to the filter.

"Asia," I reply, my voice cold.

She cocks her head to the side and gives me one of those looks she uses to so skillfully manipulate the men around her. "Now why can't you act happy to see me? It's been *so long*."

"Not long enough."

She sticks out her lower lip in a pout. I can't believe I once fell for that. "Fine. Be that way."

I cross my arms and give her a pointed look, waiting.

"Baby, it's cold out here. Aren't you going to invite me in?"

"I don't want you anywhere near my house, let alone inside it."

As if I flipped a switch, her face hardens, all that affected sweetness disappearing in a blink. "Some things never change, and I see you're still a dick."

"Tell me what you want. I don't like being this close to you."

She stands carefully, dropping the cigarette to the porch floor and stomping it out with the toe of her red high heel. "I need some money."

"Not gonna happen." I pull my keys from my pocket, ready to go inside and lock her out. I don't need to hear whatever sob story she has for me. I've fallen for her shit before, and I won't again. Not this time.

"The last two years have been so hard on me," she says. "I was so depressed I could hardly get out of bed most days. I used up all my savings just trying to pay my bills."

I snort. The "savings" she's referring to is the nest egg I set her up with when I thought she was going to have my baby. If Asia had a penny in the bank before she pissed on a stick for me, I'd be surprised. I shove the key into the lock and push open the door. "Go find another sucker."

Her eyes flash with anger but her voice is coy again, the sweet, ever-suffering Asia. "You can't just ignore me. Not when you're the reason I'm so depressed."

When she hangs her head dramatically, I look over my shoulder to see who she's performing for and, yeah, sure enough, Mrs. O'Neil is on her front porch watching us.

"Everything okay, Sam?"

"Don't push me away, Sam," Asia says dramatically. She blinks a few times and produces a few tears. "Not without talking to me first."

"Sam?" Mrs. O'Neil calls again.

"Everything's fine," I reply. "Do you want to talk about this in the house?" I ask Asia. It's all I can do not to spit the words.

Asia gives me a satisfied smile—"As a matter of fact . . ."—then strolls right into my house.

I'm a pretty easygoing guy, and there's a very short list of people who aren't welcome in my home. Asia Franks is at the top of it. And yet here she is.

I pull the door closed behind me. "I'm not giving you any money."

"Sure you are," she says, sauntering into the house and surveying the open-concept space. "You're going to give me whatever I want, because you don't want my story ruining your happy little life."

Her eyes scan the room, and I know what she's looking for—anything of value, anything to prove to her that the world is unfair and some people get everything while she gets nothing. Anything to justify her blackmailing me.

I cross my arms. "You don't have a story that anyone wants to hear."

She sticks out her lower lip again. "Why do you hate me so much?"

Because you stole something that was mine.

"I think a lot of people will be interested in my story. Especially now that your daddy is running for governor. I understand he has some stiff competition in the primaries."

"His son got drunk and screwed a stripper. The voters have forgiven worse."

She sighs heavily. "What I think they'd find interesting is the part where you made me . . ." She looks me dead in the eye and blinks those fake-ass tears back into her eyes. "The part where you made me get an abortion. I would have done anything to keep my baby."

Rage screams through me so fast and so hard that I've taken three long strides toward her before I force myself to stop and clench my hands at my sides. "You fucking cunt. What did I ever do to you?" Anger and hatred drip from my voice.

Her eyes go hard, and she pulls something from her pocket. When she produces a tiny recorder, I stumble back a few steps. I know exactly how our exchange will sound to anyone she shares it with. And I know she won't hesitate to share it with anyone who can give her something she wants.

"What do you want from me?"

She closes the distance between us and runs her hands down my chest. I don't move her hands because I'm afraid of what I might do if I let myself touch her. I've never hated anyone in my life as much as I hate her. I've never wanted to hurt a woman, but I want to hurt her. "I can't forgive you for that, you know," she whispers. "You made me think . . ."

That line is for the recording, no doubt. "How much?"

"Ten thousand will get me out of your hair."

"And if I refuse?"

"I'll come forward with my story."

"I'll tell them the truth."

She trails her fingers down the buttons on my shirt, one at a time. "Obviously you'd lie to protect your father from scandal. Just like you paid me to have the abortion to protect your family from scandal."

I grab her wrists and squeeze. "Ten thousand, and then you're out of my life."

"Of course. I'm not asking for more than I need to get by. You don't know how hard it's been for me." Her gaze flicks to her wrist where I'm squeezing. "I think you're bruising me. What will people think?"

I release her and step back. "I'll get you the money."

"I'm glad we understand each other." She swings her hips as she walks to the door.

I'll never forget that night two years ago when Asia showed up at my house. My head was already buzzing from Liz showing up at my office, and then there was Asia, waiting to grant my wish, telling me she'd have the baby.

I was so stunned and grateful I had to remind myself to breathe. I cupped Asia's face in my hands and studied her. "You promise?" I don't know what I was looking for there, but I stared at her until I was sure I could believe her.

"I promise."

Then I kissed her—not because I loved her or planned to make a life with her. I kissed her because I understood she was giving me a gift.

After she left, I showered and dressed and went back to Lizzy's house. I'm a private person, but I wanted to tell Liz about Asia and the baby. I was venturing into unknown territory and I needed a friend. I wanted Liz to be that friend, to be part of my life.

When I got to her house, she was different somehow. More distant. Almost like she was embarrassed to look at me. I took her on a walk and stared at the changing leaves as I tried to figure out what to say. I'd never asked a girl to go steady with me, I'd never wanted to, so I had no idea how to start with Liz.

When I finally broke the silence, I said, "I know we said it was just a fling ..."

She smiled at me, a strained, tight expression. "No strings, no attachments, no expectations. You're not here because you've changed your mind on me, are you?"

Something in the back of my mind warned me that *this* was the real reason I'd never asked a woman for more than sex. *She doesn't want you*, it warned. "I—" And when I told her another woman was going to have my baby? Did I really expect that to help my cause? "A friend gave me some news this morning and I wondered if I could take you out. Talk to you about it."

"I'm kind of busy." She looked away. "No expectations, Sam. But that goes both ways, okay? I don't want this to be all awkward now."

She'd taken what I offered, but she didn't want more. I swallowed hard, wanting to say something more than goodbye. "You're special, Rowdy. Sometimes I get the feeling you don't actually know that."

"I'm just a girl who needed a good lay. Thanks for that."

Her words were dull and sharp all at once and sawed their way into my chest like a rusty serrated blade. "I don't even know what to make of you."

"Do you really need to know?" She shifted awkwardly then. "Can you do me a favor? Don't tell anyone about our little . . . indiscretion? I'd like to keep it our secret. I don't want people getting the wrong idea about me."

I wish I could say that was the first time in my life a woman had made me feel cheap, like a dirty secret she didn't want the world to know about. I wish she'd been the first to make me feel I had no purpose to her outside the bedroom. Maybe if I hadn't been so adept at that kind of relationship with women, I would have fought harder for her. Maybe she would have been my girl and last summer would have never happened. "Who would I tell?" I asked.

And so I went to the gym and I had a long, sweaty workout, pushing myself until the ache in my gut transformed into a throbbing protest from screaming lungs and exhausted muscles. I never told anyone about my night with Liz, and I never told anyone about Asia, never told a soul that I was going to be a father and that I was thrilled and excited and terrified all at once.

I didn't have to tell anyone because Asia used my money to get herself some new furniture, and a nice little cushion in her savings account, and the next time I heard from her, she was calling to tell me she'd had the abortion and that she didn't want to hear from me again.

CHAPTER THREE

Liz

W<small>HEN</small> I <small>GET HOME</small>, the house is eerily quiet. Most nights I miss the days Hanna and I lived here together. She's my twin sister and best friend. We grew up sharing a room and went on to share a dorm and then this house in college. I miss having her here, but tonight, I'm glad for the privacy because I have an anonymous stranger who wants to chat when I get into bed.

I take a shower, shampoo my hair, and wash the smell of bar and Harry off my skin. Instead of the yoga pants and sweatshirt I typically choose in the winter, I put on a thin black slip that slides over my skin and makes me feel sexy as hell. He won't be seeing me, but that doesn't mean I don't want to feel good—sexy is a state of mind, after all.

I grab my laptop and climb into bed. Even though we both have the chat client on our phones, we do the majority of our chatting from keyboards; it's so much easier to type out significant chunks of text that way.

I wriggle into my pillows and power up my computer. My chat client opens immediately, and I can't help but smile when I see the green light by his name.

Tink24: *Wait for me long?*

Riverrat69: *It was worth it. How are you feeling?*

Tink24: *Better since I showered the reminder of tonight's date off me.*

Riverrat69: *That doesn't sound good. Do I need to find this guy and kick his ass?*

Tink24: *Ha! Thanks for the offer, but it was nothing like that. I'm just feeling . . . frustrated.*

Riverrat69: *Romantically or sexually?*

Tink24: *Both, to be honest.*

Riverrat69: *It blows my mind that a girl like you doesn't have guys lining up outside her door.*

Tink24: *A girl like me? What does that mean?*

Riverrat69: *Funny. Smart. Sexy as fuck.*

Tink24: *You've never seen me. How do you know I'm sexy?*

Riverrat69: *You can tell a lot from a girl's hip . . . and the kind of panties she wears.*

Tink24: *Well, my looks have never been my problem. I'm not saying I'm a knockout, but there are always guys willing to sleep with me if that's what I want.*

Riverrat69: *But you want . . . something more.*

Tink24: *I do. I won't apologize for that. Why don't you?*

Riverrat69: *I did once. It didn't turn out like I'd hoped.*

Tink24: *What does that mean?*

I squeeze my eyes shut, full aware of what a mind-fuck I'm putting myself through by having this conversation with Maybe Sam, trying to read too much into everything he says.

I exhale slowly and open my eyes to see the cursor

still blinking at me—no reply from him. I should back down from my too-personal question.

Tink24: *You don't have to answer that.*

Riverrat69: *No. It's okay. I'm just not sure how to answer. Don't settle, okay? I know you're looking for a meaningful relationship and it can be frustrating, but don't settle for someone who doesn't make your heart race.*

Sam makes my heart race. *You make my heart race,* I type, but then I hold down the delete key until the words disappear.

Riverrat69: *Tell me about your dream guy. What's he like?*

I stare at my computer for a long time, my heart pounding. Once, I'd thought Sam was my dream guy. I wanted him for so long, and when we finally got together, it was . . . perfect. Hot and sexy, but also intense in a way I would almost describe as emotional. I have no one to blame but myself for any expectations I had after that night. Sam warned me he wasn't interested in forever.

"I don't do emotional strings."

And silly, naive me. I thought he wanted me to save him, to be the one who changed that about him.

I went to his house and saw him with her. Some woman I didn't even recognize. It wasn't fair to be hurt by what I saw. He hadn't made me any promises. But the way he held her. The way he was *looking* at her.

He hadn't wanted me to fix him, but he was looking at her like she *had*. And seeing that broke my heart.

Riverrat69: *Never mind. That's stupid.*

Shaking my head, I put my fingers back on my keyboard. I want to type: *Is this Sam Bradshaw?* But I don't. I'm not ready to know for sure yet. More, I'm not ready for him to know who I am.

Tink24: *It's not stupid, just not an easy question to answer.*

Riverrat69: *Try?*

Tink24: *My sister's fiancé bought her a dog. Not a puppy—they have two infants, so a puppy would just be cruel. He bought her a dog. Her name is Nana, like the dog in Peter Pan. She's a sweet thing and she's used to kids, but her original owner realized their child was allergic, so they needed to find a new home.*

Her fiancé is a good guy, and I always liked him, but when he brought home that dog, I think I fell in love with him. What woman wouldn't love a man who buys her a dog?

Riverrat69: *So you want a man who will buy you a dog?*

Tink24: *I want a man who knows when I need a dog.*

I frown. These obscure, personal-but-vague conversations have become the norm for us. The sad thing is, even without personal details and even while trying to protect my own identity, I feel more connected with this man than I have with any of the dates I've been on in the last eight months. That scares me. I'm starting to wonder if I'm doomed to be single forever.

Riverrat69: *I hope you find him. I do.*

Tink24: *Enough about me. How was your day?*

Riverrat69: *That picture just about killed me this morning. Do you have any idea how hard it is to finish a business meeting when a beautiful woman sends you a picture of her ass?*

Tink24: *Sorrynotsorry?*

Riverrat69: *You're the whole package. Brains, body, humor. You make me . . .*

Tink24: *What?*

Riverrat69: *You make me believe there could be more. You make me want something more.*

Tink24: *You've always been clear on the score.*

I hesitate for a minute, and then type.

Tink24: *What if we know each other? I mean, outside of Something Real.*

I hold my breath as I wait for his response. Either the oxygen deprivation makes time slow to a crawl or it takes longer than usual for him to reply.

Riverrat69: *New Hope is a small place. It's possible we do.*

I start to type *Do you live in New Hope now?* but I erase it before I can send it. The question would break our unspoken agreement to keep this anonymous. And, if I'm honest, there's part of me that likes the anonymity. Almost as if knowing his name makes him real, and once he's real I have to let him go to make room for the real relationship I promised myself I'd find.

I roll to my stomach and, settling the laptop in front of me, reposition the screen so the camera is aimed right at my exposed cleavage. I attach the pic to a new message and send it, my way of reminding myself exactly what this is and what it isn't.

Riverrat69: *Jesus. You're killing me.*

Tink24: *I like thinking of you looking at me. Even if*

only one tiny piece at a time.

Riverrat69: *This morning, when you sent that picture, all I could think about was taking those panties off you. My dick was so hard, I could hardly focus at my meeting.*

Tink24: *Tell me what you were focusing on.*

Riverrat69: *How I want to tie you to the bed and undress you while you watch. I want to taste every inch of you—starting at your neck and working my way down. I'd kiss your breasts and your belly, and when I finally reached your legs, I'd spread them wide so I could look at you before I pressed my face between your thighs.*

Something feels off for a minute—the coldness of the black words on the white screen—but then I close my eyes and imagine *Sam* whispering those words in my ear, and I have to squeeze my legs together to shut out the ache there. The movement only makes it worse. This is torture. I need to stop or I need more—to meet him, to know his name, to take him up on all the suggestions he's made over the last few weeks.

Riverrat69: *Sleep well, sexy. I'll talk to you tomorrow.*

I watch the little green light by his screen name change to gray and then stare dumbly at the screen for a few moments. I close my computer, bury my face into my pillow, and scream.

***

A girl could gain five pounds just by walking into this bakery, and I would gladly grow a gut and a couple of extra chins if it meant that I got to continue this early-morning tradition for the rest of my life.

The bell rings as I push through the glass doors and into my twin sister's bakery, Coffee, Cakes, and Confections. Our oldest sister, Krystal, is working behind the counter this morning, organizing the coffee filters or something. She came in last Christmas and started managing the place for Hanna while Hanna had to be on pregnancy bed rest. When Hanna came back after the twins were born, she kept Krystal so she could focus on the baking and take more time off. And, honestly, Krystal's good at running this place—better at it than I was, not that Hanna ever complained.

"Good morning, Liz," Krystal says. "Coffee?"

"Please. And could you dump, like, half a cup of that caramel sauce into it?"

Krystal, ever the health-conscious one, raises an eyebrow but does as I ask. I help myself to a chocolate croissant. Life is too short to not eat Hanna's chocolate croissants. Seriously.

"I heard you had another date last night," Krystal says, handing me my coffee.

"Where did you hear that?" I ask around a bite of chocolate and pastry dough. Jesus, this crap is good.

"*New Hope Tattler*," she informs me.

I scowl. "Why do they care about my love life? Is there seriously nothing more interesting happening in this town?"

"There was a full spread about Hanna's wedding too," Krystal says. She shrugs. "It's New Hope. What's there to say?"

"Is the bride-to-be in the back?"

"Elbow deep in fondant," Krystal says.

"Nowhere else I'd rather be," Hanna calls from the kitchen.

Grinning, I take my coffee and croissant and follow the sound of her voice. "Isn't there a rule about how brides shouldn't make their own wedding cakes?" I ask when I spot her rolling a thin sheet of fondant icing. I used to hate the crap, but that was because I'd never tried Hanna's.

"If there is, it's a stupid rule," she says. She's glowing today. Come to think of it, she's been glowing every day since Nate moved to town, and then her radiance tripled after she had her twin girls.

My heart tugs with the potent cocktail of envy and happiness I've grown accustomed to feeling every time I'm near her. There's no one in the world who deserves happiness as much as my twin, and I could kiss Nate's feet for giving it to her. But I so badly want a little of what she has. I want it so much it almost hurts.

"How was the date last night?" she asks.

"So you didn't read about it in the *Tattler*?"

She rolls her eyes. "I did. Right before I read about how Taylor Swift is rumored to be one of my bridesmaids."

I snort. "Fair enough, so the *Tattler* isn't always *accurate*, but anything horrible it said about my date with Harry was sadly probably true."

"It said he was a fifty-two-year-old carpet salesman from Terre Haute," she says with a cocked brow.

I wrinkle my nose. "He *said* he was thirty-four, but he may have been fudging by a couple of decades."

"That bad?"

I shrug. "It's not really about his age. I could go for a George Clooney older-man type. But there was absolutely no spark."

"You tried to find a spark?"

"He cornered me when I came out of the bathroom. Shoved his tongue down my throat in case I was hiding it there." I shake my head. "Then Sam appeared out of nowhere."

"Where were you again?"

"Brady's."

"You've gotta stop taking dates to Brady's if you don't want to run into Sam."

But maybe I *want* to run into Sam. Maybe I miss Sam. But I shake my head and take another bite of my croissant. Hanna knows about what happened with my Super Summer Screw-Up, and how much it changed my relationship with Sam. Not that there was a relationship to change . . . exactly. I wish he'd be more rational about it, but when it comes to Della, Sam isn't the analytical thinker he is every day at the bank. When it comes to Della, Sam is one hundred percent protective big brother.

I chase my pastry with sugar-laced coffee and finally feel a little better.

"How's the job hunt going?" she asks.

I'm going to make a T-shirt that says, "Nope, still don't have a boyfriend, still don't have a job." It would be for everyone else to reference, of course. Hanna's allowed to ask. "Nothing. How sad is it that I'm twenty-four years old and still don't know what I want to be when I grow up?"

"You can work here," she offers.

"You're the best for offering, but I'm determined to make it on my own. I'm a big girl now."

"It's too bad Della had to let your personal issues poison your business relationship. You were a great preschool teacher."

"Can I borrow those rose-colored glasses of yours?" I ask. "Because I was a terrible preschool teacher, and I pretty much hated it." I scrub my hands over my face. Sam's sister, Della, and I both have Elementary Education degrees, and last year when we couldn't find jobs, we decided to open our own preschool. It was all fine and dandy until she decided I was a harlot who must be thrust from her life.

Truth be told, I miss Della and our friendship more than I miss the preschool. As much as I always thought I wanted to work with kids, I found myself watching the clock every day, anxious for the minute I could leave the school and tell dirty jokes and curse like a sailor—in other words, be myself.

"You'll find something," Hanna says. "I know you will."

"Are you all set for this weekend?" I ask to change the subject.

Hanna beams. "I think so. I can't believe it's finally here."

"Well, let me know if you need anything. I've got plenty of free time on my hands." I press a kiss to Hanna's happily flushed cheek and then head back to the front of the bakery, where I find Mr. Bradshaw, Sam's father, standing at the counter, a cup of coffee in his hand.

"Mr. Bradshaw. How are you this morning?"

"It's a beautiful day. I think I smell the first snow in the air. Haven't seen your mother around headquarters much, Elizabeth. Where's she been keeping herself?" He hands several bills to Krystal, who blushes prettily under his attention. "Keep the change."

"She's been busy helping with my nieces," I tell him. "Between having twin girls and running a business, Hanna needs all the help she can get. But I know Mom's a supporter, and you have her vote."

He smiles, and his eyes crinkle in the corners. My mind goes to Sam. Will he age like this? The distinguished salt-and-pepper hair, the deep voice that gets huskier with age? Suddenly, I'm struck with the image of waking next to Sam when we're in our fifties, and my heart squeezes a little.

Stop making him out to be something he's not, I warn myself, but I've been getting a lot of those thoughts lately. I've been catching myself thinking of him in relationship terms, which is absurd, since he hates my guts. It's just everything with River makes me think maybe Sam might . . .

No. Nothing but hurt down that road.

"Della said you resigned from your position at the preschool," he says. "I hope she wasn't the reason."

I stiffen a little, but hopefully he can't tell. "Of course not," I lie. "It really wasn't my thing. I wanted it to be, but the truth is I still don't know what I want to be when I grow up. I need to find that thing I'm good at, I guess."

"Sam tells me you helped write the grants for the preschool and the new playground equipment."

Sam told him that? "That's true."

"Well, I was on the committee that selected the recipients, and your application was far and away the best we received." He studies me for a minute, then shifts. "You know, when you volunteered at the office last spring, I always admired the perspective you brought to getting my message out to the public. I was sorry not to see more of you."

"Oh, I've just been busy." I made myself scarce after the Super Summer Screw-Up, but since we all agreed to keep it quiet, Mr. Bradshaw doesn't know why I stopped volunteering.

"Well, it takes a village to run a gubernatorial campaign. I'll tell you what," he says. "Come by headquarters if you're interested. We'll put you to work and see if you're a good fit."

It surprises me that he thinks I might make a positive contribution to his campaign. Everyone assumes I'm ditzy, but this respected politician thinks I'm good enough to be part of his team. "I would love that." Seriously. Just like that, my day goes from meh to amazing.

"Great," he says, giving that charming politician grin. "You'll be working with my son-in-law. You know Connor, right?"

CHAPTER FOUR

Sam

I'M TWENTY-SEVEN YEARS OLD and still intimidated by my old man. Facing him for the first time since Asia walked in my door and threatened to destroy his campaign, I feel like the little boy who shattered a window with a baseball. Only worse. Because I don't have ten grand, and if I want to get Asia off my back, I'm going to have to get the money from my father.

I'd stand in line to get punched in the nuts before volunteering to have this conversation.

"You wanted to talk?" Dad asks when I step into his office.

I close the door behind me. My father pours us each two fingers of brandy and hands me one before sitting down.

"Thanks." He has no idea how much I need this. I take the seat across from him and swallow half of mine down, while he messes with his phone. "I have a problem."

If he was distracted before, I have my father's full attention now. He's that kind of dad. He might have one hundred and ten too many obligations on his plate at any given moment, but any time one of us kids has a problem, we get his absolute attention. Normally, I'm grateful for that, but right about now I'd like to be invisible while I confess what I've done.

"What is it?"

I roll back my shoulders, preparing for battle. Might as well rip off the Band-Aid. "A couple of years ago, I got a girl pregnant."

Dad stills and his face goes serious. "Didn't I teach you to always, *always* wear a condom?"

"Yes, sir." As much as I want to look at my feet or my drink, or anything but the disappointment in his eyes, I hold his gaze. He did teach me the importance of wearing a condom. And he taught me to hold a man's gaze while speaking. So I do. "I was drunk and maybe it broke, or maybe I forgot. I honestly don't know. I don't . . . remember."

"I suppose she's back to collect money for the baby now, huh? Jesus. Why didn't you tell me sooner? We could have had this taken care of."

I'm not sure what he means by that—not sure I *want*

to know what he means. "There is no baby. She got an abortion."

He closes his eyes and exhales, muttering something that sounds a lot like *Thank God.* Not exactly a moment potential voters would find charming. Then again, I'm not a potential voter. I'm his son.

I make myself breathe. I inhale and clench my hands into fists, exhale and release them. It's all I can do not to jump out of my chair and start shouting, but my father isn't the enemy. I know he's only thinking of me.

"I didn't want her to get an abortion," I finally say when I have my anger under control. "I begged her to keep the baby. I told her I'd take care of her. And at one point, I thought she was going to. She told me she would. But she ended up getting the abortion anyway, and now she's threatening to go to the media and tell them that I forced her to do it, that I coerced and threatened her. None of it's true, but she knows about your campaign and she wants money."

"Who is this woman? Someone local?"

Now it's harder to hold his gaze. "A stripper from Indy."

Dad's face hardens with sharp but fragile lines of disappointment. "You fucked a stripper and got her pregnant."

My throat is thick. There's nothing worse than disappointing my father.

"How much does she want?"

"Ten thousand dollars."

Dad settles his elbows on his desk and rests his head in his hands. I finish my brandy and stand to pour myself more.

"I'm sorry, Dad." I study the amber liquid. "I never thought my mistake could come back on you like this, but I should have known."

"We'll take care of it. I'll get my guys on it. We need to find out some facts first—was she really pregnant, was an abortion actually performed? She can't prove much, and with a woman like that, there's a good chance it wasn't even your baby, but she knows this will look bad, even if we can't prove a thing."

I nod.

"In the meantime, don't talk to her. Don't take her calls and don't let her get you alone. Give her information to Connor, and we'll damage-control this situation as best we can." He downs the rest of his brandy and studies me. "Is there anything else you need to tell me? Any other skeletons in your closet I should be prepared to have jump out at me?"

"No, sir."

"I'll see you at the house tonight. Your mom wants all her kids there for dinner."

I nod in agreement and leave his office, ready to put this shit day behind me.

Liz

"Weddings make me horny."

SOMETHING RECKLESS

My younger sister Maggie chokes on her beer, and my friend Cally giggles into her martini. A few middle-aged women at the table behind us turn to cast disapproving looks in my direction. Screw them. Weddings probably make them horny too, but after years of granny panties and stool softeners, they're too insecure to admit it.

We're at The Wire, where Mom invited all the out-of-town guests for cocktails. Tomorrow we'll caravan to Brown County for the wedding weekend.

Tonight, it's more than my sister's upcoming vows that are doing a number on me. That would be enough—there's something about one man promising forever to one woman that leaves me craving smexy times with the nearest male. But tonight, the general go-get-'em attitude of my sex drive has less to do with marriage vows and more to do with the promises made to me by a complete stranger. Last night's chat with River was cut too short for my liking, leaving me all tense and wound-up and needy. My body was disappointed when it had to settle for my hand to take care of business when my brain had been weaving all kinds of fantasies promising . . . *Sam.*

"What?" I say when my friends and sisters keep staring at me. "It's been a while. I'm glad I can still *get* horny. If I go much longer, my coochie is in danger of drying up."

"A while? Really?" Nix cocks an eyebrow in disbelief. "How long?"

I bite my lip and study her. She doesn't believe I've actually been abstaining. "A few months," I say.

She lifts a brow. "You had sex a few months ago and you're looking for sympathy from me?"

"You have *my* sympathies," Maggie says.

Cally chimes in with, "Mine too."

I scowl. I don't want to talk about this. Not really. Not when Cally, Maggie, and my own freaking twin are on their men like marathon bull riders. "Eight months." That's how long it's been since my Super Summer Screw-Up. "If we're talking actual *peen-meets-vag* sex, longer."

Nix taps her foot. No sympathy. "How long?" she repeats.

"Fourteen months," I say under my breath.

Maggie and Cally's jaws drop.

"Lizzy!" Nix screeches. "You're saying you haven't had sex since you hooked up with Sam at Will and Cally's wedding?"

"Quiet down!" I grind between my teeth, but Club Disapproval at the next table is shooting me evil looks again. "Your math skills are remarkable," I mutter to Nix.

"Jesus," she says. "Even *I've* had sex more recently than that. Are you sure you aren't forgetting a hookup?"

"I haven't had sex in *I'm-at-risk-of-growing-a-new-hymen* months, Nix. Trust me. I wouldn't forget."

Maggie snorts. "I think abstinence is starting to get to her too," she says to Nix. "Yesterday, I caught her eyeing the bratwurst in my fridge."

"It was a really nice bratwurst," I say, "and I was . . . hungry. Who am I kidding? Sex. I need some."

"Take your pick," Nix says, motioning to the various

men hanging around the bar. "There are any number of eligible bachelors here who would love to go home with you."

"Right. I'm sure," I mutter, running my eyes over the selection. But I'm not actually tempted. I don't want to have sex with just anyone. I don't need to be engaged or in love or anything, but it needs to be worth it. It's like eating a slice of deep-dish pizza. I'm no stranger to high-calorie foods—bring 'em on—but there's nothing worse than eating a thousand-calorie slice of pizza that leaves you thinking you could've had a V8. Sex is the same way. I don't just want penetration. I want bed-rocking, guaranteed-to-blow-your-fucking-mind sex. Can-I-haz-more-please? sex.

No. I don't just want sex. I want sure-to-be-amazing, wake-the-neighbors-and-make-the-dogs-howl sex. Any noble thoughts of waiting to meet my true love are off the table at this point. I want something reckless.

As if on cue, my phone buzzes. I hide it under the table so the girls don't see it before I read the message.

Riverrat69: *God help me, I can't stop thinking about you.*

"You *are* looking hot tonight," Hanna says.

I grin. Because of the message I just received and because Hanna's right. Tonight I wore red—the color that looks best with my pale skin and blond curls. I pulled my hair off my neck and donned my highest heels. None of this would come as a surprise to anyone who knows me—I don't like to leave the house unless

I'm "camera-ready," as Mom would say. For evidence of what's on a woman's mind, you need to look beyond her clothes to what she's wearing underneath.

And anyone who could see what I'm wearing under this dress—and how very little—would know that Lizzy Thompson has a secret. *Boy, do I.*

Biting back my smile so they're not suspicious, I hit the button to close the chat client that the object of my fantasies uses to talk to me.

"Look at you." Maggie chortles. "I see it in your eyes. You already have something planned. Miss Abstinence isn't going to hold out much longer."

"I'm not that lucky," I say, but I wink at her as I take a long drink while mentally composing my reply to the message.

"How's the search for Mr. Right going?" Cally asks.

"I get trying online dating, but I can't believe you're trying that new service," Maggie says. "What happens if you hit it off with someone and there's no physical attraction when you meet? Isn't that going to be awkward? 'Sorry, George. You have a great personality, and I thought I liked you, but I fancy six-pack stomachs, and you're sporting more of a keg.'"

I snort and shake my head. Ever since I signed up for Something Real, the girls have been questioning my sanity. Nix is the only one in the group who knows what it's like to be single. The others are so high on happily-ever-after that they've forgotten how lonely it is being single.

"I think you can find love in unexpected places," Hanna says. "Why not a website?"

"I figured it couldn't hurt to try," I say. "The traditional way wasn't working out for me."

Maggie frowns. "Just be careful. There are so many creeps out there."

"Truth," Cally says. "I don't like the anonymity aspect. Like, what if you found out you were talking to Kenny Rawlins?" She shudders.

"Isn't he married?" Nix asks.

Maggie snorts. "Never slowed him down before . . ." She trails off, distracted as Asher crosses the bar, his eyes locked on hers. Her husband looks fine as fuck tonight in black dress pants and a matching button-up dress shirt.

"Ready to go home?" he asks her when he reaches the table. Anyone with functioning eyeballs can see in his eyes that "go home" is just code for "go fuck like bunnies." Hell, you don't need eyes. The two of them practically reek of pheromones.

"Thought you'd never ask," she practically purrs. She abandons her beer and takes his hand.

Cally scans the room until she finds her husband. William Bailey is on the other side of the bar, talking to my mother, who is still mourning the fact that Will married Cally instead of one of her daughters. "I think I'll go too. My sister's watching the baby, and I don't want to keep her out too late on a school night."

"Same here," Hanna says, her eyes seeking out Nate. "I want to get home to the girls. Thank you for coming tonight, ladies."

We all say our goodbyes, and Nix and I watch the happy couples retreat.

"Bitches," Nix mutters when we're alone.

I grin, because I know she says it with affection. "Seriously unfair, isn't it?"

"Can I tell you a secret?" she asks.

"Of course."

Her shoulders sag as she sighs. "Before moving here and meeting you all, I didn't think I wanted to get married. Like, *ever*. In my experience, men are good for one thing, and if you expect anything more than sex from them, you're going to be disappointed."

I try not to look shocked, but that's quite a strong opinion and I've never heard her say so before. "Not all guys are assholes."

She nods. "Yeah, I know that now. It didn't take much time around Asher and Will to prove me wrong."

"They're good guys," I say. "Nate and Max too." I cock my head. "Huh. Maybe I should set you up with Max."

She throws up her hands, palms out. "No way. The last thing I need to do is let myself fall for a guy who's still hung up on Hanna."

"Fair enough." She's right, but I still hate seeing Max alone. If I ever doubted Max was a stand-up guy, the last year has proven it. He deserves someone good.

Nix grabs her purse. "I'm going to go, but I'll see you at the wedding tomorrow."

I stand and give her a hug before she goes, then I grab my own purse and open the chat client to type a reply to my favorite stranger.

Tink24: *I've been thinking about you, too. You do*

know how to put ideas into a girl's head.

Understatement of the century, but it'll do. I slide my phone into my purse, say my goodbyes, and head for my car. I'm unlocking my door when my phone buzzes again.

Riverrat69: *Would you think I'd lost my mind if I told you I wanted to meet you?*

CHAPTER
FIVE

Sam

"S<small>AM</small>!" Dad calls when I walk in the door. He has his campaign face on. *Hey, look at me! I have children and I'm so proud of them.* To be fair, Dad is proud of us even when potential voters aren't involved, but the effusive praise is saved for the masses. "Come in here," he says, ushering me to the conference room. "I want you to see what Connor has mocked up for the next wave of social media images."

I step into the room and freeze. Liz is working at a laptop on the big oval table that sits in the center of the room. Liz, with her sweet smile and big blue eyes. Liz, with her wet dream of a body and infectious laugh. And Connor is right behind her, his body too damn close to hers, his mouth by her ear as he points to the screen.

Jealousy shoots through my blood, and I have to remind myself to breathe. She's not mine.

But she sure as fuck isn't his, either.

"I don't have to introduce you to the newest member of our team," Dad says, gesturing to Liz. "I'm going to put Liz's writing skills to work for a while, see if she's a good fit for our campaign."

Liz looks up, happiness all over her face, then she sees me and falters for just a moment, something like regret flashing in her eyes. Does she regret that night, or do I just wish she would? If we hadn't slept together, this would be a hell of a lot less awkward. Then again, I'm not the only guy in this room she's fucked.

"You didn't tell me," I say to Liz. "Congratulations."

"I didn't know until yesterday. And thank you. I'm thrilled that your father is giving me a chance."

"You'll do great." I'm not just appeasing her. It's true. She can write. I've seen the grants she's written, and those skills will be an asset to my father's campaign. I'm just not sure how I feel about her working so closely with my family. With Connor.

"She's a good fit," Connor says.

"Connor," I say with a nod. I force a smile for the benefit of everyone in the room, but we're all faking it here. The only one this isn't awkward for is my father, and that's because he's clueless.

"Thanks for coming over to talk with us on your lunch break," Dad says. "Connor, would you join Sam and me in my office?" He ushers us back and closes his office door behind us before taking his spot behind his desk.

Connor takes his spot in one of the leather-upholstered chairs opposite Dad, then motions to me. "Have a seat."

My stomach cramps. I don't know exactly why my father called me here today, but I have a pretty good guess. I resent that Connor is going to be part of this conversation. Plastering on my polite smile, I lower myself into the damn chair.

"We've come to an agreement with Asia," Connor begins carefully. He avoids my eyes. *Pussy.* "We don't anticipate she'll be a problem."

"Good," I manage, dislodging the word from where it wanted to stick in my throat. Connor is my sister's husband. He used to be my friend. No matter what I may think of him and his piss-poor choices, no matter how unworthy I think he is of Della, he's not the enemy. "Thank you."

My father gives Connor an approving nod, and Connor clears his throat before continuing. "On the off chance that she decides to come forward anyway, we'd like to take some proactive measures to protect you."

"*Protect* me? I don't need protecting from Asia. She's a lying, manipulative—"

Dad holds up a hand to stop me. "Exactly. And the image you maintain will make her lies all the easier for the public to swallow."

"What *image* do I maintain? I'm not the politician. I don't have an image."

"Everyone has an image," Connor says. "And yours

is that of the consummate playboy."

Well, fuck. "My love life is irrelevant to my father's campaign."

"*Should be*, maybe," Connor says. "But you know as well as I do that the press is going to be watching your every move, and with the primaries coming up in May, we can't afford to have a wild card like Asia and whoever else you might have an unsavory history with. We can't let her run loose without hedging our bets a little."

I curl my fingers around the chair arms, since I can't strangle the father of my unborn niece. "You think I have a long line of strippers who aborted my children against my wishes? Is that what you're suggesting?"

Connor drops his gaze to his notes, and my father sighs audibly. "Drop the victim act, Sam. We're not suggesting you get married or anything so dramatic."

I inhale slowly. Exhale. I fucking hate this. "What are you suggesting, exactly?" I shift my gaze to my brother-in-law. "Connor?"

To his credit, he meets my gaze. Fucker still insists he did nothing wrong. "A steady girlfriend. Find a girl, woo her, play nice, and otherwise keep your dick in your pants until we get your father into office next November."

"Governor Guy's daughter is still single," Dad says.

Right. For half my life, Dad has been trying to hook me up with Sabrina Guy, and I'm so profoundly uninterested in the sweet, soft-spoken thing that I could fall asleep just thinking about her. Never mind the *other* reason I couldn't bring myself to date her, but Dad doesn't know about that, and I won't be the one to tell him.

"Connor," my father continues, with his polite smile, "may my son and I have the room, please?"

"Of course." Connor gathers his things and stands, nodding at me before he leaves me with my father.

"I understand that I'm asking a lot of you," Dad says when we're alone. "But you have to understand that I'm not just trying to protect my campaign. I'm trying to protect you, and I apologize that it's necessary."

I take a breath. "This isn't just a ploy to get me to settle down?"

Dad smiles ruefully. "I can't say I'd object to that. You're my son, so of course I'd like to see you settle down and find someone who makes you as happy as your mother makes me." He leans back in his chair and crosses his legs. "I know that has to happen on your own terms."

"You just want me to date someone. Regularly. No photo ops or grand gestures for the media to coo over."

"Not unless you want to make them."

Shit. I think he's right. Honestly, it's not much of him to ask of his oldest son. "Does it have to be Sabrina?"

He cocks his head. "You've always objected to her. Do you mind sharing why?"

Fuck yes, I mind sharing. "Does it really matter? I'm not interested."

My father nods, accepting that. For the moment, at least. "Okay, so it doesn't have to be Sabrina, but no strippers. Understood?"

SOMETHING RECKLESS

I stand. I am so over this meeting. "Understood," I mutter, heading for the door.

Lizzy's working at her laptop in the conference room, and something in my chest snags at the sight of her. Her hair's pulled into a messy knot at the top of her head, and she chews on the end of her pen as she considers something.

"See you tomorrow?" I ask.

She jumps and her eyes go big. "What?"

"At Hanna and Nate's wedding?"

"Oh. Yeah. Yeah, of course. It'll be good to . . . have you there." Her smile is the least believable thing I've seen all day, and I'm immediately suspicious. Is she hiding something? Was I wrong when I told Della there was nothing to worry about? Have Liz and Connor rekindled something since she started working here? It's not like Della's in a position to take care of Connor's . . . *needs*.

Fuck. Nothing good down that road. I return her fake smile with my own.

I need to go back to the bank, where I can drown out the sound of my jealous thoughts with numbers and memos until my eyeballs ache, but I can't seem to take my eyes off Liz.

It's one thing to want to protect my sister from the likes of Connor. It's quite another to make myself crazy with jealousy concerning Liz. She's not mine. Never has been, never will be.

***

Sam
Eight Months Before . . .

"Your girlfriend is here," I warn as I knock on the door to Connor's apartment.

"Get out of my way," my sister says. She shoves me, and I back up as she punches her key in the lock and pushes the door open. We both draw in a breath at what we see on the other side.

"Fucking bastard," I breathe. Connor's sleeping on the living room floor in a tangle of sheets and blankets, a woman in his arms.

"You cheating scum," Della cries. "How could you?"

Connor jumps up and scrambles for his pants. "Della, what are you doing here?"

"I came to see my *boyfriend*."

That's the moment the girl in his bed rolls over, and I see who spent the night with Connor. She pulls the sheet under her arms and sits up, groggy and beautiful as all hell with those blond curls messy around her sleepy features.

"Good morning, Liz," I say. For my sister's sake, I pretend I'm not the one who has been betrayed here. I pretend I'm not the one who's dying inside at seeing them naked together.

Liz blinks at Della. "Della? What are you doing

here?"

Della lunges for her, and I wrap my arms around her waist to stop her. "You fucking slut. You fucking bitch cunt slut."

"Della," Connor says. "I'm sorry, I thought—"

"I'm *pregnant*, Connor. I'm *pregnant,* and you're fucking another girl."

I tear my gaze away from Liz—seeing her like this hurts too much, anyway—and turn my anger on Connor. "You got my sister pregnant?" I let my disappointment in Liz fuel my brotherly protective instinct. "You're a piece of shit."

"You're pregnant?" Connor's face goes pale and he bends at the waist, as if someone just sucker-punched him. I'd like to be next.

Liz hops up and tries to take the sheet with her, but it snags under the corner of the couch, exposing half her body. I look away. This isn't how I imagined I'd see her naked again. Fresh out of Connor's arms. My heartbroken sister calling her names. She yanks at it as she turns to each of us in confusion. "Connor? I thought you said . . ." Finally the sheet breaks free, and she stumbles back.

"How do you sleep at night?" Della asks her. "Are you really so selfish that you don't see what you're doing?"

"Liz," Connor says, "could you please go? We'll talk later."

Liz gapes at him, but then she wraps the sheet tightly under her arms and leaves the room without another word.

"You too, Sam," Connor says, apology in his eyes. "I need a minute with Della."

Della runs to him and falls sobbing into his arms, and I back out of the apartment and head to my car, mind spinning, angry at the world. A few seconds later, Liz joins me in the hall, still wrapped in that sheet, her clothes wadded under her arm. She closes the door, then sinks to the floor, curling into herself as if she's trying to disappear. She's drawing in choppy breaths, and she looks small and vulnerable.

The last thing I want right now is to feel sorry for her, and when the sympathy surges up, I stomp it back down.

"What just happened?" she whispers.

"What did you expect? That he'd send his girlfriend away for the cheap fuck?"

Anger contorts her features, washing away the vulnerability. "Don't put this on me. I didn't do anything *wrong*."

"How do you figure?"

"They were over. He was moving on."

"They were broken up? Officially? He told you that?"

Red creeps up her cheeks as shame takes its rightful place in this conversation. "I thought . . . It seemed like . . ."

"You're better than this." Then, because I can't look at her anymore, I walk away.

CHAPTER
SIX

Liz

Riverrat69: *Have you thought about it?*

THE WORDS MAKE my heart triple its pace. Last night, River asked me to meet him. I think I reread the message at least fifteen times, simultaneously hoping it said what I thought and praying I'd misread it.

On the one hand, after fourteen months of abstinence, I am so fucking game for meeting my anonymous friend, for doing all the wicked things he's described.

I've been good—*so* good and *so* patient and *so*

abstinent while searching for my something real. But this weekend my twin sister is getting married, and not only am I single, I'm sex deprived. In a nutshell, my plan isn't working for shit.

Letting this anonymous stranger end my dry spell seems like the best possible coping mechanism for dealing with my loneliness. Only, I'm afraid—or is it hopeful?—this isn't so anonymous. And I know I wouldn't be tempted in the slightest if I didn't hear River's words in Sam's voice.

On the other hand, if River really is Sam, I don't know how he's going to react when he finds out he's been talking to the one woman in this world he detests. Have I thought about his invitation to meet him?

Tink24: *I'd be lying if I said I hadn't.*

A lot. I've thought about it more than I want to admit. I'm not a dumb girl. My mom taught me never to take candy from strangers, and my big sister taught me never to take an unopened drink from a man in a bar. I'm pretty sure meeting a stranger for hot, anonymous sex falls firmly in the same category. I want to meet him. I want to end the secrecy. But I shouldn't.

Riverrat69: *I didn't mean for it to go this far. You deserve better than what I'm offering, but if I let this end without meeting you . . . without touching you . . . God, I'm not sure I could forgive myself.*

I never thought it would come to this either. Those

early days we joked around about the concept of Something Real, and I'd tell him about the guys I'd meet from the other sites. River and I talked about nothing and everything. It didn't start like this—the dirty talk, the rule-breaking pictures, the longing. That came with time. I never would have imagined we'd meet.

But what good could come of it? He doesn't want the things I do, and if he's Sam, learning I am Tink24 might make him walk away forever. The truth is, I'm afraid to lose River.

But I can't deny that I want to meet him, either. I can't deny that he makes butterflies dance in my stomach.

Tink24: *And what exactly are you offering?*

Riverrat69: *Pleasure. As much or as little as you want.*

Taking a deep breath, I carefully compose another reply.

Tink24: *I want to, but it's complicated.*

Riverrat69: *Nothing complicated about what I want to do to you.*

Tink24: *What if you're not attracted to me?*

Riverrat69: *I swear to you, I've seen enough to*

know that won't be a problem.

Tink24: *I have a lot to think about. Can we talk tomorrow?*

Riverrat69: *Of course. Don't do this if you're not ready. I don't want to pressure you.*

Tink24: *Good night, River.*

Riverrat69: *Sweet dreams.*

Sam

"Is it true?" Shit. Della looks pissed—ready-to-cut-off-someone's-balls pissed. "Daddy, is it true?"

Ryann rolls her eyes. "Watch out, Dad. She's pulling out the big guns and *Daddy*ing you."

My father wipes the corners of his mouth with his napkin. "What's the problem, Della?"

"Is Liz Thompson working for you?"

"On a trial basis, yes." He frowns. "Is there a problem?"

She looks at me, eyes pleading, then whispers, "I just don't like her." I wonder if she'd bring it up at all if Connor were here, but he's off on some campaign errand for Dad tonight.

"Della," Mom scolds, "don't be ridiculous. You and Liz used to be great friends. Just because things didn't work out with the daycare doesn't mean she can't work for your father."

Della's eyes are wide and wet, but she looks down at her plate to hide her tears. She doesn't want them to know the truth about why she hates Liz so much. If my parents knew the truth, they never would have let her marry Connor.

"I will say I was surprised," Mom says. "Liz doesn't seem like the serious type. She comes off as a little too ditzy for politics."

"She's not ditzy." I say it before I think, and Della glares at me. I shrug. "She's not. Just because she's a peppy blonde doesn't mean she doesn't have a brain."

"He's right," Dad says. He puts another serving of salad on his plate. "I think people underestimate her. She has a lot to learn about campaign work, but she's been helping Connor with my speech for the gala. I have to say, her early work has some real potential."

I nod, satisfied that my dad is giving Liz a chance. I shouldn't be. I shouldn't want her anywhere near my family after what happened with Connor, but maybe what happened between them wasn't as cut and dry as I wanted to believe.

Mom smiles at me. "Do I sense a *romantic* interest in the Thompson girl? You two would make a beautiful couple."

"You should have seen the way they were dancing together at Cally and William's wedding last year," my little sister, Ryann, says. "Pretty sure you could have found the meaning of life easier than the space between their bodies."

Della turns on me and scowls, and Mom says, "Really now?"

Heat creeps up my neck, and I shoot a warning look to Ryann. "We were just dancing."

Della glares at me one more time for good measure. "I don't feel well, Mom. I'm going to go lie down."

"Of course, darling." Mom smiles as Della hoists herself and her massive stomach up from her chair and leaves the room. "Maybe you should bring Liz to the gala fundraiser next week," Mom says to me.

"What about Governor Guy's daughter?" Dad asks. "I thought Sam could take her."

I bow my head and mentally count to ten.

Dad turns to me. "I think she really likes you, and more importantly, Guy likes you."

Across from me, my little brother, Ian, smirks. "I'll go with Sabrina if Sam doesn't want to."

"As if she'd want you," Ryann says.

Ian makes a face. "Oh, and I suppose *you* have a date?"

"I don't want a date. I'm a young, independent woman."

"Code for *can't find a date*," Ian says.

Dad clears his throat, trying not to laugh, and Mom shakes her head. "You two cut it out." She turns to me. "Sam, I think it would be lovely if you wanted to take Sabrina. You know how important their family is to ours. That said, if you'd rather take Liz, I'd support that too. If she's working on the campaign now, it would probably be best if Liz came there anyway."

"I'll let you know." I push out of my seat. "I'm going to check on Della."

As I leave the dining room, I hear my mom saying, "I can't believe how invested he is in this pregnancy. I think he's finally ready to settle down."

Their voices are fading as my father says, "That's why I want him to give Sabrina a chance. She's good for him, and it would finally join the Guy and Bradshaw families in a more official way."

My father loves me. He loves all of us. But when your parent is a politician, your identity is never as simple as that of a beloved child. We're props and collateral—something to be positioned to make him look better and bartered to better the family's influence.

When I open the door to the nursery, Della's sitting in the rocking chair in the corner, tears rolling down her cheeks, her hands on her belly.

"Del," I whisper.

She offers me a wobbly smile. "I don't want to hate her, you know. I know Connor chose me, he married *me*, but I'll never know if he would have chosen me if it hadn't been for the baby."

"He loves you."

She nods. "I know. And I'm trying to get over it, but the idea of them working together every day makes me crazy."

You and me both, sis.

"But what choice do I have, right?"

I exhale slowly, then breathe in the clean scent of the nursery. As much as my parents' meddling has made us all crazy, this is the kind of people they are—the kind who set up a nursery in their home for their grandchild.

"You could tell them," I say. When Della swore me to secrecy about what happened that night, I thought I was agreeing to protect her. Now I realize I was compliant with her cover-up, because part of me wanted to protect Liz from the ramifications of her own poor decisions. If you would have told me eight months ago that any of my decisions were motivated by the desire to protect Liz, I would have called you a liar, but I can see it now. "You could tell Mom and Dad the truth about Liz and Connor's history, and they'd put Liz off the campaign."

Her eyes go wide, terrified. "You think I should?"

"No. Not really. It would hurt everyone involved, but if you can't live with her working with Connor, you do have the choice."

"I can live with it," she says, but she sounds less like she's sure and more like she's trying to convince herself. She studies me for a minute. "Are you really taking her to the fundraiser?"

I shrug as if I'm not a giant tangle of emotions around everything that involves Liz. "It crossed my mind."

"Take her," she says, surprising me.

"Seriously?"

"Woo her. Distract her. Fuck her for all I care, but keep her away from Connor."

"She's not going to mess with Connor. You're *married* now. It's not like before, when you two were having troubles."

She crosses her arms over her chest and sets her jaw. "Are you going to help me get through this or not?"

I sigh. Della needs reassurance and I need a girlfriend to improve my image. Maybe the solution is just that simple. "Yeah. I'll help."

CHAPTER
SEVEN

Liz

SAM VISITS CAMPAIGN HEADQUARTERS again on Friday morning, and again he gives me that look—like I don't belong and he'd really prefer I wasn't here.

I watch him in my peripheral vision as he chats with his dad over coffee, but I try not to stare. I try to pretend that we don't have a history, that he doesn't hate me, and that there's no way he's the man who's been talking dirty to me online, but I'm not that good an actress, and when he's on his way out the door I can't handle it.

I hop out of my seat, grab him, and pull him into the

supply closet. Then I feel stupid because it's dark in here and I can't even see his face.

"I really want this job," I blurt.

"Okay."

Not only is it dark in here, the space is smaller than I anticipated, and every time I inhale, my chest brushes against his. I can smell his soap and his aftershave. I close my eyes and give myself to the count of three to revel in the things the smell does to my insides—very, very good things—then I do my best to plead my case. "I'm sorry if it makes you uncomfortable or if you hate me or . . . whatever. But this is the first time I've had a job I was this excited about. I love it. Please don't ruin this for me."

"You're worried I'm going to tell my father what happened between you and Connor? You think I'd do that to my sister?"

"I never meant to hurt her," I whisper. "I care about Della, even if she won't talk to me anymore, and you know I care about Connor—not *that* way, but he's a friend, and—"

"Shut up, Liz." His voice is deep, and the husky tone in his command slingshots me back in time to our nights together, his hands on me, his rough voice whispering commands in my ear.

Obeying, I bite my lip to keep myself from saying more. There's a time to argue in your own defense, and there's a time to cut your losses.

Sam's hands settle on my shoulders then slowly, oh-so slowly, he sweeps his fingertips down my arms and to my waist.

I swallow. Hard. Because right about now, a little make-out session with Sam—in a dark supply room or anywhere—sounds so damn good. It would be a poor decision. Been there, done that, got the heartache to prove it. But damn if I don't want it anyway.

That last time I had sex? Actual going-*all*-the-way sex, not that drunken blow job that happened with Connor last summer? No, the last time I had actual sex was good. Great. O-mazing (which is like amazing, but with more orgasms). I found bruises the next day—hickies on the side of my breast and my inner thigh. What self-respecting grown man leaves hickies on a woman? But Sam isn't self-respecting. He's just Sam. And he's damn good in bed and knows it. We hooked up for the first time two years ago and then again at Cally's wedding last October, even though I'd told myself sleeping with him was a poor decision.

Maybe poor decisions are underrated.

He's barely touching me, his fingertips resting on my hips, but I want to sway toward him. Hell, I want to rub against him like a cat.

"Rowdy?"

"Yeah?"

"Do you have a date to your sister's wedding?"

"No."

"Wanna be mine?"

I actually gasp, a horrifyingly desperate little sound. "Really?"

"Really."

"Wh . . . why?"

He chuckles softly and then I feel his lips on the

shell of my ear. "Maybe I'm fond of what happens when we find ourselves at weddings together. Will you be my date?"

"Yes," I breathe.

"Good. See you there."

Then there's a click, and I squint as light pours into the storage closet and Sam heads for the street.

"See you there," I whisper, but he's already gone.

Headquarters is rocking with activity today, and I've been so busy since Sam left this morning, I've barely had time to think about what happened in the supply closet. We have a load of new volunteers who need training, and everyone is in high gear preparing for the fundraising gala next week.

"It's not that we don't appreciate your offer to sing Christmas carols throughout dinner," I tell Mrs. Patrinsky. "It's just that Mr. Bradshaw already arranged for a string quartet."

"If it's been decided, who am I to change your fancy plans?" Mrs. Patrinsky says. "But I was once told that my voice could call the angels home."

"More like wake the dead," Connor mutters in my ear when she's gone.

I bite back a giggle. "She can't be that bad."

"The ladies at St. Catherine's started a petition to get her to stop singing during mass. It's that bad." He winks at me then turns back to the stack of volunteer packets we've been preparing all morning.

Something tugs in my chest. Connor and I used to be good friends, but we screwed that up. Now we never talk because it would hurt Della, but that doesn't mean I don't miss him.

"What does Della think of me working here?"

He stills but doesn't look at me. "She doesn't like it."

I'm sure that came as a shock to no one. "So why haven't I been let go?"

Slowly, he turns to me, but first he looks over his shoulder to make sure we're alone. "She never told her parents about what happened between you and me." He takes a breath, his regret clear in the grimace on his face. "She doesn't want them to know."

"I don't understand. You didn't do anything wrong, Connor. You two were broken up. She was moving out of your apartment."

"In Della's eyes, I betrayed her." He shrugs. "But that's why you're still here. She doesn't want her parents to know. And as long as they don't, both of our lives will be better."

I hang my head. "I hate feeling like your dirty secret."

He steps closer. "Liz . . ."

I look up and sigh. He's so tall and lanky and adorably goofy. And I'm still not sure Della deserves him. "What?"

His Adam's apple bobs as he swallows. "I just want you to know—"

"How are those changes on my speech coming?" Mr. Bradshaw asks, making Connor and I jump.

"Changes?" I ask.

Connor steps back and shoves his hands in his pockets, looking guilty as hell. That's the kind of guy he is. He always feels guilty and takes the blame, even when he's innocent. "I emailed some notes to you last night," Connor tells me. Then he turns to Mr. Bradshaw. "We've been busy with volunteers all morning and haven't worked on it yet."

"Let me know when you have a new draft," Mr. Bradshaw says. "I'll be in my office."

"Okay, sir," I squeak. "Absolutely."

Connor immediately goes to the conference table and boots up his laptop.

"What were you saying?" I ask. I sit down on my side of the table and retrieve my laptop from its case. "Before we were interrupted."

Connor exhales heavily and shakes his head. "Nothing."

With a sigh, I boot up my computer, preparing to load my email and see what changes Mr. Bradshaw wants to the speech. The Something Real chat application loads automatically, and my computer dings with a chat notification from River.

Riverrat69: *Tell me what you're wearing today.*

Crap. I shouldn't have this on at work. I flick my gaze to Connor, but he's got his headphones on and he's absorbed in whatever he's working on. A quick reply wouldn't hurt.

Tink24: *Black dress, pink heels, pink sweater. I'm fucking adorable.*

Riverrat69: *I don't doubt it, but I'm more interested in what you're wearing beneath all that. Or you could just send me another picture if you prefer.*

I squirm and make sure Connor's still absorbed in his work. Then I close my eyes and picture Sam at his desk at the bank, typing those words. That's all it takes for my body to go warm, flushed all over.

Tink24: *No pictures today, naughty.*

Riverrat69: *Fair enough. It will only make me want you in the flesh that much more.*

Tink24: *I dreamed about you last night.*

Riverrat69: *Anything good?*

Tink24: *All of it was good. Except the waking up alone part. That part sucked.*

Riverrat69: *Feeling a little frustrated, are we?*

Frustrated is an understatement. Abstinence hasn't been good to me. Maybe it's just all the pressure of making sure I find the *right* guy, but it's almost as if the moment I decided I was holding out for *the one*, every guy I've connected with has failed in the physical connection category.

Tink24: *I miss sex.*

Riverrat69: *Surely with all these dates you've been on, you've gotten a few moments of satisfaction?*

Tink24: *You overestimate the men in this town. This last guy I took home . . . he was a good kisser—usually you can tell by their kisses. Then he invited me back to his place and got his hand in my panties and I swear he thought he was trying to prime a lawnmower to start, the way he kept pressing on my clit. Jab, jab, jab. Is that supposed to do something for me?*

Truth be told, it wasn't his total lack of finesse with the female anatomy that crossed him off my list. It was that being around him did nothing for me. He was nice enough, just bland. Every man who hasn't been completely objectionable has felt bland to me. With two exceptions: Sam and Riverrat69. Or is that one exception?

Riverrat69: *You're exaggerating. We're talking fingering here, not rocket science.*

I bite back a laugh, and Connor looks up from his computer and cocks his head. I clear my throat. "Just an email from my sister," I lie. "She's hilarious."

Riverrat69: *They should make straight boys take a class on pussy. I remember back when my brother hit puberty and cornered me with questions . . . God bless him, he was trying to figure it out, but I lost sleep for weeks worrying about the poor girl he got to third base with the first time.*

Tink24: *What would they teach in your proposed pussy class?*

Riverrat69: *Not to jab at the clit like it's a primer, for starters. You're not drilling for oil, for Christ's sake. Pussy 101 would focus on foreplay, technique, patience, and execution.*

Tink24: *If you put this on Kickstarter, women everywhere would donate to the cause.*

Riverrat69: *It's a matter about which I care very deeply. Very.*

I look up at Connor again, and his brow is wrinkled as he watches me. I hurry and close out the chat application and pull up my email. God, I haven't even been here a week and I'm already having risqué chat conversations on the clock. Not that I'm getting paid by the hour, or much at all for that matter, but still. I want to keep this job.

The email with the suggested speech revisions is

waiting for me, and I put my head down and get to work.

CHAPTER
EIGHT

Liz

"Oh my God. Oh my God. Oh my God." I tap on my screen wildly as if there's some magical swipe-tap-hyperventilate combination that can take the text back. Or, more specifically, the *picture*. Nausea rolls over me and I drop my phone to the counter and press my hands to my hot cheeks. It's over. It's done. The picture is out there.

"Liz?" I look up to see my mom standing in my kitchen, frowning at me. Her hair is extra coifed tonight, and her frown extra condemning. Which, if you know my mother, is saying something. If a frown can say, "Anything that's wrong in your life, you brought on yourself," Mom's does. She doesn't *mean* to be a judgmental harpy where all of her daughters are concerned, kind of like clowns don't mean to be creepy. Intent is pretty much irrelevant.

I drop my hands from my cheeks. "Hi, Mom."

"What happened?"

"Nothing. It's just hot in here. I'm feeling a little woozy." I'm not about to tell my mother that I accidentally sent a naked picture to Sam Bradshaw.

I want to meet River in person. I haven't been able to get it out of my mind since he suggested it. But given my complicated history with Sam, I decided that River/probably Sam needed to know exactly whom he was meeting. When I sent the picture, I was so busy thinking about what Sam's reaction would be, I sent it to Sam via text message, rather than to River via Something Real chat—a picture of myself in nothing but a purple lace thong, black heels, and a smile.

Fuck, fuck, fuckity fuck, fuck, fuck.

It shouldn't matter, but now instead of the picture being the way I tell River/probably Sam that I am Tink24, the picture is on its way to Sam's phone from my phone. Even if it's really the same thing, it's not the same thing at all.

"You're not wearing that, are you?" Mom asks. She narrows her eyes so disapprovingly at my fuzzy candy-cane sleep pants and white tank that, for a moment, I consider it. Just because it would get Mom's hackles up, I want to wear my pajamas to Hanna's wedding rehearsal. Hanna wouldn't care. She's so sleep deprived from taking care of the twins while Nate's been on tour that she probably wouldn't even notice.

"I'll go change," I mutter, turning toward my bedroom.

The second my bare feet hit the carpet of my room, my phone buzzes, rattling against the kitchen counter. I spin and run all in one motion and reach for the phone at the exact moment as Mom's fingers wrap around it. "I got it."

She lifts a brow but doesn't release my phone. "Are you hiding something? If you're doing something you don't want your mother to know about, you probably shouldn't be doing it."

"I'm not a little girl anymore, Mom. There are plenty of things I do that I don't want you knowing about." With a tug, I snatch the phone away and tuck it into my pocket. If she knew what I did moments before she'd arrived, she would be so disappointed. Of course, I don't think she'd be less disappointed if I'd sent it to the anonymous stranger it was intended for.

"We're going to be late," she scolds.

I rush into my room, close the door behind me, and lean against it before withdrawing the phone from my pocket.

Sam: *Nice shoes.*

That makes me smile. Damn. I needed that.

I click into the text box and stare at my phone, but I can't think of a reply.

Instead of texting Sam, I pull up the chat application

SOMETHING RECKLESS

I use to talk to River. I already depleted my short supply of courage sending that picture the first time, so I'm not going to send it again.

Tink24: *Do you still want to meet me?*

Riverrat69: *More than anything.*

Tink24: *When? Where?*

Riverrat69: *Can you get to Brown County tomorrow night?*

I put my hand to my mouth. I'll be staying in Brown County tomorrow after Hanna's wedding. And so will Sam.

It really is him. It has to be.

Tink24: *Yes. It will have to be late. I have an event.*

Riverrat69: *5429 Water Pointe Blvd. I'll wait up.*

Tink24: *I'll see you then.*

Riverrat69: *I've never actually ripped a woman's clothes off before, but I might have to with you. I don't think you'll make it past the foyer before I bury my face in your pussy.*

The thrill that buzzes though me at his words settles hard and hot between my legs.

Tink24: *You have to promise not to rip my dress. It's too pretty for that.*

Riverrat69: *Then you have to promise to take it off as soon as you step in the door.*

"Elizabeth!" Mom calls.

Snapping out of my stupor, I toss the phone on the bed. "Just a minute!"

I need to focus on getting dressed in something sexier than my Christmas pajamas. I don't know if Sam's coming down for the wedding festivities tonight or tomorrow, but I want to look my best. Just in case.

I pick black thigh-high stockings, a black skirt that's almost inappropriately short, and a red sweater that hugs me in all the right places. Perfect. Sexy, without being over the top. In five minutes, I've dressed, applied lip-gloss and mascara, and am heading out the door with Mom.

I wouldn't typically carpool with my mother, but she can't drive for shit in the winter, and I agreed to take her. Hanna and Nate are getting married in this gorgeous mansion in Brown County. The ten-bed, ten-bath home they rented has a ballroom and massive gourmet kitchen, and is nestled into the wooded hills of Brown County. They rented the whole place, as well as half the rooms at the inn down the street, for their guests. With the dusting of snow on the trees, it's going to be a gorgeous Christmas wedding. Maybe the happiest day of my twin's life. And the way things are shaping up, it might not be such a bad day for me either.

This is a mistake, some rational part of my brain warns. I signed up for Something Real because I wanted commitment. Sam has never offered that—as himself or as River.

In fact, my relationship with Sam can be broken down into a series of defining moments that I realize, in an isolated list, make me look like Slutty McSluttypants.

1. The night I tried to seduce him and he turned me down because I was a seventeen-year-old virgin.

2. The night I decided to "cheer him up" at a mutual friend's wedding and ended up inviting him back to my place.

3. The night of Cally's wedding when I slept with him *again*, even though I'd promised myself I wouldn't.

4. The morning early last summer when he and Della walked in on Connor and me together.

I'm not proud of that little list. It doesn't leave me feeling particularly warm and fuzzy about the choices I've made. And I can't help but wonder if this weekend is going to leave me with nothing more than another item to tick off when I think of Sam.

I was ready to tell River I wouldn't meet him. I was too afraid to lose him once he found out who I was. Then Sam asked me to be his date for the wedding, and that changed everything. If he wants to be my date, maybe he won't be so disappointed when he finds out I'm the woman he's been talking to online.

My phone buzzes with a text message, and not knowing what it says kills me. If I were alone, I'd probably pull over to read it, but since Mom's in the car, I wait until we arrive at the cabin.

Sam: *I can only assume that picture was my Christmas gift. I must have been a very good boy this year.*

Sam

Liz: *This is so embarrassing. I meant to send that to the other guy who uses me for sex.*

Thank God I was alone when the picture came through. I'm in my office at the bank and haven't been fit for company since. It's bad enough that I can hardly sit at my desk without remembering the time she came here two years ago, nude under her skirt. She let me spread her legs and touch her while I whispered dirty words in her ear. It's one of my favorite memories, though it would definitely rank higher on the list had I simply disabled the damn camera and fucked her on the desk like she wanted me to.

It seems like I have so many regrets where Liz is concerned. I look at the picture again and literally bite my knuckle. Because *damn*. It shows all my favorite parts—the spot at the top of her leg right under the curve of her ass, the flat of her belly, her pert tits, just waiting for my mouth. Fuck. Yes.

This is torture. I'm not going to sleep with her this weekend. That would be a terrible idea, but it's going to be the hardest part about being her date at the wedding. Every time we hook up, she shuns me for months afterward, and if I'm going to date her to calm Della's nerves while Liz works alongside Connor, I can't have her shutting me out of her life. Never mind that sleeping with her when I'm using her to improve my reputation seems like a complete shit thing to do.

I consider my response carefully before sending.

Sam: *Saying that I'm using you for sex implies that you're not using me right back.*

Liz: *We wouldn't want to imply any such thing.*

Sam: *See you tomorrow, Rowdy.*

Liz: *I'm looking forward to it. I feel like the whole evening might turn out to be . . . enlightening.*

What does that mean?

"Hey, handsome."

I look up from my desk at the sound of my office door clicking closed and find Sabrina Guy leaning against it. "Sabrina." *Fuck.* "To what do I owe the honor?"

She sticks out her lower lip in a pretty pout. She

looks so much like her mother it floors me sometimes. The same wild red hair, the same patrician nose, the same killer curves. They could pass for sisters. "Mom wants me to go to the fundraiser dinner for your father next week, and I don't have a date. Would you let me spend the evening on your arm?"

I shift uncomfortably in my chair, grateful to have the desk hiding the effects of my conversation with Liz. "I'm sorry to disappoint you, Sabrina, but I already have a date."

"So cancel," she says sweetly. She wrinkles her nose. "Just kidding. Kind of."

"What brings you to town?" As much as I'd like to hustle her out of my office, I know I'm expected to play nice with the Guy family, so I'll make polite if I have to. Anything short of faking some romantic interest in Sabrina that I just don't have.

She sinks into the chair across from my desk and crosses her long legs, exposing a generous amount of skin between her knee-high boots and the hem of her skirt. She's beautiful. I can't deny that. But for reasons I can't tell my father, there are lines I can't cross. Sabrina is firmly on the other side of most of them.

"I'm here to campaign," she begins, and I sit back in my chair, preparing for a long discussion of politics and family gossip.

CHAPTER NINE

Liz

THE CEREMONY WAS PERFECT, and the reception is a dream. White lights and tulle are draped everywhere, adding a magical quality to the already majestic feel of a ballroom that boasts two entirely glass walls overlooking the hills of Brown County. Candles flicker from every available surface, and bouquets of deep red roses sit at each table.

Nate and Hanna are on the dance floor. Nate's eyes seem to be constantly trained on her, as if she's a precious gem he thought he'd lost. No one has ever looked at me like that. Probably never will. I don't inspire that kind of tenderness.

Sam is fucking delicious in his tux. He's tall and broad and fills the tux like a dream. But that's nothing compared to what I know is underneath. He's even sexier with his clothes off than on. And his package? Jesus. I call him *cocky* for a reason. I've barely talked to him since our bodies were pressed together in the storage closet together yesterday. I've been too busy with bridesmaid duties. But for the rest of the night, I get to be Sam's "date," whatever that entails, and later . . . later, I'll be River's.

The tangled mix of nerves, hope, and anticipation I feel at that thought is so potent that even the wine can't seem to tame it.

From my spot at the head table, I watch Sam. He's sitting a couple of tables away with William and Max. William has his arms full of chubby baby boy, and Max is settling his daughter into Sam's arms.

Next to me, Cally sighs. "Is there anything more appealing than a handsome man holding a baby?"

"Nothing," I whisper.

It's too easy to imagine Sam holding his own child, totally enraptured with the little fingers and squeaks. Despite his claims of not wanting to do the whole marriage-and-family thing, I think he'd be good at it. He comes from a big family, and he's a natural with kids.

Stop it, my rational self scolds. That's not going to happen, and I need to stop those thoughts before they go any further.

"Go on," Cally says, nudging me. "Go dance with

him."

No use pretending I don't know who she's talking about when I've been staring at him for the last five minutes. I slip my feet back into my heels and make my way to Sam's table.

"You have company," Max says, taking his daughter from Sam. "You two go have fun." He winks at me.

Sam's face goes serious as he gives me a once-over, his eyes sliding down my body so slowly and deliberately that my face heats with embarrassment and arousal.

"It's good of Max to be here tonight," I say when we get to the dance floor. I place one hand in Sam's and put the other on his shoulder, dancing in a way that keeps the most distance between our bodies.

"Between you and me, I think it killed him a little to watch her marry someone else."

I look over Sam's shoulder and see Max gathering his things to leave. "Then why did he come?"

Sam's face is serious, cautious. "That's just the kind of man Max is, Rowdy. He'll sacrifice part of himself just to make the woman he loves happy."

"He still loves her?"

"He's trying not to," he says, "but he does. Of course he does." Taking my hips in his hands, he pulls our bodies together then brings his mouth to my ear. "I don't really want to talk about Max and Hanna right now." The heat of his breath against my ear—oh hell, this is gonna be good.

"What do you want to talk about?"

"I was going to give you a hard time about that guy

feeling you up by the restroom the other night, but if you'd been there with me and dressed like that, I'd have done the same."

My stomach flip-flops. "You talk a big game, Bradshaw."

He grins. "Unlike you, I guess. Never sleep with a guy on the first date?"

"Never," I lie.

"And so what happened after Cally's wedding . . .?"

"We never went on a date," I explain, and that much is true.

He raises a brow. "Ah, the loophole. So clever. I guess it's a shame we're on a date tonight then. Because I sure enjoyed those not-dates."

"Me too," I whisper, my teeth sinking into my lower lip.

"But you're not interested in not-dating anymore, are you, Rowdy? I hear you're an active member of Something Real."

"Where did you hear that?"

"It's all over the *New Hope Tattler.*" He pulls his phone from his pocket and taps a few times on the screen before handing it to me.

Lizzy Thompson Trying It All to Find Love

So much for anonymous. "Fuck me," I breathe.

"I could arrange for that," Sam says as he takes back his phone and returns it to his pocket. His voice is low, and that seductive bass line that makes me . . . want things.

From inside my very slutty panties, my girlie parts seem to be screaming, *Yes, please, old friend! Stay awhile?*

As if he can hear their desperate, horny-girl cries, Sam grins and brushes my cheek with his knuckles.

Is he trying to confirm my membership in Something Real because he wants to tease me about using the site or because he suspects I'm Tink24? I so badly want it to be the latter. I don't like the idea of Sam being here with me now while planning to meet a stranger for anonymous sex in just a few hours. I feel almost jealous. Of myself. Which is ridiculous. "Why are you doing this?"

"Doing what?" His gaze drops to my mouth, and I could melt right here in his arms if my brain weren't going two hundred miles an hour trying to solve this puzzle I've gotten myself into. "Why am I dancing with you at a wedding? Isn't that what we do? Some of my best memories are of me and you at weddings."

"After last summer. After Connor . . . you hate me."

He's quiet for a minute as he studies me. "I hated seeing you in his arms. I hated thinking about him touching you. I could never hate you."

It's the first thing he's said about last summer, the first time he's acknowledged out loud that he cared for any reason other than Della's hurt feelings. "It was a mistake. But we didn't have sex. We weren't lying about that."

Connor and Della broke up, and he'd called me over. His heart was broken. He needed a friend. And I had just watched Nate propose to my sister. I was lonely and wondering why I never gave Connor the chance he probably deserved. Add vodka and a little desperation, and *voila*—the makings of a mistake bordering on disaster.

Sam's hand slides from my hip to my ass as he groans against my ear. "I don't care if you're using the clinical definition of sex or the Clintonian definition. You were naked in his arms. I wanted to cut off his dick."

"Liz, can you help?" Hanna calls, saving me from trying to come up with a response.

"Bridesmaid duty calls." I pull out of his embrace and meet his hot gaze for three thundering beats of my heart. When I walk up the stairs, I feel his eyes on me every step of the way.

I follow Hanna to the master bedroom at the top of the stairs.

"You sure you don't want to run away to Hawaii?" I ask as I help her out of her dress. "I'll watch the girls."

"Not even a little bit," she says with a grin. "There's no honeymoon I want as much as I want two weeks with Nate home with me, Collin, and the babies. He travels so much. All I really wanted was some time for our little family to be together, everyone who matters all in one place."

My heart tugs. *I* want that.

"I saw you dancing with Sam," she singsongs. "Anything happening there?"

"Probably not." Helping Hanna out of her wedding dress reminds me why I enrolled in Something Real to begin with. That whole thing where I want someone, someday, to look at me the way Asher looks at Maggie. The way William looks at Cally. The way Nate looks at

Hanna. I want forever as much as the next girl.

But would it really hurt to put forever on hold for a night?

"Will says Sam really likes you."

I nod and hang her dress as she changes into jeans and a sweater. "So true. He likes my tits, my ass . . ."

Hanna snorts. "Good point."

When I turn around, she's dressed and beaming. "Do you need anything else?"

She shakes her head and straightens her dress. "I think we're going to sneak out. We don't get much sleep these days and we're both tired. But you guys can stay and party as long as you like."

That she's trying to blame her twins for the fact that she's leaving her own reception early so she and her husband can fuck like bunnies? So cute. "Get out of here. Send me a text when you get to your room, or I'll worry."

"Sure thing." She hugs me then rushes down to meet Nate.

I collapse onto the bed and close my eyes. Sam doesn't hate me, which means he might not hate learning that I'm Tink24. Which means agreeing to meet him tonight might be the best decision I've made in months.

My phone buzzes with a text.

Sam: *I have to get out of here. Thanks for the date.*

My stomach sinks and dances all at once. He's ditching me. So he can meet Tink24? Oh God. It's true.

I'm seriously jealous of myself.

***

I can't believe I'm doing this. I've done some crazy shit in my life, but this takes the cake.

I look at the message again and a shiver of anticipation races up my spine, followed by a healthy rush of what-the-fuck-am-I-getting-myself-into fear. Equal parts nerves and anticipation have my body fluttering all over, but I am nothing if not determined.

This is the address. Tonight is the night.

I'm not sure I should be here. Aren't there rules for meeting people for the first time? I didn't even tell anyone where I was going. Truth be told, I was too embarrassed to tell them. "Hey, I'm going to go meet a man I've been talking to online. No, I don't know his name or really anything about him. Nope, not sure when I'll be home, but I'm pretty sure he plans to tie me up and fuck me three ways to Sunday. Good plan, huh?"

This is stupid. *So stupid.* Even though I'm ninety-eight percent positive Sam is River, going in there without confirmation is a risk no female in her right mind should take. It seemed reasonable when he suggested it—it already feels like he knows me so intimately—and if he is Sam, God knows I know *him* intimately. But suddenly, I'm seeing my decisions as if through someone else's eyes, and I'm not feeling very good about them.

I grab my phone and stare at it. This is why Sam left the reception, isn't it? To meet Tink24?

Part of me—the sane, rational, sensible part—needs assurance that I'm not off base here. I need to know I'm about to meet a man I can trust. Instead of using the chat client to message Riverrat69, I text Sam.

Liz: *Tell me you're the one waiting inside that cabin.*

I stare at it a minute before sending, contemplating. I don't have to do this. I could go back to my room at the inn and tell River I couldn't go through with it. But I don't want to. I want to go inside this cabin, look Sam in the eye, and strip away all the anonymity from the last two months. It's time.

You make me believe there could be more. You make me want something more.

Would he have said that if he knew I was the one of the other side of the conversation?

I wait, staring at my phone, willing Sam to text me back. Nothing.

The digital clock on my dashboard clicks past one minute, then two. My stomach sinks.

Then the front door opens, and a dark silhouette shadows the porch. When the porch light comes on, I gasp, shocked to see the very thing I've been promising myself is true.

It's Sam.

CHAPTER TEN

Liz

I'M MOVING TOWARD the front porch before I even realize I've gotten out of the car, and he's walking down the steps to meet me. It's as if our bodies are magnetized, pulled together without our consent by irresistible attraction.

We meet at the bottom of the steps leading to the cabin's wraparound porch. He's still staring at me. Still not touching me. I don't know how to do this. Do I tell him I hoped it would be him? Do I want to know if he is surprised to see me here? What if he wishes I were someone else? I don't want to risk knowing that I might be a disappointment to him. I don't think I could handle knowing that. Do we spend the night talking, or do we—

His mouth on mine cuts off my thoughts. The kiss is hard, heavy, hot, and I don't want to talk at all.

I kiss him back, take his face in my hands and slide my tongue between his lips. He tastes like a man. I don't know how else to explain it, but there is something distinctly masculine about Sam's taste. It's clean and crisp without being sweet. Earthy. Real.

He moves his way down my neck, his hands tangled in my hair. He tugs, pulling my hair and drawing my face up to look at the stars to give him better access to my neck. My moan echoes off the trees and his attention turns from sweet to rough. His mouth opens and he nips at the tender skin with his teeth, sucks and tastes. I'll have marks tomorrow, but if the price of this sweet torture is a couple of weeks of turtlenecks, I'll gladly pay.

It's too dark out here for me to see what's in his eyes, but when he pulls away, he's breathing hard—not at all like a man disappointed in the identity of his anonymous lover. Is it just lust there or something more?

Stop thinking.

"Come inside," he whispers. Then he takes my hand and leads me into the cabin, where he surveys me in the low light of the foyer. He's still in his tux pants and dress shirt, but his jacket is gone and his tie hangs loose around his neck. "You look amazing in this dress. I've been pretending all night that there's something I want to do more than get you out of it."

"What would you do with me if you got so lucky?"

"I'd keep you up all night, for starters." He slides a hand into my hair and traces the side of my neck with his thumb. His groan rumbles through me. "Tell me what you came here for."

I thought that was pretty clear. "I'm wearing extremely slutty underwear. What do you think?"

His nostrils flare and his breathing goes thready. "I think I'm going to have to up my game, because now I want to see it."

I have to bite back a smile. "Good," I say. My heart thumps out a beat, probably Morse code for *please* and *thank you.*

"How slutty is this underwear of yours?"

I lick my lips. "Oh, it's damn near whorish."

"Let me see it, Liz."

I lift my chin and prop my hands on my hips. "Seriously? That's all the seduction I get? *Let me see it?*"

He steps closer until I have to crane my neck to look at him, and holy hell he smells good. "What game are we playing here, Rowdy?" he murmurs against my ear. "Is this the one where we pretend we don't want each other and sleep alone . . ." His fingers skim down my shoulder and my eyes float closed. "Or is it the one where I make you come so hard you scream my name and tomorrow you act like you want nothing to do with me?"

"Are those my only choices?" I ask, but I keep my eyes closed, focusing on the feel of his rough fingers dancing across my skin. The truth is, I don't want to play either game. I'm done playing games when it comes to Sam. I'm done pretending I don't want him when I do, and I'm done pretending our annual one-night stand is enough for me.

"Tell me you aren't going to run away in the morning. Promise me you won't shut me out again."

I don't know what that means, and I'm too scared to analyze it. My eyes are still closed when he takes my chin in his fingers and tilts my face up to his, still closed when he brushes his lips over mine and when I open under him because I'm helpless to this man's kiss.

"Promise me," he repeats.

"I won't run away." Then I unzip my dress and let it fall to the floor in a puddle, and my boldness is rewarded. Sam's lips part and his breath escapes him in a rush.

He steps back and takes me in. The bra is strapless, black lace demi-cups that lift my breasts until they threaten to spill out. The panties—what there is of them—are a thong in matching black lace. Their fine lace straps sit in a sharp *V* high on my hipbones.

A ringlet of hair escaped my up-do, and he takes it between his fingers and twirls it around. I deserve a medal for not melting right here at his feet.

He hooks his index finger under the black bow between my bra cups. "Did you wear this for me?" His voice is a husky whisper that I can't deny.

"Yes."

His fingers skim my belly, trace over my hip, following the lace of my thong behind me to where the straps meet at the small of my back. My breath catches as he takes the fabric path over the curve of my tailbone and down, his fingers bringing every nerve ending to life as they pass. Electric pleasure whips through me.

"Fourteen months since I've touched you," he says. "Fourteen months since I've gotten to hear the way you breathe when you're turned on, since I've gotten to listen to you scream as I make you come. Tell me you haven't thought about it."

"I'd be lying."

"Don't lie," he says, eyes hot and intense. "Just tell me you want me."

"I want you."

He kisses his way down my neck, slowly at first, then his mouth is hot, open, hungry at the juncture of my neck and shoulder, and he's taking both of my hands behind my back, cuffing them in one of his. He steps forward, parting my thighs with his knee and positioning his leg between them.

When his mouth drops to my breast and sucks my nipple through the lace of my bra, I arch my back to bring him closer. I pull at my hands and find them already bound behind my back, and I gasp.

He lifts his head. "This is what you wanted, isn't it? Isn't this why you're here?" His eyes are darker than before, but they're also seeking permission. I could say no. I could ask him to untie me. I don't want to end this. I want to give him the control he craves.

"I—" *Can't breathe for wanting you so much.* For wanting this. Slowly, I trail my gaze down his chest and to his belt. "How am I supposed to unbutton your pants?"

He groans but doesn't take the hint. Instead, his hands find my breasts and tease my nipples, making them tight, aching peaks that he watches intently. Not being able to touch him is pure torture—I want to feel the hard planes of his chest under my fingers, want to find my way down to his belt and cup him through his tux pants.

His mouth opens against the bare curve of my shoulder and he nips at the skin and nibbles a path toward the peak of my breast. I whimper at the pain-laced pleasure and take two steps back. He's breathing hard. His hands are clenched at his sides, as if he has to keep himself from coming after me.

"Did I hurt you?" he asks.

I answer him by dropping to my knees. "I need you in my mouth," I whisper. He stares at me, eyes dark. "I'm waiting."

Sam

Liz Thompson on her knees in front of me, hands bound behind her back as she waits for my dick in her mouth. This is it. The fantasy. The basic facts of this situation have me so impossibly aroused I can't wait to free myself from my briefs and feel her tongue on me.

She's so fucking beautiful. Those blond curls have

fallen in soft wisps around her neck, and the way I have her hands bound behind her thrusts her breasts out toward me, those sweet pink nipples visible through the sheer black lace. I can't resist the request in her eyes.

Stepping forward, I slowly unbuckle my belt and pull it from my waist. The metal buckle clunks as it hits the floor, but she doesn't flinch. Her eyes are full of trust and need. I take another step, release the button on my pants, and free my dick from my boxer briefs. Her tongue darts out to wet her lips at the sight, and I about lose my shit.

Keep it together.

A final step, and her mouth is right there, a breath from my cock. Her lips part.

"Open wider for me, Rowdy."

She obeys, parting those plump, pink lips for me. But more than knowing what's about to happen, I'm turned on by the pulse thrumming wildly at the side of her neck as she waits for me. I love how much being bound turns her on. "Please?" she asks.

More blood pulses into my already impossibly hard dick. I wrap my fist around the base of my shaft and guide it toward her lips.

She leans forward, closing the distance and pressing her open mouth against my hip. She licks her way to the other side, dipping down toward my cock in the middle, only to come back up again. "Your body is so gorgeous," she whispers.

I can't reply because she's found me with her mouth, her tongue stroking along the underside of my cock. I fist my free hand at my side, determined to let her take her time. She licks the head, pressing her tongue against the bead of moisture at the tip. Her moan buzzes pleasure through me, and when she opens and slowly takes me deeper, I release my grip on my cock and my hands find their way into her hair. Her moan vibrates against me.

Giving head turns her on—or maybe giving *me* head. I can see it in the flush of her cheeks, feel it in the way her throat opens to take more of me, the way her body sways toward mine, wanting to get as close as possible. She's damn near the base of my cock, and I tug lightly on her hair, urging her back. "You don't have to go so deep, baby."

She sucks in response. Hard. Damn hard. And instead of moving her back, I'm bucking my hips and giving her more. My control snaps and I rock into her face, fucking her mouth. She moans her approval and sucks harder, working me over with her lips and tongue with every stroke.

"I'm gonna come, Liz." She doesn't hear my warning or doesn't care, and the vibration of her moan takes my last thread of control, and I come, filling her throat as my hands curl into her hair.

When she finally pulls back, her lips are swollen and her cheeks are flushed. Her hair is a mess, half of it tumbling around her shoulders. I want a picture of her like that, turned on, lips swollen, eyes hot. But I don't need one. I never forget a single second of my nights with Liz.

CHAPTER ELEVEN

Liz

HE HELPS ME to my feet. His eyes are all over me—my face, my breasts, my hips, the tops of my thighs. My skin heats everywhere his eyes touch, and I wait for his hands to follow, but they don't. All I have is the heat of his hand holding mine.

"Do you feel okay?" he asks.

I nod. I feel incredible, as if every cell in my body has been hibernating, waiting for Sam, and now I'm buzzing as they all wake and stretch their arms. "What about you?"

He groans, a long, low sound that comes from his

chest, and wraps his arms around me. "I haven't felt this good in months."

Something tugs in my chest, and I have to remind myself that he's talking about the sex. He's not talking about how it feels to hold me or look into my eyes or be with me. *This is just sex, Liz.*

He tugs on the tie binding my wrists, and my arms fall to my sides. Taking my hands in his, he brings my hands to his mouth and kisses the inside of each wrist. "Come with me."

He leads me by the hand farther into the cabin and through a vaulted-ceiling living room to a massive bedroom with a four-poster bed, cedar plank walls, and big windows. There's nothing but darkness beyond the windows now, but I'm sure there will be quite a view when the sun rises.

"This place is gorgeous."

"It's been in the family for sixty years. Dad led the charge in renovating it and adding the second story a few years back, but we all use it. Sometimes I come here and just spend the whole weekend in silence, looking out at the hills. Connor uses it a lot too— especially when Della's in a mood." His smile falters, as if he's remembered my history with Connor. He looks as if he wants to say something else, but he just shakes his head. "Wait here a minute."

"Don't be long." After he leaves, I climb into the bed and slide under the fluffy down comforter. Now that he's not touching me, I'm too cold to be in nothing but my underwear.

When Sam returns, he's armed with a bottle of red

wine, a corkscrew, and two glasses. "Not much to eat here, but there's always plenty of wine in the cellar. Is Cabernet okay with you?"

"Sounds perfect."

He pops the cork and fills both of our glasses before handing one to me. "You cold?"

"It's okay," I say, but my shiver betrays me.

"I'll start a fire."

I sip my wine and watch as he goes about the work of making a fire in the stone fireplace that faces the bed. The muscles under his shirt bunch and flex, and he adds wood and gets the flames burning to his satisfaction.

When he returns to the bed, he's smiling. He lifts his glass. "To weddings."

I giggle and tap my glass lightly to his. "To weddings."

The wine is dry but smooth. Any tension I felt melts away as the alcohol spreads warmth through my chest and limbs.

I take another sip, then a full drink, drowning out the demons that tell me this will end after tonight. It always ends after the hookup. It has to.

I drain my glass and cling to the words he typed. *You make me believe there could be more. You make me want something more.* Now that he knows it's me, does he still feel that way? And what is *more*? Commitment? Family? Or just more than a random hookup once a year?

"I'm glad you came tonight," he says softly.

I have so many questions—like what he thought when he realized it had been me all this time, or if he knew before I stepped out of the car—but he's pulling back the covers.

"If you're going to be in bed with me, I want to be able to see you."

"Did you . . . want it to be me?" I ask. I shouldn't. There's a rule about asking questions if you don't want to know the answer. "When I pulled into the driveway, did part of you . . . Did you think I'd be the one coming here tonight?"

"You surprised me, I guess. Why?"

I shake my head, too insecure to explain why I need to know. I didn't just want River to be Sam. I wanted Sam to want Tink to be me. When we'd exchange dirty messages, sometimes my whole body would go cold. Something about it would feel wrong. Off. But it was the thought of Sam that brought me back, that made the exchanges hot instead of mechanical. Arousing instead of creepy. But if that wasn't the case for him—if spending the night with me is no different than spending the night with any other woman—I'm not sure I want to know. "Never mind."

He's studying me, brow wrinkled but a half-smile curving his lips. Like I'm a curious puzzle he's trying to figure out. "Tonight, you were the only one I wanted to be with." With his index finger, he traces the line of my jaw and the column of my neck, and a shiver races down my arms, leaving goose bumps in its path. His gaze dips lower and finds my breasts, my hard nipples, but then he looks me in the eye again and says, "I think about you. A lot."

I bite my lip but I know he can still see my smile. "I

think about you too."

"You're still cold."

I nod.

"How about we check out the hot tub while that fire warms up?"

"Hot tub?"

He grins and nods to the French doors. "Right out there."

Slowly, he removes my bra and peels my panties from my hips. Then he climbs out of bed, and I watch him as he undresses. My mouth waters at the sight of all that hard muscle and bare skin. I want to touch him. Taste him.

He offers me his hand. "Come with me?"

Sam

Liz waits for me in the hot tub as I gather our wine glasses and a few candles to put around the edge of the spa that sits into the covered deck. There are lights on the deck, but I don't want to turn them on and sacrifice our privacy. Tonight it's just us, Liz and me, and the rest of the world is the silent darkness beyond. It'll be waiting for us in the morning, and until then, we can ignore it.

"This is romantic," Liz says as I climb into the gurgling spa. Candlelight flickers across her features, and the steam that rises from the spa has made the tendrils of hair around her face curl. If it's possible, she looks even more beautiful now than she did at the wedding.

I hand her a glass of wine and watch as she takes a long drink and moans softly. I settle into a spot across from her, but I can't take my eyes off her—her flushed cheeks, the rise and fall of her breasts just above the water. I didn't believe I'd ever get another night with Liz. But here we are.

She sets her wine glass on the edge and swims across to me. "You're too far away."

"Is that so?"

She climbs onto my lap, straddling me and wrapping her legs behind my back. "That's better."

I groan as she shifts her hips and settles against the hard length of my cock. "Better and worse," I breathe. Because it makes me want more. I could lift her by the hips and bring her down on me, could fuck her right here with the water bubbling around us and no protective barrier between me and all that hot, tight flesh.

I kiss her softly, nibbling at her lips and sliding my hands into her hair. More pins fly loose and her hair tumbles into my hands. My chest fills with a tenderness I can't handle, and I deepen the kiss, knot my hand into her hair and pull until she cries out.

"God, please," she murmurs as I latch on to her neck.

That tenderness inside me won't scatter. *Don't let me use you, Liz.* But this moment—in the steam of the spa, shrouded in night—this isn't about the campaign or my appearance to the press. This is just about me, and Liz. It's just about this undeniable chemistry we've always had. It's about pleasure and need and nothing else.

I cup her breasts in my hands and dip my head to give attention to each nipple, laving one, then the other, before I return to the first and suck it between my teeth. Her hands are in my hair and she presses my face to her breast, silently begging for more.

She rocks her hips against me, and even though it's torture, even though she's pushing me to skate on the edge of my control, I pull her closer. Wrapping my hands around her hips, I squeeze her ass and continue to torture her nipples—sucking, licking, biting.

Her moans turn to desperate, louder cries, and the rocking of her hips turns to grinding as she climbs toward her orgasm.

"Ride me, baby." Pain laces my words. I'm fighting the need to slide inside her. "I want to hear you come." I bring my hand to her nipple and pinch, and she spasms, at once arching toward my touch and away. She breaks, falling apart in my hands, her scream echoing off the snow-covered trees.

I kiss her shoulder, her neck, and her temple. She catches her breath against my chest, circling her hips every few seconds as she rides the receding tide of her orgasm back down. Then, her feet still locked behind my back, I wrap my arms around her, lift her out of the water, and carry her inside.

I lay her down in front of the fire, watching the light

of the flame flicker in her eyes and make her skin glow. She parts her legs and watches me slide on a condom, and reaches for me as I lower myself to the floor. I take her hands above her head and hold them there as I slowly slide into her.

She moans and then cries out at the intrusion, but when I try to withdraw, she whispers, "Please," and I'm lost.

CHAPTER TWELVE

Sam

ELIZABETH THOMPSON IS my downfall. My temptation. My shouldn't-want-it-but-can't-stay-away.

I could watch her sleep for hours, memorizing the shape of her face, the flat of her stomach, the curve of her hipbone. I could lose track of time inhaling her scent. She's beautiful, and when she sleeps, all that beauty is raw and unguarded.

Dappled morning light is coming through the leafless trees outside and into the windows. The heater hums as it cycles on. I should get out of bed and start a fire so it's more comfortable in here when she wakes up, but I don't want to leave her side.

Once upon a time, there was a guy who kept his heart locked away in a box. One night, when he was in a darker place than he'd ever been in his life, she showed him light. She made him laugh. She turned him on. She looked so fucking beautiful when she came that it was hard for the guy to imagine his heart needed protecting, that it could be pulverized.

That first night with Liz was a wave of sunshine in the middle of a dark and ugly time. It changed something about me, made me consider things I'd seen as fairytales before.

I've never been a romantic. That doesn't mean I'm an asshole, but I've never been the kind of guy who believes in happily-ever-after. My parents are making it work, but at what cost? And are they really happy, or is the secret to a happy marriage really just lying to yourself every morning, telling yourself there's nowhere you'd rather be?

Obviously, there was somewhere Dad would've rather been. *Jacqueline* wouldn't have happened if Mom had been enough for him.

When I tell a woman that I'm a no-strings-attached kind of guy, I mean it, and I've never been tempted to be anything else—except for with Liz.

Last night, I confessed that I think about her, but that was a watered-down version of the truth. The truth is that Liz has a hold on something so much deeper than my thoughts, even deeper than my fantasies. I crave her. I have since she came to my house at Notre Dame. She'd gotten drunk and climbed onto the bar in the basement, and every guy in the room had been captivated. I'd wanted to punch them all—because she was only seventeen. And because she was *mine*.

That possessiveness where she's concerned has never gone away, even if it doesn't make any damn sense. But if my father is going to insist I see someone, why not her? Why not the woman who occupies so many of my thoughts and fantasies? It's the perfect solution. I appease Dad and set Della's mind at ease. And maybe by the time the election rolls around, I'll finally be able to let her go.

She moans as she rolls away from me and slowly sits up.

Without looking at me, she climbs out of bed, gathers her underwear off the floor, and tiptoes to the door. I could stay here and let her leave. It would send the message that this is just sex, and that I'm still the guy who has nothing more than that to offer.

And that's exactly why I climb out of bed, pull on my boxer briefs, and follow her into the living room. I find her standing there in nothing but her panties, her arms behind her back as she clasps her bra.

Stalking to her quietly, I wrap my arms around her from behind, pinning her hands to her sides.

She moans as I drop my mouth to her neck. "I have to leave. My family will be expecting me at breakfast."

I cup her breasts in my hands, finding her nipples through the lace of her bra. "Tell them you're sleeping in," I murmur against her throat, and she melts into me.

"Can't," she whispers. "My mom would come to my room."

SOMETHING RECKLESS

I snake my hand down her stomach and let my fingers brush the lace of her underwear. She draws in a long breath, fighting for control in a struggle I intend to see her lose. "I'm not done with you yet."

My fingers slide under the lace. She sighs and covers my hand with hers, urging me further south.

Instead of obeying the silent plea, I spin her around, grab her by the hips, and hoist her onto the back of the couch. I spread her legs and step between them as I draw her closer.

She grabs a handful of my hair and draws my mouth to hers, and I kiss her. She tastes like breath mints and temptation.

She locks her ankles behind my back and squeezes me with her thighs. I drop my mouth to her breast and latch on, sucking at her through the lace until she cries out.

My fingers replace my mouth, and I toy with her nipple. Her lips part and desire sweeps across her face in waves.

I love how Liz resigns herself to pleasure. She doesn't fight for it or against it like some women. She lets it wash over her, accepts it as the natural process that it is. She rides the wave, cresting with the highs and wallowing in the lows.

"I need to feel you," I hear myself whisper. Half a step back, and I slide my hand between our bodies and cup her wet heat in my hand. I feel her, hot and slick through her panties, and it's not enough. Tugging the lace to the side, I sink two fingers into her. She's ready and wet around my fingers.

"Yes. Please," she whimpers. Her head falls back and her nails bite into my arms.

"I love the way your pussy squeezes my fingers," I whisper in her ear. "Hot and tight and greedy—Jesus, Liz." I swear, if she so much as grazed her fingers over me right now, I'd be at risk of going off in my briefs. She's just that sexy.

I rotate my hand slightly and find her clit with my thumb, grazing it lightly as I grit my teeth and hold back my own need. I want to peel off my boxers and bring her down on my shaft, cradle her ass as I take her against the wall.

Suddenly, she stiffens in my arms and starts smacking my hands away.

"Sorry!" The squeaked apology comes from behind me. "Oh, God! So sorry!"

***

Liz

I hop off the couch and scramble away from Sam. I feel like a teenager who just got caught letting her boyfriend get to third base.

"Jesus, Ryann," Sam growls. "Heard of knocking?" He's standing there in nothing but boxers, his hard-on clear as day.

Ryann, his younger sister, is standing with her back to us now. "I didn't know you'd have company. Trust me, I didn't want to see that. Ever. I'm going to have to take a scouring pad to my brain."

My cheeks heat with embarrassment. "I'll go get dressed," I mutter.

"Um . . ." Ryann grabs my dress off the foyer floor and holds it out to the side between two fingers without turning to look at me.

"Thank you," I mumble. As I grab it, my phone buzzes from my purse where I left it by the door last night. I frown. That tone is the sound for the chat client, and no one but River uses that to contact me. *No one but Sam,* I mentally amend. I hurry into my dress then grab my phone from my purse to open the message.

Riverrat69: *I'm sorry I had to bail on you. I had a family matter and couldn't get away. I hope you can forgive me.*

I blink at the message then look up at Sam, expecting to see his phone in his hand, but he's standing in the living room in his boxer briefs, no phone in sight.

"What?" he asks. "Who is it?"

My phone dings again.

Riverrat69: *Can you meet tonight instead? I can't stop thinking about getting you tied up. Sucking on your clit until you come.*

I close the robe tighter around myself as my stomach flips with horror. *Oh my God.*

I rush to the bedroom, and Sam follows me. "What's wrong? You look like you've seen a ghost."

Yesterday, that message would have turned me on, and I would have replied with something equally risqué, but Sam couldn't have typed that message, and that makes me sick to my stomach.

Oh my God. What have I done?

CHAPTER THIRTEEN

Sam

"She's cute," Ryann says to me between sips of coffee. "She's got a certain goodness about her that's a little incongruous with your typical conquests. I'm not sure what she sees in you."

Liz is gone. She scrambled out the door in her bridesmaid dress minutes after Ryann caught me feeling her up on the couch. Not that my sister walking in on us like that didn't also horrify me, but I was surprised how Liz reacted. She couldn't get out the door fast enough. Or maybe the problem is that I wasn't surprised. I knew this would happen if we slept together again. She always runs.

I pour myself a cup of coffee. "Why are you here?"

"Della had the baby last night," Ryann says. "A girl. She's beautiful."

I grin, happy to hear the news. I was beginning to worry that Della was going to do something drastic if that baby didn't come soon. "And you came out here to tell me that?"

She shakes her head. "No, I sent you a text to tell you. I came out here to check on the house. The neighbors called Mom and said there was a flower delivery here yesterday. They got the flowers from the porch but thought that was odd since no one was here. Apparently they didn't realize you were setting the stage for seduction."

"I didn't order any flowers."

Ryann snorts. "Right. I kind of already saw what's up between you two. No need to hide it."

"Shut up. You're a child. Scrub what you saw from your brain."

"Trust me, I intend to order a case of Brillo pads the second I get home. But I'm *not* a child." She narrows her eyes and crosses her arms. "You really didn't order the flowers?"

"I wasn't even planning to stay here. I had reservations at the inn." I rub the back of my neck and try to get my mind straight.

It wasn't supposed to happen like this last night. I intended to have her be my date, to have any pictures that were leaked to the press show me with Liz on my arm. I left the wedding because I knew I'd take her home with me if we danced anymore. And I knew it would be *déjà vu*. We'd touch. Kiss. Fuck. And nothing we did would change what happened last summer. Nothing would change my reasons for asking her to be my date.

But then she followed me here. I hadn't expected that.

I ran from temptation, and temptation followed me right to my door. I'm weak—at least when it comes to Liz. "Let me get dressed and we'll go to the hospital."

In the master, I close the door behind me, and my gaze catches on the tangle of sheets on the bed and I miss her already. *Damn.*

She got away too soon. Again.

I grab clothes from my duffle and head into the bathroom to take a quick shower and dress. The second I step under the hot spray, I'm struck with the image of Liz in her shower our first night together, her arms stretched above her head, tied to the showerhead, her pussy against my face. My dick goes so hard it aches, and I have to turn the water cold and force myself to think about something else.

Liz

"Liz?" Hanna cocks her head at me and approaches slowly, much the way one might approach a feral animal.

Maybe that's because she can see the horror and guilt all over my face. Or maybe it's because I'm sitting in my bridesmaid dress in the corner of her bakery with a bowl of her famous Everything But the Kitchen Sink cookie dough in my lap, and a nine-inch spatula in my hand.

My twin sister is a goddess in the kitchen. Give her flour, sugar, and an oven, and she'll create something that will make you forget there are pleasures other than food.

And that's why I'm sitting here. I'm trying to forget.

"What happened, sweetie?"

I look up at her and swallow a mouthful of dough filled with homemade peanut butter cup pieces, toffee, chopped walnut, a generous dash of skinny-is-overrated, and a sprinkle of bring-on-the-heart-attack. I've eaten enough that my stomach hurts, and yet it hasn't *begun* to numb the horror of this morning's discovery.

"You're supposed to be doing the newlywed thing," I say. "Shouldn't Nate be bringing you breakfast in bed or something?"

She sinks onto the floor next to me and steals my spatula. "Already did."

"Then aren't you supposed to be fucking like bunnies?"

"Already did."

"Snuggling?"

She wraps her arm around my shoulders and leans her head against mine. It's then that I realize I'm crying. "I'm a hot mess," I whisper.

"I noticed."

"I don't think Sam wants me." Then I start sobbing again—chest-shaking, heart-aching, snotty sobbing. It's as if my body has been poisoned by hope I knew better than to have and it has to wring it out of me.

Hanna doesn't ask questions or get on the phone to yell at Sam for hurting me—which is good, since Sam would have no idea what she was talking about. She knows what I need better than I do, so she sits, stroking my hair and murmuring in my ear until I get all the ugliness and self-hatred out.

When my breathing steadies and the tears are gone, she takes the bowl of cookie dough from my hands and says, "Start at the beginning."

I nod, take a deep breath, and begin. I tell her about meeting Riverrat69 on Something Real. I tell her how I believed it was Sam and how things escalated until last night when we were supposed to meet.

"Stop right there for a minute," Hanna says when I tell her I agreed to go to the cabin.

"I know." I squeeze my eyes shut, too embarrassed to look her in the eye.

"Liz, what if he was some crazy guy? What if it was someone who lures women to the country to skin them alive?"

I shake my head. "I know, okay? That's why I sent Sam a text when I got there. I don't think I would have agreed to meet him if I hadn't believed it was Sam. I'm not *completely* stupid." Then I add in a mumble, "Only mostly stupid."

"So it *was* Sam?" she asks, confused.

"Instead of messaging River, I sent Sam a text to see if he was the one inside the cabin, and then he came out. I made sure it was him before I even got out of my car."

Hanna presses her hand to her chest and lets out a breath. "So what happened next?" she asks. When I sniffle and arch a brow, she says, "Okay, I can guess what happened *next*. What about after the dirty sex?"

I thought I was out of tears, but my eyes fill again. "This morning I got a message from River apologizing that he couldn't make it last night."

Hanna frowns. "That doesn't make sense. Why would Sam try to mess with your mind like that?"

"It wasn't Sam. Sam was right next to me when the message came through. Sam isn't River. I just . . . I just wanted him to be."

"Wait." She rubs her temples. "You're telling me that this anonymous stranger invited you to meet him, and the place he invited you happened to be Sam's cabin, and Sam happened to be there? That doesn't even make sense. What did River say?"

"I haven't replied to his message this morning. I panicked and took the messenger app we've been using off my phone. I'm freaking out here."

"That's understandable. Holy crap. This is a mess. Are you sure you were at the right place? Maybe you transposed some numbers in your head and ended up at the Bradshaws' cabin when you were supposed to be somewhere else?"

"I rechecked the house number on my way out. This

is no coincidence, Hanna. River, whoever he is, invited me to the Bradshaws' cabin."

"Maybe he's a friend of the family, or maybe he was going to meet you there and then take you to his cabin further out."

I nod. These are all real possibilities, but they don't address what hurts the most. "I really wanted it to be him," I whisper.

"I thought you *didn't* want to be with Sam." She's frowning at me, and I know she's hurt that I haven't been completely honest about how I feel.

"I don't *want* to want to be with him," I say, as if that explains anything. "I like him, I want him, but if I could control my feelings I would neither like him nor want him."

"Okay." She nods as if I'm not irrational, bless her heart. "There's a difference."

I sigh and shrug. "We aren't 'forever' kind of material. But I've always liked him. A lot. Remember when I hooked up with him after Will and Cally's wedding? I told you it wasn't the first time."

"Yes . . ."

"It happened the year before that too. He'd warned me it was just a fling, and I thought I was okay with that, but then I saw him with this other woman later and . . ."

"That was the day you painted your room that ugly beige," she says. Leave it to Hanna to know that. No one knows me better.

I draw in a ragged breath. More tears are coming. I can feel them. "I am such an embarrassing cliché, but I really wanted to be the one who changed him. Like in the movies where the girl's hoo-ha is so spectacular, the player guy is blind to all other hoo-has after one taste of hers. I wanted to be the one with the magical hoo-ha." Shit. I'm crying again. Hard.

"You're not a cliché. Nate promised me nothing more than sex too, and I fell in love with him. You're not the first woman to think she can handle it and find herself falling for the guy anyway."

"It was my fault." I bring another bite of cookie dough to my lips then drop it when my stomach heaves in protest. "The way things were after that first time. I insisted I only wanted sex as much as he only wanted sex. So it became this joke between us. He'd tease me and flirt, thinking he was playing by my rules, but the whole time I was dying a little inside."

"Liz, you should have told me." She strokes my hair. "We're supposed to talk about this stuff."

"When I started talking to River, it was nothing, but then I started thinking he might be Sam and things escalated. Now I just feel . . ." I bite down on my lip, but the tears come anyway. "I feel like a fool who wanted something so much she was hellbent on seeing it."

CHAPTER
FOURTEEN

Sam

Dᴇʟʟᴀ ɪs ᴛʜᴇ ᴍᴏsᴛ beautiful mother in the world. I've never seen her happier than she looks with her new baby in her arms. The little bundle is wrapped in a blue-and-pink striped blanket, and happiness radiates off everyone in the room. Connor stands beside her, beaming at their new daughter, and something unrecognizable twists inside my gut.

Envy.

Jesus. I never thought I'd feel that, not about kids. I'm not supposed to feel it. I've never been anxious to get married or settle down, and I'm sure as hell not ready for kids. But something about seeing Della hold that baby makes some primal part of me respond.

"Hello," I say to announce my presence. Everyone's so entranced by the baby that I could probably stand here for hours before they noticed.

Connor looks up first. "Sam! Thanks for coming!"

I cross the room and shake my brother-in-law's hand. "Congratulations. She's beautiful."

"Her name is Avery," Della says. "After Grandma."

Connor hands the baby to me, and I cradle her in my arms. The baby blinks and then seems to lock her eyes on mine. I don't know if she can make out my face or not, but it feels like she can. Like she sees me and recognizes me.

"You're a natural."

I turn and shake my head at my mom, who apparently entered the room while I was caught under Avery's spell. "A natural *uncle*," I say. "I get to spoil her rotten and send her home."

Mom looks to Della. "When is he going to find himself a wife and give me more grandbabies?"

"Hey, greedy, how many grandchildren do you need?" I ask.

"I bet Liz Thompson would make grandbabies with him," Ryann singsongs as she joins us. "I caught them in quite the compromising position this morning."

"Lizzy Thompson?" Mom says, her face splitting into a grin. "Really?"

I squeeze my eyes shut and feel Della's scowl burning into me. Apparently she's already forgotten her request in favor of hating all things connected to Liz.

Next to me, Connor shifts awkwardly.

"Lizzy Thompson?" Della says, parroting Mom, minus the happiness. "Really?"

"What?" Leave it to Ryann to pick up on Della's tone. "What's wrong with Liz? I think they're freaking adorable together."

Della doesn't reply. She won't. She swore me to secrecy the day she told me she was pregnant with Connor's baby and was going to marry him despite what had happened with Liz. Della, Connor, and I are the only people in this room who know the truth. Anyone else would think Liz would be a great match for me.

"Della doesn't think anyone is good enough for her big brother," Mom says as she steals Avery from my arms. "But Lizzy is a sweet girl."

"She's a slut," Della says under her breath. Her serene, motherly glow is fading fast.

"Watch it," I say. "Bitch is not your color, sis."

Connor winces and flashes me an apologetic smile before turning back to his wife. "Del . . ." He squeezes her hand and then sinks into the chair next to her bed, and whispers something in her ear. Della's stiff posture relaxes, and she sinks back, but not before flashing me a look that communicates just what she thinks of the woman I spent my night with.

"She has been dating around a lot," Ryann says, giving me a pointed look. "According to the *Tattler*, she's looking for a husband."

"Oh, I saw that." Mom beams.

I turn up my palms. "Seriously, Mom? You're

reading the *New Hope Tattler* now?"

"People link to it on Facebook all the time." She shrugs, all innocence and poise. "I can't help it if the previews put part of the article in my newsfeed."

Ryann looks green. "You read the *Tattler*?"

A few weeks ago, the *Tattler* named a bunch of high school girls seen at a college party. Ryann and her best friend, Drew Fisher, were on the list. Ryann already got a piece of my mind about that. I may despise the *Tattler*, but if knowing her whereabouts might be seen by our mother is going to keep my little sister out of trouble, then I could get behind the trashy website.

Mom cuts her eyes to Ryann. "I see enough."

"Well, it's just a bunch of gossip," Ryann says. "Half of it is lies, anyway."

Mom smirks. "Mmm-hmm."

Thankfully, the topic shifts to Della's labor and delivery as the baby is passed around the room, and before I know it, it's five in the evening and the nurses are shooing us out the door so the new mother and baby can both rest.

I say my goodbyes and Connor follows me out.

"Can we talk for a minute?" he asks when we're alone in the hall.

I stop walking and shove my hands into my pockets. Connor used to be one of my best friends. We met in college, and for a couple of years I shared a house with him and William Bailey and a couple of other guys. My friendship with Connor changed when he started dating my sister. It ended when he broke my sister's heart. Now he's no longer my friend. He's my brother-in-law, and I accept that—Della's life, Della's choices—but that doesn't mean I have to like the guy. "Yeah. Sure."

"Was Ryann telling the truth? You spent last night with . . . Liz?" He doesn't look angry, but the way he says her name sounds a little pained.

"That's not really your business, Connor."

"I know but . . ." He props his hands on his hips and looks at the ceiling. "I'm thinking about your sister," he finally says with a sigh. "You know if I could go back and change what happened, I would. But I can't do that, and I don't want you doing anything that's going to rub the past in Della's face."

My whole body has gone rigid. "Like what?"

"I know you and Liz . . . hook up sometimes."

"What's your point?"

"I'm just hoping she's not the one you're thinking of dating throughout this campaign. I don't think she's the right choice."

It doesn't matter that I'd come to the same conclusion on my drive here. My thoughts and emotions are too tangled where Liz is concerned, and twelve months of dating isn't going to improve that situation. But anger surges through me the second Connor vocalizes the very thing I was thinking. Slowly, I count backward from five before saying, "I don't remember asking you."

"Governor Guy will be in town tomorrow. Sabrina's already here. *There* is a good choice. Hell, almost anyone would be a better choice than Liz."

My whole body tenses. "My sister just gave birth to your child, and you're seriously going to stand there and be jealous of my relationship with Liz?"

"Lower your voice," he says.

"Stay out of my business," I hiss. "She isn't yours, Connor, and I'll date her if I want to."

"You'll fuck her and you'll break her heart," he mutters.

I take a step closer. I look down on most guys, but Connor's my height and we're eye to eye. "Say that again."

He exhales slowly. "Just . . . whatever. But don't bring her home. That wouldn't be fair to Della."

When angry words fill my mouth, I keep my jaw locked shut so they can't escape. I've said my piece to him more than once. Della made her choice. Time to let go and move on. The thing is, when it comes to Liz, I've always found letting go to be harder than it should be.

"Thank you for thinking of my sister," I finally say. "But just because you fucked a girl once doesn't mean you get to decide if I bring her home."

Liz

At home, I face my closed laptop as if I'm afraid it might attack me.

I took the app off my phone, but I know the Something Real messenger client is going to load the minute I start up my computer, and I'm going to be faced with a deluge of messages from him.

Or maybe I won't. Maybe he hasn't sent me a single thing since he apologized for bailing on me last night.

My stomach flips and nausea rolls over me. How long have I been convinced that it was Sam I was talking to? I kept telling myself that it was, but now that I'm forced to accept that it wasn't Sam, I feel . . . violated.

That's not fair. River never claimed to be Sam. That's on *me*. And yet now that I know, I wish I gave heed to all those moments we'd been chatting and I'd grown cold, all the times I'd get that *off* feeling in my gut. Any time I found myself questioning who my anonymous friend was, I'd remind myself of all the reasons I thought he was Sam. River was looking for an investment; *Sam* does investment banking. River likes to talk dirty; *Sam* likes to talk dirty. River has a little brother; *Sam* has a little brother. River wants to tie me up; *Sam* likes to tie me up.

But maybe that's a more common fantasy than I realize. And the other things? A background in finance, a little brother? What an idiot am I? There have to be thousands of guys who fit that description.

Holding my breath, I open my laptop and turn it on. As it does with every startup, the messenger client loads and my missed messages fill my screen.

Riverrat69: *I don't blame you for being pissed. The ball's in your court now, just know I would have rather been with you last night.*

I press my hands to my hot cheeks. How can I tell River what has me so upset? How can I tell Sam?

I shake my head. I can't. Telling Sam would be suicide. There's nothing between us and no reason I should hurt him by admitting I went to the cabin to meet someone else.

"But I only went because I thought that someone else was him," I whisper. God, what a convoluted mess I've created.

I place my hands on the keyboard to reply to River. But instead of replying, I scroll back through our message history, to a month ago around the time when things started crossing the friendship line.

Riverrat69: *Tell me what turns you on.*

Tink24: *Kissing. Secret meetings in dark corners. Strong men who pursue what they want but aren't too proud to ask for permission before taking it. What about you?*

Riverrat69: *Blondes, beautiful women in short skirts, sassy-mouthed vixens.*

Tink24: *Oh, so I turn you on?*

Riverrat69: *Yes. You do. But you already knew that.*

Tink24: *I hoped. Anything else?*

227

Riverrat69: *So much. The curve of a woman's ass. Hearing her scream my name as I drive into her. The way she stops breathing just before she comes. Your turn.*

Tink24: *This conversation turns me on. And if the moment is right and I feel safe . . . being tied up.*

Riverrat69: *I would love to tie you up. I've fantasized about it more than once.*

It was after that conversation that I'd begun to convince myself Sam was the one I was talking to. Somewhere along the way, I forgot how that all played out. I remembered it as him bringing up bondage first. But it had been me. And wouldn't most guys play along if a woman said she'd like to be tied up?

The doorbell rings, and I jump.

After closing my laptop, I hurry toward the door and look out the window. Hanna, Nix, Cally, and Maggie are standing on my porch, their arms loaded with grocery bags.

I open the door and my throat goes thick with tears. I am so grateful for my friends. "What are you guys doing here?"

"Cheering you up," Hanna says, pushing past me.

Cally follows her to the kitchen and chimes in with, "Pretending to be something more than a diaper-changing milk machine for a few minutes."

Maggie wraps me in a hug. "Hanna said we needed a girls' night. So here we are."

"Yeah, here we are," Nix says with a grin.

My smile wobbles. "You guys are the best."

"We know," the girls say in unison.

I follow them to my kitchen, where Hanna is producing the ingredients for chocolate martinis. When she was going through everything with Nate and Max last year, this was how we cheered her up. Since Cally and Hanna both have babies at home now, martini nights are a rare occurrence. "It means a lot to me that you guys came," I say as we gather in the kitchen. "Now give me vodka."

Hanna pours dark brown liquid from the martini shaker into a glass then thrusts it in my hand. She makes more for the other girls as I drink.

"So I've decided this is the creepiest thing ever," Nix says after draining half of her martini. "You need to tell Sam about this Riverrat guy so you can get to the bottom of this."

Cally shivers. "Someone was meeting at you at *their cabin.* Nix is right. That's just creepy."

I can't disagree. The whole thing is just too coincidental and weird. I might think that it was some big scheme to trick me, and Sam was in on it, but that doesn't make sense. What would he get out of that?

"I don't want to tell Sam," I say. "It would only hurt him, and there's no reason to tell him when nothing is going to happen between us."

"You don't know that," Hanna says. "I still believe he really likes you." When I give her a look, she says, "Likes you for *more* than sex."

"To be fair," Maggie says, "whether or not you have

a future with Sam, you need to figure out who this guy is."

"He still wants to meet me," I say. "I could agree to that."

Hanna shakes her head. "I don't know if I'm comfortable with that. Why can't he tell you who he is *then* you can meet?"

"He doesn't know who I am either," I say. "God, I'm glad I accidentally sent that picture of me to Sam through text when I meant to send it to River through Something Real Chat."

Nix frowns at me. "What are you talking about? You can't send pictures through Something Real."

"Sure you can," I say. "I sent River pictures before."

"You did?" the girls screech in unison.

"Not of *me*, exactly," I say. "I was only *bending* the rules, not breaking them. I'd send pictures of tiny parts of me. My hip, my toes . . ." My cheeks heat. "You know . . ."

Nix folds her arms. "That's so weird. There's no way to send pictures from my account."

We all turn to her. "You have an account with Something Real?" I ask.

She looks away. "You made it sound pretty cool, so I thought it was worth a try. But trust me, there's no picture sending." She pulls her phone from her pocket and messes with it for a minute before showing it to me.

She has the chat application pulled up and, sure enough, there's no option to send pictures.

"I guess I thought it was pretty trusting of them to let us have that when we were supposed to be anonymous," I admit. "But it's in beta testing, so maybe it's just a glitch."

"Back to River not knowing who you are," Maggie says. "Why does that matter?"

I shrug. "I could end it. I could just delete my account and the program and never talk to him again. It's gotta be someone who lives in the area, so it's better that we don't know each other, right?"

"But you *liked* him," Hanna says. "That's gotta mean something. Why not find out who he is and then see if you can make it work?"

Maggie shakes her head. "But that's gonna be all sorts of complicated if it's someone connected to the Bradshaws."

"Or if it's one of the *actual* Bradshaws," Nix says. "It is their family cabin."

"It's the *Bradshaw* family cabin," I repeat, but I'm starting to get hysterical again and it comes out in a squeak. "Sam even told me last night that Connor uses it a lot to give Della space when she's in her moods. Connor." I lift my hand to my mouth. I feel sick again. "Oh my God."

"Liz?" Hanna says. "Tell me what you're thinking."

I draw in a ragged breath, but it's hard. My lungs are too horrified to accept air. "What if I've been having this online relationship with *Connor*?" I shake my head. "No. He wouldn't. He's married now, and regardless of what you guys think about what happened last summer, he's a *really good guy.*"

The girls all exchange a look, then study their nails, the counter, their drinks, anything but my face.

Cally's the first to speak. "Did River say *why* he didn't show up last night, Liz?"

"He said he had a family matter come up and he couldn't get away." I shake my head. "Connor's a good guy. I'm a bitch for even thinking for a second it could be him. It's not. He wouldn't do that."

Hanna meets my eyes and grimaces. "According to the *New Hope Tattler*, Connor's wife gave birth to their daughter last night."

"The birth of a child would definitely keep him from meeting with his online mistress," Nix says.

"No," I whisper. It makes sense. Too much sense. But I'm more miserable than ever.

CHAPTER FIFTEEN

Sam

So completely fuckable. And she needs to be mine.

Since Liz started working here, I've been to campaign headquarters more than ever before. I used to hate this place, but now when I walk in the door, I actually smile. Because it means I'm going to see Liz.

Liz is standing on the sidewalk in front of campaign headquarters, staring at the door as if she's trying to work up the courage to walk through it. Her hair's pinned into a knot at the top of her head, and she's wearing black tights, boots that come up to her knees, and a pink polka-dot coat that ties at her waist and makes her look like one of those glamorous women with pinup curves from the forties.

I'm suddenly struck with the image of her coming to my house in nothing but that coat and a pair of matching heels. I'd lift her onto the kitchen counter and untie the belt while—

"Sam?" Connor says behind me. "Did you hear what I said?"

Not a word.

"I'm wondering if you're bringing a date to the gala on Saturday? Operation Make the Player Look Like a Good Guy?"

"Yeah," I grunt without taking my eyes off Liz. "I'll have a date."

"Who?" Connor follows my gaze out to the street, then clears his throat. "Maybe run that by your dad?"

Reluctantly, I give Connor my attention. "Why's that?"

"This is his political career you're affecting. I'm just thinking that someone else—"

"Liz is going to be my date," I say, though in truth, I still have to ask her. The more Connor attempts to push me away from her, the more determined I am to keep her close. I like her, but I don't know if I trust her. I know better than anyone that those two emotions don't go well together—not if you're looking for a happy ending. But I'll keep her away from Connor and close to me because I've never expected a happy ending anyway.

"We shouldn't have hired her," he mutters.

I turn to him and narrow my eyes. "Excuse me?"

He sighs then shakes his head. "You don't think with your brain where Liz is involved."

"Guess that makes two of us."

***

Liz

I have to quit my job. I barely slept last night trying to think of a way around it, but I can't keep working alongside Connor. It's bad enough that I had an online relationship with a married man, bad enough that we had very dirty conversations through the course of that relationship, bad enough that we almost met in person, but add to all that my history with Connor and the fact that I was the key player in what his wife sees as his biggest betrayal, and if this relationship gets out, we're screwed. Della would hate me more than she does now. She'd divorce Connor. And Sam . . .

In some weird way, I feel like I just got Sam back. I'm not foolish enough to think Saturday night was the start of some new romance between us, but it was something. I thought maybe we could be friends again at the very least. But if he knew, he would go back to hating me.

Taking a deep breath, I push through the doors and into headquarters. As luck would have it, Connor's the first person I see. "How's the baby?" I can only pray he can't tell how forced my smile is.

Connor beams. "She's beautiful. Not letting her mom and dad get much sleep, but worth every second of torture."

"I'm sure," I whisper. "And Della?"

He shakes his head in wonder. "She's so amazing. She was meant to be a mom. She's a natural."

He looks so happy. Is that the face of a man who would cheat on his wife? I won't be the reason Connor and Della's marriage falls apart. Last night the girls did their best to convince me that I'm not the one responsible here. There was no way I could have known that River is a married man, and his decision to engage in an inappropriate online relationship is his betrayal alone. So, yeah, maybe he'll find someone else when I stop replying on Something Real, but at least if he crosses that line and cheats, *I* won't be the one responsible.

"Hey, Liz."

I gasp at the sound of Sam's voice, as if he could hear my thoughts. I shake away the silly worry. "Hi." He's handsome today in his banker's clothes. Some men look uncomfortable in a suit and tie, but Sam owns it and it looks as natural on him as jeans and a T-shirt look on other guys. "How are you?"

"Good." He slides his eyes down my body and back up, and I have to reprimand my girly parts when they start in with a celebratory cha-cha.

"I need to talk to your father," I blurt.

"Sure." He takes my arm and leads me back to his father's office, but when we're in the middle of the hallway he stops and pins me against the wall with a hand on either side of my head. "How are things with Connor?"

"Wha . . . what?" *He found out. He found out about River.*

"Is it weird?" he asks, his eyes dipping to my mouth. "After what happened between you?"

"Oh. No. Not weird," I stammer. He's looking at my mouth still, and instead of thinking of a good way to answer this question, I'm thinking about how much I want him to kiss me. Why does my brain take to the hills every time Sam's around? "I . . . think I need to quit anyway, so it won't be a problem."

He frowns. "Quit? Why?"

Why, indeed. I was so busy figuring out *what* I needed to do, I never bothered to come up with what I would say when I did it. What *am* I going to tell Mr. Bradshaw when I resign? *Hey, I've been having an inappropriate online relationship with a man who is probably your son-in-law, so I'm guessing I shouldn't be working here.*

"It's because of what happened between you two last summer, isn't it?" Sam asks. "Did Della get to you?"

"No." I shake my head. "This isn't because of Della. I've just had second thoughts . . ." Well, hell, the history is already there. I might as well run with it. It's not like I'm admitting to anything new. "I've had second thoughts about working so closely with Connor."

"Don't worry about him."

"So, you're okay with me working here?"

He smiles and steps back. "Why wouldn't I be? Tell

me you aren't going to quit."

There's a click, and Mr. Bradshaw's door opens and he steps into the hallway.

"Mr. Bradshaw," I say. I straighten and try my best not to look like I was wishing his son would kiss me against this wall. "Good morning."

"Call me Travis," he says. He knows I won't. He's been telling me to call him Travis since I was fifteen years old and having sleepovers at his house. He grins, little wrinkles appearing around his eyes. Sam's father is one of those men who aged so well every woman in town swoons over him—from my mom to my little sister, Abby. The whole George Clooney thing he's got going on really serves him well as a politician.

A woman follows him out of the office—tall and slim, with long red hair. "Governor Guy," I squeak.

The governor smiles at me, then nods to Sam. "Good morning. It's a beautiful day in New Hope, isn't it?"

"Christine," Sam says, surprising me by using her first name. I guess their families have known each other for a long time, but I'd still expect him to use her title. "I'd like you to meet my father's newest campaign worker, Elizabeth Thompson."

I offer her my hand, more pleased than I want to admit that Sam introduced me as *Elizabeth* and not *Lizzy*. "It's a pleasure, Governor. It's an honor to tell you in person how much I appreciate the work you've done during your two terms. When I was in high school and you were running for your first term, you were my idol. I wanted to *be* Christine Guy when I grew up."

The governor turns to Mr. Bradshaw and arches a

brow. "I *like* her, Travis." When she turns back to me, she's smiling. "Does this mean you have plans to be Indiana's second female governor?"

I duck my head. Politicians have things like their SAT scores go public, and how they were caught cheating on the ISTEP in grade school. Politicians who smoked pot when they were young claim they didn't inhale, but I don't think there's a fix that easy for proof of stupid. "I've wised up since then, I guess. No one wants to put a perky blonde in a powerful political office."

She frowns. "And what asshole put that idea in your head?"

The idea came from my political science professor during my first year at Sinclair, but I wave away her question.

"You know, they told me no one wanted to put a widowed ex-beauty queen in office, but here I am, finishing up my second term and making a bid for president of the United States."

"You're an inspiration," I say softly, but I know the words do little to communicate how very much I mean them. "As for me, I've learned I'm happier behind the scenes. I don't think I'd like living in the spotlight every day, but I do love helping someone as worthy as Candidate Bradshaw get there."

"She's quickly becoming an asset around here," Mr. Bradshaw says. "She's got a way with rhetoric, this one."

Governor Guy nods. "Maybe I'll let Travis here teach you the ropes, and then steal you away for my own campaign after the primaries."

My breath leaves me, and I can't find it in time to respond. Mr. Bradshaw and the governor start discussing the gala, and Sam winks at me. Mr. Bradshaw walks the governor to the door and leaves Sam and me alone in the hallway again.

"Well done," he murmurs, stepping closer. "Governor Guy doesn't impress easily, but she liked you."

"Do you think she was serious about joining her campaign? I could actually do that?"

"If you don't mind working for shit pay," Sam says.

"I don't mind. I mean, it would be worth it. Don't you think?"

His face goes serious. "I think it's amazing that I've known you all this time and I never knew you liked politics so much."

"When I started at Sinclair, my first major was political science. I was encouraged to . . . *rethink* my decision."

He studies me for a minute, something changing in his expression. "Prove them wrong, Liz. If this is what you want, I think you should go after it. You have an in with Christine. Most people who want a future in politics could only dream of having a connection like that. Do it."

"Help the first female governor of Indiana become the first female president of the United States?"

"Yeah. Why not?"

Because I need to quit. Because I screwed up again, and this time it could ruin a marriage.

"Don't quit," Sam says. "Stay on and work for my dad, and if a few months of being overworked, underpaid, and barely appreciated doesn't scare you away from the grunt work of politics, join Christine."

"I should quit," I say quietly. I can hear Connor's deep voice up front as he laughs and talks with Mr. Bradshaw. "I was an idiot to take the job and think last summer wouldn't matter."

"You weren't an idiot. You were after something you wanted. Don't give it up because of him."

CHAPTER SIXTEEN

Sam

"Do you understand what this could do to your life?" I ask, jabbing my finger at the computer screen. "Do you get it?"

Ryann lifts her chin and her eyes go a little harder. She's a stubborn little shit, kind of like me. And kind of like me, she's not really good at admitting when she's wrong. "You're overreacting," she says, tossing her pretty blond hair.

"What if they'd gotten pictures, Ryann? What if there were pictures proving that you were having an affair with a man more than twice your age?"

"Calm down, Sam. There aren't pictures, okay? I'm not an idiot."

I rub the back of my neck, where my tension has been gathering since Hanna sent me the link this morning. Hanna's used to keeping her eye on the *New Hope Tattler*, since her rocker fiancé is one of the pseudo-tabloid's favorite topics. But this morning, the website wasn't reporting on Nate Crane for once. Instead, it was dragging my sister's name through the dirt, implying that she's sleeping with some old art professor at Sinclair University.

The second she arrived at the bank for her teller shift this afternoon, I called her into my office.

"What are you going to do if Mom and Dad see this?"

"Deny, deny, deny. I come from the same family you do. I know how to play the game." When I glare at her, she shrugs as if she doesn't care, but her eyes change and I know the truth. She's terrified of our parents finding out. "It's not like *you* didn't do it at my age."

I freeze for a minute. "What do you know about what I did at your age?"

"Enough. Trust me. *More* than enough. Yuck."

I didn't think anyone knew about that, but that's a conversation for another day. "This is different."

"Yeah, because I'm a girl. Why is that fair?"

I sigh and sag into my chair. I'm not sure it is fair, but the idea of that skeezy old man touching my little sister still makes my stomach churn. Mom and Dad are all about keeping up appearances. Can't be the most influential New Hope family if people don't respect you.

"Our lives aren't our own anymore, are they?" she asks.

"No. They never were, even before his gubernatorial bid."

"How's it going with Lizzy?"

I haven't seen her all week. She's been avoiding me. She sends my calls to voicemail and keeps her text replies brief. "I'm twenty-seven years old and I've never had a real relationship before. I'm afraid I don't know how."

Ryann snorts then throws her hand over her mouth. "Oh. Sorry. You're serious."

"I'm serious," I grumble.

"Well, have you asked her out, stupid?"

"Yes, she was my date for Hanna's wedding."

She rolls her eyes. "Not have you asked her to go with you to an event you have to go to anyway. Have you asked her on a date that is just about the two of you? A real date. She volunteers at the animal shelter tomorrow. You should come by, help her walk the dogs, and ask her on a date."

"Think she'll go for it?"

She shrugs. "She seems to like your ugly mug, so probably, but you're kind of missing the point."

"What point?"

"You want a relationship? You have to put yourself out there and risk being rejected."

***

Liz

The Humane Society of New Hope is full of old strays unlikely to ever be adopted. The signs on their cages are like the descriptions on real-estate listings, trying to make them sound fancier than they are. *Shepherd-Lab mix*, *Husky-Corgi mix*, *Poodle-Lab mix*. In all cases, *mutt* would be more honest. These are dogs without homes. A lot of them were simply dropped here—people like to come to the country to drop dogs. It makes them feel better about abandoning them. As if they're just trying to give the dogs a good life, when the truth is they found the dog to be too inconvenient or their infatuation wore off once they weren't cute puppies anymore.

"Welcome back," Ryann says when I walk in the door. "They're waiting for you."

She hands me the keys that open the locks on the kennels and a pair of leashes, and I enter into the loud hallway lined with kennels of the older dogs. There are a few puppies around the corner in the next room, but the puppies get plenty of playtime and attention. These raggedy old mutts, though? They need me.

"Hey, Princess," I whisper, coming to the first dog's cage. The sign says *Black Lab mix*, and that's probably accurate enough. Part black Lab, part something that makes her nose squished, and something else that makes her tale fluffy and curly like a Husky's.

I open the cage and slip on the leash. Her tail swishes back and forth in the universal dog sign for love, happiness, and dinnertime.

A lot of the dogs I can walk two at a time, but Princess needs special treatment. It's almost as if she gets sad to have to share my attention with anyone else, so I've taken to walking her on her own.

I wrap my scarf around my neck, and we go out the back door and through the play area to the gate. The snow crunches under our feet as we walk. The air is frigid, but the sun is shining today and the sky is blue. More snow is coming in this weekend, pretty much guaranteeing we'll have a white Christmas.

"When are you going to adopt that dog already?"

I turn at the sound of the voice and find Sam walking behind me. He must be walking home from work. He has a long, heavy coat on, but it's only partially buttoned, and underneath I can see he's still dressed in a shirt and tie. "Oh, hey."

His eyes warm with his smile and he lengthens his stride to catch up with me. "Mind if I join you?"

"I—of course not." *Dear Heart, Chill the fuck out. M'kay? Thanks.* Because my heart can't be doing somersaults at the sight of Sam anymore.

If Sam found out about River . . . about Connor . . .

My stomach mimics my heart and does a somersault of its own—but the sick kind, not the happy, fluttery kind. "How was your week?" I ask to end the silence.

"It was okay. I've been . . . distracted most of the week."

We stop as Princess sniffs at a tree, then does her best to water it. "Distracted? Why?"

He cocks his head at me, and the corner of his mouth quirks in a self-conscious smile. "Weren't *you*? Even a little?"

My cheeks heat. Right. *Distracted.* Because we spent Saturday night and the better part of Sunday morning having wild and crazy monkey sex. And it was so good, really, who could think of anything else? Only a woman who has some terrible secret to hide, that's who.

"You're fucking adorable when you're embarrassed, Rowdy."

"I'm sure," I say. Then I give Princess's leash a gentle tug to pull her back onto the sidewalk and we resume walking.

"Be my date to the gala on Saturday," he says.

"What? Why?"

"I can think of a number of reasons, but I don't want to say them out loud and embarrass the dog." He tucks his hands in his pockets and smiles softly. "Besides, I'm told I look pretty irresistible in a tux."

"Haven't we already hit our one-date quota for the year?"

"My sister interrupted us, so that constitutes a do-over. I need a date, Liz. Be my date."

"I don't know if that's a good idea." *I'm sure that's a terrible idea.*

"It's a great idea."

I've spent most of the week rewriting Mr. Bradshaw's speech forty different ways and trying to

247

decide what to do about my job. I can either quit—cut line and run before Connor finds out I'm Tink24 or, worse, someone else finds out what's been going on between us online. Or I can stick it out for a little longer and have a chance at the greatest opportunity of my life. I don't want to lose a chance to work on Governor Guy's campaign, so I don't want to quit. If I'm going to keep my job and avoid Connor, wouldn't it be better to do so with Sam by my side?

"Come on," he whispers, sliding his hand around my waist and dipping his mouth to my ear. "I don't think I can handle another one of these dinners without you next to me."

"And how will I help?" I ask, but I already know I'm going to go with him. "What difference will it make having me by your side?"

"I'll get to spend it thinking of all the filthy things I'm going to do to you after."

CHAPTER SEVENTEEN

Sam

I'M NERVOUS. Fucking nervous about taking a woman to dinner. This isn't like me. Being so damn distracted I can't work isn't like me. Wanting to bring her home and hold her all night isn't like me.

If only it wasn't so complicated.

I slap my steering wheel. "Fuck you, Connor."

Because the things Liz makes me feel don't come easily for me, but her history with my brother-in-law makes them that much more difficult. I couldn't even take Ryann's very simple advice to ask Liz on a date that *wasn't* an already-scheduled obligation. Liz isn't ready for that yet. She's too busy putting up her walls, and I don't know what it is about me that makes her do that. We touch, we fuck, it's so damn good, and then she's guarded all over again.

When she steps onto her front porch, all that noise melts away. God, she's beautiful.

She's wearing a little black dress, a short thing that shows her long, toned legs and hugs her hips. It highlights every curve and reminds me of all of my favorite places to touch and taste.

I climb out of the car and walk around to her side to open her door. "You look amazing," I tell her as she steps in front of me.

A blush creeps up her cheeks. "Thank you."

Then, because I can't resist and because I want her to know she's mine tonight, I slide my hand behind her neck and lower my mouth to hers. When I slip my tongue between her lips, the taste of her slingshots me back in time to the first time we kissed. She feels so soft and nervous that for a moment I contemplate what I'd do if I had a second chance at the night she came to Notre Dame. Maybe I'd crawl into bed after her and hold her while she slept. Maybe when she turned to me in the middle of the night and offered me something I knew I didn't deserve, I'd take it anyway.

When she climbed on my lap that night, I knew what she wanted. She wanted me to take her virginity when I already believed it to be mine. *She* was already mine. I just had to wait another year, maybe two. I had to make sure she was ready. I had to make sure I didn't hurt her or scare her away.

That she gave herself to Connor that first time, I could forgive. I had no business expecting her to wait for me. But when I found her in his bed last summer . . .

Yes, if life gave second chances, I would do that night in college differently. I would do a lot of things differently. The first kiss, the first night we had sex, and the way I handled it when Asia showed up in my living room and told me she would keep the baby.

Liz has always been there. This fixture in my life that always felt out of my reach. And I helped put her there. She stayed beyond my grasp because she was scared to trust me with her heart. I see that now. I don't know how to make her trust me, and I don't know how to trust her, but I want to figure it out.

I don't know how to tell her that, how to explain that I don't really like the man I've become but I'm not sure I can be anyone else. I don't know how to warn her that having her on my arm tonight started as a political move intended to make my father look good, but already means more to me than that. So I slant my mouth over hers and kiss her deeper, and she softens under me and moans into my mouth.

When I pull back, her tongue sneaks out to her lip, as if she must collect the memory of the kiss there, and I feel myself fall down a couple of rungs on a precariously tall ladder. I'm terrified of what I might find if I fall all the way to the bottom, but for her maybe the risk is worth it.

SOMETHING RECKLESS

✳✳✳

Liz

"What was that for?" I ask.

"Do I need a reason to kiss the most beautiful woman I've seen all day?"

Don't say things like that. I've already spent the last two days reminding myself that this date with Sam is a matter of convenience for him. He needs a date, and I'm handy. But when he makes me feel so much more precious than that, it's hard to remember. If he keeps putting on the charm, I'm going to be in trouble. "Thank you." I climb into the car self-consciously, and he closes the door behind me before coming around to his side and getting in the driver's seat.

Sam's broad shoulders seem to overwhelm the small space inside the car, and for a moment I think about what I might do if we were a real couple. Maybe I'd lean my head against his shoulder or we'd hold hands between our seats.

"I'm nervous," I say, forcing my mind to think about something other than my endless litany of Sam-related what-ifs. "I'm proud of what I wrote, and I know your father liked it, but the idea that so many people are going to be listening to my words, that what they take from those will affect what they think of your father's campaign and how they talk about it . . ." I shake my head. "It's intimidating."

He tilts my chin up with his index finger and looks into my eyes. "My father wouldn't read anything that wasn't perfect. Trust me. He is unwavering in his high standards."

I bite my lip and nod. "I just need to think about something else."

He drags his gaze over me slowly, his grin growing. "I think I can help you with that."

Judging by the way he's looking at me, I assume I know what he means, even though he doesn't explain. But then he turns the key in the ignition and starts driving without any of the thought-dissolving touches I'm anticipating.

"What should I expect?" I ask when we're merging onto the highway.

"Lots of people. Lots of money. Lots of bullshit. Most of these people are my dad's supporters, and they won't give you any trouble. The only ones you need to watch out for are the journalists. They'll try to trick you into talking, saying more than you should."

I tense at the idea of someone trying to get me to spill some campaign secret, and Sam puts his warm hand on my thigh.

"Just smile and stay by my side. I won't let anyone bother you." His hand shifts, finding its way under the hem of my skirt as he curls his fingers around my thigh.

The muscles between my legs squeeze at the nearness of his hand. My breath catches and I instinctively scoot my hips toward the edge of the seat, silently urging his hand closer to where I want it. He doesn't give in.

SOMETHING RECKLESS

The whole drive there, we chat intermittently about who will be there and what to expect, and every so often his fingertips sweep over my inner thigh, but never any higher.

When he pulls into the valet parking line, he turns to me. "Your cheeks are a little flushed, Liz. You feeling okay?"

"Yeah, well . . ." I drop my gaze to where his hand is still positioned under my skirt and then look back to his face.

He grins and brushes the center of my panties. After a forty-five-minute drive thinking about exactly that kind of touch, it's all I can do not to grab him by the wrist and beg for more. He removes his hand. "Not nervous anymore, are you?"

Someone opens my door, and I stare dumbly at the red-vested man offering his hand.

"I think this is the part where you get out of the car," Sam says.

Sam

"That's what I see for the future of this great state," my father says from the podium on the stage. "The workers, the innovators, the believers—they're the ones who will bring the jobs back to Indiana, and if you elect me, I will help them make it happen."

The audience breaks into applause, and my father smiles and waves before exiting the stage.

Beside me, Liz is pale. I'm not sure she's taken a single unnecessary breath in the last fifteen minutes. In fact, I'm pretty sure she skipped a few essential doses of oxygen.

"Well done," I whisper in her ear. I help her to her feet, since everyone else is already standing to applaud, and that seems to snap her out of it. She claps with the rest of us until my father returns to our table and kisses my mother hard on the mouth before taking his seat.

"That was an amazing speech," Sabrina tells my father.

"Agreed," Governor Guy says as we all take our seats. "I'm afraid my opening speech paled in comparison."

"Your speech was fantastic, Governor," Liz says. "The part about Hoosier pride and the two Indianas—small town and city—and how we need to work together so both can thrive? That was spot on."

Christine beams. "Why, thank you, Elizabeth. I thought that might resonate with this crowd. But don't be modest. Travis tells me you're responsible for his speech tonight."

"I can't take all the credit," Liz says. "Connor and Mr. Bradshaw each played a big part in getting it right."

"She flatters us," my father says. "Connor and I tweaked, but Liz was the mind behind the speech. Quite the wordsmith, this one."

The string quartet starts to play, and my father and mother excuse themselves for the dance floor.

When they're gone, Christine leans across the table toward Liz. "Have you applied for a position on my campaign yet?"

"What?"

"Don't look so shocked. I've known Travis a long time, and he has an eye for talent. You should apply for a position with my campaign. It would be an amazing experience for you."

Sabrina rolls her eyes. "Mom, Liz is a small-town girl. I'm sure the last thing she wants to do is be stuck on the campaign trail with you. Am I right, Liz?"

My stomach knots as I wait for her to answer. I want her to prove Sabrina wrong, because her presumption is insulting. On the other hand, I don't want Liz to leave. Maybe this started as a cover, an attempt to appease my father and help my image while keeping Della's jealousy at bay, but it's more than that now. It's more than a campaign move and it's more than sex. At least, it is for me.

"Home isn't the place you never leave. It's the place where you return. New Hope will be here after we get Governor Guy in the White House."

And as much as I hate the idea of her leaving, I'm proud of her answer. "Christine, don't corner her now. She'll think about it and get back to you. Come dance with me," I say to Liz.

She sinks her teeth into her bottom lip and nods. Taking her hand, I lead her to the dance floor and pull her into my arms. *Where she belongs.* She settles against me.

"You're amazing, you know that?"

She shakes her head and avoids my gaze. "I'm not amazing. Your *family* is amazing. Look what they're doing for me."

"I already told you my father doesn't tolerate anything but the best. He's not doing you any favors, Liz. You're talented. Now, do something for me."

"What?"

"Take a deep breath. You've been holding your breath all night and I'd rather not lose you to oxygen depravation just yet."

She laughs a little and her body softens incrementally. "No one ever took me seriously before. To be fair, that's my fault. I'm not smart like my sisters, and I suck at taking tests, so I always told myself that my brain wasn't important. People liked me just fine for other reasons, until your dad brought me into his campaign and pushed me to write his speeches, and *rewrite* his speeches. I would have thought having someone push me like that would be draining, but it's just the opposite. I'm energized. I didn't realize how exhausting it was to dismiss my own mind."

I slide a hand into her hair, letting the soft tendrils curl around my fingers. "Why do you say you're not smart?"

"Because I'm not. I wasn't good at school. No one cares that you can write if you can't take tests." She stops and shrugs as if that explains everything, but I wait, knowing there's more, and eventually she gives it to me. "My mom pulled strings to get me into Sinclair. She never admitted it, but I know it's true. It's probably for the best she did, because if I hadn't been able to go to college with Hanna, I probably wouldn't have gone at all. Everyone thought I was dumb. I guess those assumptions already come standard with the blond hair, but it's more than that with me."

"I never thought you were dumb."

She sighs. "I had to cheat to pass the written portion of my driver's test. Seriously, the only thing I can do is write."

I pull back so I can look in her eyes. "I never thought you were dumb," I repeat. "Lots of people don't test well, and, frankly, that's a pretty arbitrary measure of intelligence. I've always thought of you as smart and talented."

Something flickers in her big blue eyes and she steps out of my arms. "Thank you. I really appreciate that." She points toward the table. "Excuse me. I'm going to go get a drink."

Just like that, she slips from my arms, and I find Sabrina sliding into them.

"Hello, handsome," Sabrina says.

I want to go after Liz, but my father is behind Sabrina's back giving me an approving nod. Ridiculous. "Hi, Sabrina."

"Your date seems *nice*." She says the word as if it's an insult.

"Sorry to see you didn't find anyone to bring," I tell her. "My brother would have been happy to escort you."

She cocks a brow. "Ian? Is that supposed to be a joke? You think I have a thing for teenage boys?"

I sigh. It was supposed to be a jab at her

determination to marry into this family, but I don't explain it because I've been raised to be polite to the members of the Guy family no matter what.

"I have a room upstairs," she murmurs. "And some . . . party supplies. Wanna ditch the date and come have a little fun?"

"No thanks." I'm not sure if "party supplies" is supposed to be code for sex toys or drugs or both, and it really doesn't matter. I was seventeen when Sabrina's mother initiated me to the art of bondage and fucking. I don't think I could stomach taking her *daughter* to bed after that, even if Sabrina is much more age-appropriate.

Shit. Now Della's talking to Liz, and judging from the look on Liz's face, it's not good.

When Liz turns to face me, she wraps her arms around herself tightly. As if she needs to protect herself from me. I'm the one who wants to protect her. I've always wanted to protect her.

CHAPTER EIGHTEEN

Liz

"You look like *you're* having a good time," Della says when I return to the table. She's sitting there holding Avery, but everyone else seems to have left in favor of mingling at other tables or dancing.

"I'm having a nice time, thank you," I reply, ignoring the snark in her voice.

"Fair warning: I'm going to ask him to cut the act. I thought I'd rather see him with you than worry about Connor, but you're not good enough for him."

"What are you talking about?"

She grins, almost gleefully. "My father is running

for governor and needs to make the world believe that his philandering son isn't a piece of shit, and I am married to a man you have a history of seducing when he's feeling weak."

"I didn't—"

"Sam is only dating you because I asked him to and because Dad requested he work on his image by dating someone respectable."

"Right," I say. "I'm sure."

She shrugs. "Ask him. I was upset when Daddy hired you, and I asked Sam to keep you away from Connor. And then there was the thing with Asia coming back around, asking for hush money. But now that Sabrina's here, I don't think he needs you anymore. She's a better fit for him anyway."

Asia? What does she know about Asia? More than me, obviously, but that doesn't take much.

Della cocks her head and studies me. "Seriously? It didn't seem strange to you that you started working for my father and suddenly my brother started taking a real interest in you? It didn't seem strange that his ex-slut-whatever came back into town and suddenly he started asking you to be on his arm any time there's a camera around? Do us all a favor and go work for Governor Guy. She wants you. We don't."

I back away from her—this horrible woman who used to be my friend. I back toward the exit and away from the terrible things she's saying.

"Liz." Sam is dancing with Sabrina Guy, and he grins when he sees me. Is that fake too? "Are you okay?"

"I'm fine," I mumble. It's all I can do not to run, but I make my feet move slowly until I'm hidden around the corner. Then I bite my lip against the tears. I want to vomit. I want my body to reject what Della fed me. I picture her words sitting like poison in the bottom of my stomach, eating away at the lining and working its way toward my aching chest.

I don't know if my heart can survive this.

I gasp when I see Sam. I shouldn't have come this way. There's no bathroom to hide in. But by the time I'd realized that, the tears had already started and I couldn't go back out there.

"Hey," he whispers. "What's wrong?" He steps close and cups my face in his hand, running his thumb along my cheek. I love it when he does that.

I sniff and swallow back more tears. *Stupid tears.*

"Did Della say something to you? Liz?" he murmurs against my neck. God, he has such a great voice. It's a low, deep rumble that I register right in my solar plexus before it shimmies its way through my limbs and his words finally register in my brain. "Tell me what's wrong." He draws back so his eyes connect with mine.

"Nothing's wrong. No expectations, right?"

"Nothing is as it seems with you, Liz." His eyes are this brown-flecked gold. Tiger eyes that always keep their guard up. I wish I could read them, but Sam's always been a mystery to me, and I'm left relying on his words. He's like me. Too much like me. Hiding behind bravado and outrageous suggestion. "Do you want expectations? Tell me."

I part my lips to tell him exactly what I want, but

images of homes and babies and snuggling in bed on Saturday mornings fill my brain so completely that I have to step back. I want something real, and I can't have that with a man who's using me to further his family's political future. I want to rage at myself for letting it get this far, for telling myself I didn't want anything other than sex with Sam, when I wanted so much more.

I take another step back. "You want to know what I want?"

His lips curve, hopeful but cautious. "I'm here to serve."

"I want you to tell me about Asia."

He stiffens. "What?"

I lift my chin and take a step forward. "Asia," I repeat. "I want you to tell me about her."

If I thought he was guarded before, I was wrong. So wrong. His shields are completely up now and he's gone entirely unreadable. He's not even tense anymore, just . . . blank. "I don't talk about her. Ask me for anything else."

"Anything as long as it's just about sex, right?" I know I'm not being fair, but that doesn't change how much Della's words hurt me. "That's what this is about, right? So come on, let's fuck. There's a closet right there. Come on, Sam. You're using me for your image and I'm using you for sex. Della told me everything."

If I'd hoped Della was lying, that hope dissolves when he flinches. "Della doesn't know how I feel about you. Does it matter why we started this? Does it make any difference how we got here?"

"It matters."

"The only thing that matters to me is that I had an excuse to forgive you for last summer. I finally had an excuse to get over my stupid pride."

"I saw you," I say. "I saw you kissing her."

"What? Who?"

"Two years ago. I saw you kissing Asia and you'd made me no promises, so I wasn't allowed to be angry."

His face softens, as if maybe some of those defenses are coming down. "You saw me kissing her." He steps closer and skims his thumb along my jaw. "That's why you shut me out."

"I have to protect my heart." I close my eyes when the words register in my own ears. I'm revealing too much. "Can we not do this?"

"Do what?"

"This thing where you act like you don't despise me for what happened last summer, and I pretend I'm okay with this being just about sex or your image, or whatever the hell this is about for you."

"I told you I couldn't hate you. Regardless of how I feel about last summer, I don't hate you or despise you or loathe you, or any other verb shy of *want* and *crave* and kind of *dig* you." He gives a shaky smile. "This isn't just about sex, Rowdy. It never has been. Not for me. I *like* you. I like being with you and making you smile, and, yes—" He steps even closer until my body is pressed against his and I can feel his heat. He lowers his voice. "It's true. I like fucking you. But this is about more than that."

I squeeze my eyes shut. How long have I wished to

hear those words from him? And I get them now, after learning what I have about River, about Connor.

"I've seen you go on all these dates. I've watched you share meals and conversation with these men who are so unworthy of you, all for the chance that *maybe* something could happen with one of them. I wanted to punch them when they touched you. You gambled on them, why not me? I don't know what's going to happen here. All I'm asking is that you give it a chance. Give *me* a chance."

"You said you don't do strings, and I—" I study my hands and take a breath. My pride wants to get in the way of saying what I need to say. "You don't do strings, and I *want* strings."

"Strings are overrated." He tilts my face up until I meet his eyes. "I've never been any good with strings, but I'm damn good with ropes."

CHAPTER NINETEEN

Sam

Liz came home with me. Despite Della's best efforts to sabotage our night, she came home with me, and tomorrow morning, I get to wake up with her in my bed. What a lucky bastard am I?

The truth is, I'm grateful Della decided to pull out the claws tonight. Since that night I went to Liz's house to tell her about the baby and Asia, I've believed she shut me out because she didn't want me. But that wasn't it at all.

"I have to protect my heart."

A couple of years ago, I would have agreed that she

did need to protect her heart from me, but now I don't want her to. I want her to let down her defenses and take a chance. I want her to hold my hand and fall with me.

"Your family seems perfect." She shrugs in my arms.

I take her shoulders and turn her to face me. There's something strange about the way she's looking at me—as if she knows more than she's telling. "We're not perfect, Rowdy. No family is perfect."

"Well, yeah, I guess they do have you."

I poke her side, right where she's ticklish, and she curls into herself and squeals. "What was that?" I ask.

"You're clearly the black sheep," she manages between giggles.

I go after her sides again and she tries to scoot away from me, but I hold her fast, pinning her arms and rolling on top of her, my knees on either side of her hips. God, she's beautiful. Something in my chest teeters, like my heart is off balance from just looking at her.

"Your father is obviously proud of you, Sam," she says, her face serious now. "You're so much like him."

I close my eyes and roll off her. "I don't want to be like my father." Is that really my voice? That weak, small, croaking sound? It came from my mouth, but God. It doesn't feel like mine.

"Hey." She curls into me, propping herself up on one elbow, the other hand on my bare chest, her fingers splayed as if they're trying to find my heart. "I mean that in a good way. Your father is an amazing man. I wouldn't be working for him if I didn't believe that."

An amazing man. How many times in my life have I heard those words used to describe my father? How many times have I shaken the hand of a potential voter and used those words myself? I was starting to believe them too. It had been years since the ordeal with Jacqueline, and my parents worked hard—both of them—to fortify any weakness my father's infidelity caused in their marriage.

Liz is studying my face, her lower lip drawn between her teeth, and she's stroking my chest with her thumb, right between my pecs, right over my heart.

"*You* are an amazing man too," she whispers.

Rising off the bed, I take her face in my hands and kiss her hard, and she sighs and melts into me. When I break the kiss, I pull her on top of me, settling her head on my chest and her legs between mine.

"My father and I have a difficult relationship," I say. I don't know if I've ever admitted as much to anyone. Della knows, of course, but it's not something I ever had to *tell* her. She gets it because she was there. She lived it.

"I noticed. Do you want to talk about it?" she asks, her breath warm against my chest.

"No one has ever been able to read me like you do. Did you know that?" I slide a hand into her hair, toying with the soft strands and reminding myself to breathe. "He had an affair when I was in elementary school— cheated on my mother with one of the tellers at the bank." She tries to pull back, but I hold her tight, keeping her still. "Jacqueline." Saying her name out loud feels like a betrayal to my family. We agreed never to share what had happened, and even as a kid, I understood how important that promise was.

"I'm sorry," Liz says. "I didn't know."

"It was . . . ugly. Very *Fatal Attraction*. Dad tried to break it off, and she wouldn't have it. She was new to town, but we'd met her at the bank and a couple other events, and one day she came to school and got Della and me out of our classrooms, said Dad needed us. No one at the office questioned her, though I'm sure that would never happen today."

She tenses in my arms. "Where did she take you?"

"She took us to her apartment and tried to act like everything was normal." I close my eyes, remembering the smell of banana bread in the oven, the sound of Christmas music playing in the background. She'd bought me a new Transformer and a Barbie for Della. On the outside, everything seemed great, but I could see that something was off about the way she looked at us, the way she moved around the apartment, a flurry of nervous energy. "Ryann and Ian weren't in school yet, or she probably would have taken them too. They were with Mom at the preschool where she volunteered."

"What did she do?" She's holding me now, one hand behind my neck, the other wrapped around my bicep. Her touch grounds me, and her scent brings me back from the memories of the Transformer and sickeningly sweet banana bread.

"She called my dad and told him not to be late for dinner because we were going to celebrate. I remember thinking that Dad rarely made it home for dinner. He certainly wasn't going to make it here to have dinner with *this* woman." I shake my head. "I didn't realize she was the reason he was home late every night. So much of what was said, I didn't put together until much, much later. I was naive."

"You were a child."

"When my dad pulled into the driveway, she put us in the basement with the new toys and closed the door. Della and I could hear them fighting. We didn't understand, but we knew it was bad. Della started crying, and I held her until Dad came down to get us and take us home. Even though she was younger than me, Della seemed to understand. She wouldn't talk to our father. It was as if she hated him, and I didn't get that, not until later."

"That must have been very scary for you both. What happened to Jacqueline? Did she leave your family alone?"

"She committed suicide, overdosed on sleeping pills, and Della and I were told never to talk about that day at her house. It would be bad for the family and for the business. So, we didn't." I take a long, shuddering breath, surprised at how tight my chest feels at telling this old story. "Della wasn't the same after. She was sullen and quiet. She snapped at everyone and had trouble in school. Eventually, she forgave my father, but it took her a long time. He hadn't just cheated on our mother. He'd cheated on all of us."

"I'm so sorry." Turning her face into my chest, she presses a soft kiss over my heart.

"That's why I didn't want her to marry Connor," I

admit. "She has enough trouble with trust, and when Connor cheated on her with you . . ."

She stiffens in my arms and slowly pushes herself up. She sits rigid on the edge of the bed, her back to me.

My heart—that soft, mushy place that was in the center of my chest just moments ago—cools and hardens.

"It's always going to come back to that, isn't it?" She isn't looking at me. "It was a mistake, but I am *not* like your father's mistress." She goes to the bathroom and shuts the door behind her.

I press my palms against my eyelids, then I climb out of bed and go after her.

She's standing at the sink, splashing water on her face.

"You're nothing like Jacqueline," I whisper. "I'm sorry if I made it sound like there was a comparison to be made."

She turns off the water and hangs her head, and I stand behind her and take her shoulders in my hands.

"I'm just saying that my family's not perfect. We're as screwed up as the next family. The only difference is that we have to pretend we're faultless." I press a kiss to the side of her neck, then her shoulder. "Take a bath with me?"

Without waiting for her answer, I turn on the tap and set it to fill with warm water. When I offer her my hand, she follows me into the tub, but her body is still tense, her face still guarded.

"Come here, Rowdy." I open my arms for her, and she surprises me by climbing into them, straddling me, and wrapping her arms behind my neck.

"I would take that night back if I could," she says. "I hate that it's between us—that it'll always keep us apart."

"Hey." I take her chin in my hand. "Look at me. You feel this?" I wrap my other arm tightly behind her back. "We're not apart. We're together. Right where we should be."

She kisses me, and there's so much in that kiss I know she's not saying. I feel it. Something more than frustration, and even more than regret. It's long and hungry and terrified—so much like everything I feel for her.

When the kiss turns greedier and she's rubbing herself against my cock, I bring my hands to her hips to still her movement. "I need you to stop, Rowdy. Much more of that, and I'll find myself inside you without a condom."

She lifts her head, finding my eyes. "Would that be so bad?" Then she lifts her hips until the head of my cock is cradled against her entrance.

"I always use protection," I say on a choppy breath. But the protest is weakened as I lift my hips a fraction, let the head of my cock slide into her. "Are you . . ." *God.* I need more. I can't breathe or think. The only thing my body cares about is getting inside her.

"On the pill," she finishes. "Since I was a teenager."

"I'm healthy," I tell her. "I've been tested."

"Me too." She closes her eyes and parts her lips as she slides herself down my shaft.

"Holy shit." I hold her hips, keeping her still for a

moment as she adjusts to my size and I adjust to the sensations threatening to make me come before I'm ready. "You feel amazing."

She nuzzles her face in the crook of my neck, and I loosen my grip on her as she slowly starts to rock her hips. I let her ride me like that for a long time, touching her everywhere I can, kissing her everywhere my mouth can reach.

The water swirls around us and the snow falls outside. The only thing that matters is Liz in my arms.

Liz

I turn in his arms so I can look at his face, but I'm surprised to see he hasn't fallen asleep. He's watching me, and he smiles when I look at him—a soft, gentle smile for a man who just used my body.

"When did you lose your virginity?" I ask. We're in bed in our room upstairs from the gala, still nude, the sheets tangled around our legs and the pillows scattered around us. I'm not ready to think about going back to the real world.

He groans. "You're not going to do that woman thing, are you?"

I prop myself up on an elbow. "What *woman thing*?"

"The one where you ask the guy a question and he gives you an honest answer and then you get mad at him for it?"

Giggling, I straddle him so I can watch his face. I rub my hands over his chest as I talk because I really can't touch this guy enough. "I know there were women before me. I'm just curious who the lucky first was."

He watches me carefully. "I was seventeen."

"And her?"

"She was an older woman, a family friend."

I curl my nose. "Ew, as in the female equivalent of the creepy uncle?"

He runs his hands down my sides then settles them at my hips. "It wasn't creepy."

"There's a not-creepy way to seduce your friends' teenage son?"

He chuckles and takes my hands in his, lacing our fingers. "Trust me, it was consensual. I spent summers at her pool and she'd catch me watching her." He shrugs. "Turns out she liked me watching as much as I liked doing it. And then it turned out that she liked to be tied up, and I didn't mind that either." He brushes his knuckles across my cheek. "I'm rather partial to women who get off on being bound."

My whole body warms. No one knows that about me but Sam . . . And River, I suppose. But I wrinkle my nose to hide my reaction. "I still vote *icky*."

"Okay, Judgy McJudgerson, we both know I don't want to hear about your first, so tell me something else."

"Like what?"

He brings our hands to his mouth and kisses each of my knuckles. "What about your first kiss?"

I give an exaggerated dreamy sigh. "Max Hallowell, behind his grandma's house. He started to put his hand up my shirt, but I stopped him because I felt super guilty. Hanna liked him and I wasn't supposed to."

He growls, then rolls us so he's on top of me and trapping my hands over my head. "I don't like thinking of Max kissing you. And I especially don't like thinking of your sister's crush being the only reason he didn't get to go further with you."

I draw up my knees, groaning happily when the hard length of his arousal settles between my legs. This man is superhuman. It's really quite remarkable. "You asked."

"I'll choose my question more carefully next time," he says. He's running kisses down the side of my neck and he still hasn't released my hands. "Tell me about the first time you touched yourself."

"What?" I'm so distracted by the way he's kissing me. I rock my hips, trying to get him to slide into me. God, I'm ready. I should be sore. Tired. Over it. But I'm not. I don't think he could ever bore me. With him, I'm perpetually aroused.

I tug at my hands, trying to get free from his grip, and he tightens his hold and groans. "Tell me about it," he murmurs. He slides down my body and skims his lips over my nipple.

"About what?"

"Tell me about the first time you touched yourself. The first time you put your hand between your legs. *That's* a first time I want to hear about." He opens his mouth over my breast and licks my nipple before sucking hard and making me cry out.

"I don't . . . remember," I manage.

He chuckles against my breast. "Now I don't believe that. I think every girl remembers the first time she lets herself . . . explore. Were you in high school?"

My breast goes cold when his mouth leaves it, wet and exposed. "Please," I murmur, arching toward him and tugging at my hands. "Just . . ."

He holds me tight, refusing to release me or give me what I need. "I'll make you a deal, Rowdy. You tell me what I want, and I'll give you what you want." He's grinning at me, as if this is some kind of game, as if I'm not going to dissolve into a puddle of lust if he doesn't put his mouth back on me soon.

"I was in college," I say.

He groans. "A late explorer. I guess I can see that from the Catholic girl." He drags my hands to hold them at my sides, kissing my stomach as he works his way down my body.

Please, yes.

He stops at my navel and lifts his head. "Where did you do it?"

My cheeks burn with a combination of embarrassment and arousal, but I understand the game now and I want to play. I need his mouth—more, lower. "I was in bed napping."

He rewards my response by circling my navel with his tongue then tasting me there. My body shudders in response. "You couldn't have been napping if you were touching yourself," he says.

"I was half asleep. I had a sexy dream and I wanted .

. . ."

He waits patiently, and when I don't answer, he rolls off me.

"Come back here."

"Show me," he says. He takes one of my hands and settles it between my legs, and only then does he release it. "Show me what you wanted. What you did."

His voice is rough, that low, gravelly rumble he gets when he's fucking me and close to coming. Only he's not fucking me. He's propped up on his elbow next to me, his eyes trained desperately on my hand resting between my legs.

I lick my lips. I don't know why I want to do this for him. I'm not even sure why he wants me to. All I know is that the feel of my own fingers resting against my slick flesh has never been so arousing. All I know is that I want this as much as he does.

I roll to my side, facing him, but I don't remove my hand from between my legs. "I was on my stomach," I whisper. "Do you want me to roll onto my stomach or stay like this?"

"Stay like this." The command is rough, scratched out against a throat full of need. I want to kiss him, to tell him this wouldn't be so hot to me if he weren't here. If he weren't looking at me, talking to me. "You were having a good dream," he prompts.

I lick my lips and begin moving my hand between my legs. "It was easier that way," I say softly. "Being half asleep, I mean. It's not like I thought there was anything wrong with masturbation, not . . ." My breath catches as my fingers find my clit. His eyes go dark.

"Not intellectually."

"Let go, sweetheart. Just ride with it. Don't worry about me."

I watch him for a while, captivated by the way his eyes lock on my fingers as they work between my legs, the rise and fall of his chest, his audible swallow as he holds himself back. His fingers are locked around my other wrist, trapping it, adding pressure from time to time. Otherwise, he doesn't touch me at all. It's by my hand alone that I ride to that summit. I stroke my clit, pinching it lightly before softening my touch and simply rocking my hips to rub against my hand.

I let my eyes float closed and take myself there, guided by nothing but my own pleasure and the sound of his breathing.

When I come back down, I roll to my back, muscles loose, body satisfied. He kisses my collarbone.

"Thanks," he whispers.

"Thanks?"

"Yeah, that was one of the best things I've seen. Ever." His grin is so charming, and it sends a buzz of warmth all the way through my sated body.

"You know some guys don't like the idea of their woman touching herself."

He cocks a brow. "I am firmly *not* in that category."

I bring my hand to his lips. "I noticed."

Grabbing my wrist, he draws two fingers into his mouth, wrapping his tongue around them and sucking hard.

All that sleepy warmth tingles at the attention of his mouth on my fingers, and my body starts to wake.

"Let's just say that, even if it took you until college, I'm glad you finally came around." He winks. "What do you think changed?"

I snort. "I was frustrated. I'd get close when I was with guys, but they could never quite get me there. I guess I finally decided if you want a job done right, you've gotta do it yourself."

My eyes flick up to his and I watch him as he swallows, his Adam's apple bobbing. "Connor didn't . . ."

"Most girls don't their first time, silly."

"I would have made sure you did."

"Easy for you to say. You weren't there."

"I would have *made sure*," he repeats.

"Okay, Mr. Confidence, how would you have made sure?"

He lowers his head on the pillow and stares at me for a minute. I like this—Sam and me, naked in bed, bodies turned toward each other. It'd be too easy to get used to something like this.

"I would have made damn sure you got off before I ever slid inside you. I would have played with you until you had no choice but to come. And I'd have only let myself fuck you *after* I'd felt your pussy squeeze around my fingers. It's not rocket science."

I laugh. "Is that going to be part of your proposed *pussy class* for young men?"

His brow wrinkles in confusion, and I feel as if an invisible fist has punched me. Because it wasn't *Sam* who'd talked about a "pussy class." It was River. And I just confused them.

"What pussy class?"

It's not rocket science. Hadn't River said something similar? And for a minute, I forgot Sam isn't River. For too many weeks, I believed he was, and now I'm all screwed up.

I swallow hard and force a smile. "I'm thinking of someone else. Sorry. That wasn't you."

He rolls onto me and pins my hands above my head. "You're thinking of someone else while you're naked in bed with me?"

"What are you going to do about it?" I say in my best show of bravado, but he's already kissing his way down my body, showing me exactly what he plans to do.

CHAPTER TWENTY

Liz

"You're here early."

I'm setting out pastries and coffee from Hanna's bakery on the table in the conference room when I turn and see Mr. Bradshaw leaning in the doorway. "First time in my life I've had a job that made me excited about Monday morning," I say. "It's an odd feeling."

"Smells amazing," he says, nodding to the table.

"It is. My sister is the absolute best at what she does." The smile falls from my face when I see his serious expression. "Is everything okay, Mr. Bradshaw?"

He tucks his hands into his pockets and steps into the room. "I couldn't help but notice how happy you were on Sam's arm on Saturday." He grabs the *Indianapolis Star* from the table and opens it to the politics section, where there's a picture of Sam and me together. "You make a beautiful couple. The camera loves you."

Then why do you look so unhappy? "But . . .?"

He lifts his gaze from the paper and meets my eyes. "I don't want there to be a *but*, Liz."

"And yet here we are."

"Connor told me that it was more than a photo op. He said there's something going on between you two."

My stomach goes sour. "Connor?"

"He's just worried about you. And I guess I am, too. Sam doesn't exactly have a reputation for long-lasting romances, but eventually he and Sabrina are bound to end up together."

Sabrina? Mr. Bradshaw's words are a punch in the gut, and my mind fills with the image of Sam and Sabrina dancing at the gala. Was there something between them?

Mr. Bradshaw gives me an apologetic smile. "Some things are just inevitable. I don't want your efforts to help his image resulting in you getting hurt."

"You don't need to worry about me." I force a smile. "I know there's no future for me and Sam. It's not like that between us. We're friends, and sometimes we go to weddings and political events together." *And other times we fuck like bunnies into all hours of the night.*

He nods, satisfied. "You certainly impressed the governor."

"You think so?"

"I think she's going to try to steal you away from us."

"Would you forgive me?" I ask. "If I got the opportunity to work on her campaign, that is? I mean, I don't presume that I *will*, but if I did . . ."

"You keep doing such good work here," he says, "and I'll make sure she finds a spot for you."

***

To: Elizabeth Thompson
From: Something Real Reminders
Subject: You Have a Message Waiting for You

Just a reminder that Riverrat69 sent you the following message and you haven't replied:

This is me not buying you a dog. You said you want a man who knows when you need a dog. And I know you don't need a dog right now. You need a man. One who knows exactly what you like in bed and isn't afraid to deliver. One who can satisfy you. You need me. And I'm here. When you're ready.

"Liz?" Nix says. "I was at the bar and didn't see you come in. Are you okay? You look like you've seen a ghost."

I was waiting for Nix to meet me at Brady's when I

saw the email alert flashing on my phone. Like an idiot, I opened it without thinking, and now I'm paying the price in the form of guilt, and stomach-gnawing fretting. "I'm fine. I just need a drink."

"I recommend the tequila," Nix says, holding up her empty shot glass. "It's been the best part of my day. Seriously, let me go get us a round."

"I'll take two."

She goes back up to the bar, and my eyes settle on the woman by the pool tables with Sam. Sabrina Guy. She's a dead ringer for her mother, as if the governor managed to replicate instead of procreate. The fact that Governor Guy seems to have the secret of youth doesn't hurt either.

I'm tucked into a booth, and Sam hasn't even noticed I'm here. Seeing them together makes my chest ache like it did two years ago when I saw him kissing Asia. It's been a couple of years, but I'll never forget how much it hurt to see Sam being so tender with someone else right after he'd spent the night using my body in every conceivable way.

Déjà fucking vu.

Except not. Because while Sabrina's hanging on his arm tonight, he doesn't look tender, or happy, or even amused. He looks pissed.

I let him take me to the gala last weekend. I told myself it was more about work than pleasure, but he proved me wrong—*multiple* times. Then there was his dad's warning this morning, on top of my own dumb mistake remembering a conversation I had with River as one I had with Sam.

I've earned this tequila.

"Two shots," Nix says, setting the glasses in front of me. "Drink them quick and get that scowl off your face."

I tear my gaze off Sabrina and take my first shot. It hits my empty stomach like a ball of fire.

"Good girl," Nix says. "That'll cure what ails you."

"You're the doctor." I raise the second in mock salute. She sinks into her side of the booth and joins me for the second shot.

"I thought we were celebrating how well your speech went over the weekend," she says. "But you don't look very happy."

"I'm fine. This looking-for-Mr.-Right thing is exhausting me. Maybe I'm meant to be a spinster."

"I refuse to accept this as my fate or yours."

"What about you?" I ask, eyeing the empty shot glasses in front of her. "What's driven you into the loving arms of tequila?"

"Shit from home. It'll be fine, but I'm not looking forward to the holidays. If I had a husband here, I'd at least have a good excuse not to visit. What about you? Does that scowl have anything to do with Mr. Sexy over there?"

"I don't understand him," I admit. "He's this consummate bachelor, but then sometimes . . ." *Sometimes he gives me sweet speeches that make me believe we could have a future.* I shrug. "It's stupid and it doesn't matter. Let's talk about something else."

"Any dates lined up for this week?"

"Not yet." I've been so distracted by River and then

Sam that I haven't even logged into my multitude of dating sites lately. "I miss River."

Nix chokes on her drink. "I'm sorry, what?" she manages after an impressive round of hacking.

"I miss him."

"The anonymous stranger who wants to tie you up? Who may or may not be a serial killer? Who may or may not be a married man with a newborn baby at home? You. Miss. Him?"

"He's not a serial killer. He's . . . Whoever he is, he was a friend to me before any of the other stuff." I shrug. "Connor's a big idiot, I guess. But I miss my relationship with River." I miss Hanna and Cally, too. Now that they have babies, they can't come out much. It's lonely being the single girl.

"What's really bothering you?"

"Mr. Bradshaw told me he doesn't like me seeing Sam. He all but said Sabrina Guy is his *betrothed*." I roll my eyes. "God, I didn't know people even did that crap anymore."

Nix cranes her neck to look over her shoulder at Sam and Sabrina at the pool table. "It doesn't look like he's into her."

"I still haven't told him about River," I confess. "Until I come clean, I have no right being jealous of Sabrina."

"You could tell him now," she says. "He's coming this way."

"Hey, ladies," Sam says, sliding into the booth beside me, his hip pressed against mine. "How's it going tonight?"

"Good," I say, but Nix says, "We've been better."

Sam frowns and then gives me the full attention of those honey-brown eyes. "What's wrong? Did something happen?"

"Not exactly. I don't think your dad . . ." I swallow. "I don't think he approves of us dating."

He grunts and takes a sip of his beer. "Well, that's because he didn't think of it first. You may not know this, but my father's a bit of a control freak."

I shrug. "I don't want to get in the way of family matters, Sam."

He shifts his attention to Nix. "Do you think you could excuse us? I need something from her, and I think I might need a few minutes to talk her into it."

Nix quirks a brow at me, but then she slides out of the booth and leaves us alone.

"Do you have plans for this weekend?"

I shake my head. "I haven't thought that far ahead."

"How do you feel about fresh seafood, candlelight?"

"Well, I—" I stop. "Are you asking me on a date?"

"Isn't that what a guy does when he has a crush on a girl?"

"A crush?"

My confusion seems to sap his bravado, and he shifts. "I like you, Liz. I know we've done this backward, but I want . . ." He drops his gaze to his beer, then back up to my face. He looks different. Younger, somehow. Maybe because the cocky man is gone, replaced by the unsure boy. "I want to do this right. I want to cook for you and take you to fancy dinners and hold your hand." He cups my jaw and his gaze drops to my lips. "And then I want to get you naked. I *really* like you naked."

I smile, and for a second, I'm just a girl looking at a boy she's kind of always loved. For a second, it's not complicated by secretly broken hearts and online affairs.

He leans forward and his lips brush my ear as he speaks. "Let me try this the right way, and if you hate it, we can go back to our annual wedding hookup. Though, to be honest, I think we're going to need to go to more weddings, because once a year isn't gonna cut it anymore." He pulls back so he can study me, then he grins, kryptonite to the lady parts. "What do you say, Rowdy? You, me, some alone time?"

"I shouldn't," I whisper. "I know that your dad really wants you with Sabrina, and it's obvious she likes you too."

"Fuck Sabrina. I'm not interested in her. Not at all. This weekend. Say yes."

"Where are we going?"

"Two nights," he answers, surprising me. "In Chicago."

"But your dad said—"

"This isn't about my dad. It isn't about his campaign. This is about us. One weekend, two nights, just you and me."

CHAPTER
TWENTY-ONE

Liz

"I COULD GET used to this."

Sam kneads a knot under my shoulders, and I moan.
I could get used to all of it. The sex, the long baths, the
breakfast in bed, walks along Lake Michigan, the wind
stinging my cheeks, and lots and lots of naked Sam.

Tonight, we didn't even go out for dinner. We
ordered room service and watched a movie on the big-
screen TV at the foot of our bed. And as if my heart
wasn't already in his hands, he told me to roll over so
he could rub my back.

"You're so good at this," I murmur. "Where did you

learn—" My question is cut off with a gasp, because it's not his hands on my back and shoulders anymore. It's his mouth. He kisses a path down my spine and back up, and his hands find my hips and squeeze. His thumbs dig into the flesh of my ass cheeks and it's— Jesus, it's *good*. My hips arch off the bed, pushing into his touch even as my head tilts to the side to allow him better access to my neck. He withdraws for a minute, and I look lazily over my shoulder to see him gripping his thick shaft in his hand.

The sight makes my mouth water, and I start to roll over, ready for him.

"Don't move," he whispers. "Let me fuck you like this. I want to watch myself slide into you. I want to squeeze that ass as you let me take you." Then his hands are on me again, drawing me to my knees as he positions himself behind me.

His cock is nestled against me, and I arch my back, urging him inside. I don't care how—I just need him inside me as quickly as possible.

He grips my hips and slowly slides inside. God. It's so good, but he's moving so slowly it's killing me. I drop my head to the pillow and rock my hips back, and a groan rips from his chest.

"You should see yourself right now," he murmurs. "Your ass in my hands, your hair splayed over the pillow. You're so fucking beautiful."

Finally, he thrusts again, and I cry out with the intense pleasure of his cock pushing against my cervix.

His hands tighten around my hips almost cruelly, but then he smooths over the spot with the gentle, careful stroke of his thumbs. Hard and soft. Hard and soft. I bite my pillow, and he growls. "Let me hear you. Don't you dare muffle those moans. Let me hear you."

"It's so good," I whisper helplessly. Arching my back, I rock my hips to take him deeper.

"You're so beautiful like this. I want to watch your pussy squeeze around my dick as you come. Touch yourself for me."

"I don't need to. This is good." I look over my shoulder and his eyes are on me, hot and intense and demanding.

"Touch yourself."

Licking my lips, I slide my hand between my legs and find my clit. I try to keep my eyes on his, but I can't. The second my fingers close around my clit, the sensation is so much I have to close my eyes to be able to process it all. Behind me, he murmurs his approval as he pumps in and out of me and I rub my clit between my two fingers.

The orgasm hits me hard and fast, claiming me before I even realize it's coming, and I pulse around him, squeezing him as my entire body contracts and releases with exquisite pleasure.

I've hardly come back down before he increases the pace of his strokes and pulls me back into that helpless, desperate peak of pleasure. I don't want to come again—not without him. I shift the hand between my legs back a little further and cup his balls.

Groaning, he slams into me, our skin smacking with the force of his thrust, and I cry out. I can't separate the ache in my chest from the pleasure between my legs.

There's no line dividing one from the other, only this blurring of pleasure and emotion where everything feels better than I've ever known.

I move my hand, stroking him, encouraging him. His thrusts become irregular—deep and then shallow, hard and then soft, frantic and then controlled.

When he's about to come, I feel him swell inside me. My body is exhausted, but I shift my hand so my palm rubs my clit and I climb with him. His hands squeeze my hips harder and harder, and I come first, seconds before he releases.

When he withdraws, I sink into the bed, too exhausted to move, feeling used and ravaged and *whole*.

I'm faintly aware of him climbing out of bed, and the mattress shifts as he returns and places a warm washcloth between my legs.

I moan into the pillow as he washes me. He's so tender. Sweet. I thought playboys were supposed to be selfish in bed, get off and get out. Not this man. Nothing seems to drive him and please him more than my pleasure.

When he's done washing me, he lies on the pillow next to me and brushes my hair from my face. "Are you okay?"

I force my eyes to open, and nod. I'm sore but sated. Aching but exhilarated. "I'm better than okay. I think you've finally made up for all those months I suffered without sex."

"Well, I haven't recovered from my dry spell yet, so you're going to have to indulge me a little longer."

I snort. "What? As if *you've* been sex deprived since Cally and Will's wedding. Right." The smile falls off my face when I register his stoic expression. "Right?"

He rolls on top of me, settling between my legs and framing my face in his hands. "I was waiting for you to take me seriously," he whispers. "I thought I had a chance after Will and Cally's wedding, but then you shut me out again. I haven't been interested in anyone else, and I think I was waiting for you."

It feels as if my stomach is being squeezed in a hot, sweaty fist. He wouldn't say those things if he knew about River. About Connor. Why does the universe deliver everything you want exactly when you can't have it? "I thought you only wanted me for sex."

"Not even at first."

He tucks another lock of hair behind my ear before pressing a kiss to my forehead. Then he gathers me in his arms and pulls me against his chest, where I feel small and safe, where I'm surrounded by his scent and his strength, and I fall asleep.

Sam

I'm in love with her.

Maybe the revelation should leave me smiling or, at the very least, content, but instead I'm terrified.

I'm in love with Elizabeth Thompson.

SOMETHING RECKLESS

Every time we're together, it's intense and sweet and so fucking good. She leaves my body and mind buzzing. Every time I'm with her, I find myself terrified of how badly I want to keep her in my arms, but even more terrified of never holding her again.

I'm done being nothing but the guy she lets tie her up—the guy she uses for the occasional post-wedding booty call.

For two years, I told myself I was okay with that. I told myself I didn't need anything more from her, that I didn't care that she'd so easily dismissed the possibility of anything real between us. I told myself she didn't own my heart. Maybe I even believed those lies. Then I walked in on her in bed with Connor and felt as if she'd ripped my heart out.

Now, she's sleeping in my arms, those long blond curls everywhere, her pale, makeup-free lashes making her look soft and innocent. I trace her cheekbone with my thumb then the line of her jaw, the length of her neck, the delicate skin over her collarbone.

"You're the most beautiful woman I've ever touched," I whisper. My heart aches with emotion, as if it might burst if the pressure isn't released soon. I'm scared to love her. I'm scared to love anyone, but Liz more than most. She looks at me like Superman just walked into the room, and it makes me feel powerful and weak all in one confused breath. I find myself distracted by thoughts of her, and that was okay when it was about sex, when I found myself planning the next time I could get her naked and get inside her. But it's not just sex now. I find myself planning things I can say to make her smile, find myself thinking of things I want to do with her years in the future.

Last night on Facebook, I saw a picture of her holding one of her infant nieces, and I instantly imagined how she'd look pregnant, her belly swollen with a child. How she'd look holding a baby of her own in her arms. *My baby.*

I'm a rational guy. Two plus two has to equal four. I don't see how a future with Liz works. Do I take her to family dinners and remind Della of how her husband once betrayed her? Do I leave my job at the bank and go with her when she travels all over the country to work on Christine's campaign? My head sees this mess I've fallen into and knows the math doesn't add up. But my heart hurts with all this emotion I've trapped in there. Sooner or later, something's going to have to give.

She shifts in my arms and rolls over to face me. "Can't sleep?" she whispers.

I'm in love with you. But I can't say the words, so I say the next best thing. "What are you doing on Christmas?"

She blinks at me in the darkness, and I wonder if she can see it on my face—the terror and awe at realizing I've fallen in love with her. "I don't know yet."

"Will you come have dinner with me at my parents' house?"

"I didn't know there was anything going on. Is it some campaign event or something?"

"No campaign, Rowdy. No cameras. I just want to take my girlfriend home to have Christmas dinner with my crazy family."

"I—" She shakes her head, and I could kiss the moon right now because the light peeking in through the crack in the curtains lets me see her smile. "I'd like that."

I gather her in my arms, and as I bury my nose in her hair and breathe in her scent, some long-tightened knot in my chest loosens a little.

CHAPTER
TWENTY-TWO

Liz

"YOU'RE GLOWING."

I do my best to look incredulous at Hanna's declaration—I don't *glow*—but since I can't seem to wipe this idiotic grin from my face, I'm pretty sure I'm failing.

Hanna comes out from around the bakery counter, takes my shoulders, and cocks her head side to side as she studies me. Then she grins too. "I was up all night with the girls—who decided it was party time at midnight—and I didn't think there was anything I wanted to see more than my bed today, but this face?"

SOMETHING RECKLESS

Wrapping her arms around me, she pulls me into a tight hug. "I love seeing you happy."

"I am," I admit as I pull away. "Happy. I'm happy." And I'm in love. Holy shit. I don't even know how that happened. I woke up in bed next to Sam and he pulled me closer to him in his sleep, so I settled my head on his chest and inhaled his scent.

"How did it go this weekend?"

"He took me into the city. We ate and talked and made love."

"You *made love*?" Hanna asks. "Interesting."

"What, you want me to say we fucked?"

She arches a brow. "I don't *want* you to say anything in particular. I just think it's interesting that your choice of words to describe intercourse with Sam has changed. Not *bad,* just interesting."

I shrug, and I can tell that goofy grin is back on my face. "I really like him, Hanna."

"I know you do," she says softly. "I'm just not sure why it took you so long to admit it."

"I was trying to protect my heart. But that's not actually something we can do, is it?"

She shakes her head, but she looks worried now. "We don't get to choose who owns our heart and we don't get to choose who has the power to break it."

"He asked me to come to Christmas dinner at his parents' house."

"Wow."

"And he called me his girlfriend." My cheeks are starting to ache from all the smiling. "I might as well be fifteen for as happy as that word made me."

"Tell me you've told him."

"That I'm in love with him?"

"That's not what I meant, but—wow. *Have* you told him that?"

My cheeks heat with the realization of what I just admitted. "No. It's too soon. I'm afraid it will scare him off. What did you mean then?"

"About the night at the cabin? About Connor?"

If I walked into the bakery brimming with joy, her question just tapped a hole in it and I feel it leaking out of me. "How do I tell him that without ruining this? Never mind what it would mean for Connor. If Della found out, it would ruin their marriage."

"Have a seat. You need sugar." She walks behind the counter and studies the contents of the bakery case thoughtfully before selecting a new item I don't recognize. "This should do the trick." She places it on a plate and grabs a fork, a napkin, and a cup of coffee. Then she joins me at the little glass-topped table.

"What is it?" I ask. Not that I doubt her. If Hanna made it, it'll be delicious.

"Chocolate chip brioche. Pretty much sugar, eggs, butter, and a crap-ton of chocolate chips."

"Sold." I slide my fork into the flaky dough and bring the first bite to my lips. "It's delicious." But I put down my fork, because her question stole my appetite right along with my smile.

"You have to tell him, Lizzy. It's going to come out, and it needs to come from you."

Fortunately, my stomach agrees to accept a few hearty swallows of coffee. "I don't want to."

"Liz . . ."

"He's opening up to me. He's . . ." I look out at Main Street. The road is dark and the streetlights illuminate the sidewalk. "I think he's starting to fall for me."

"You *think*? Oh, Liz. He's mad about you. He has been for ages. Everyone can see it but you."

I drop my gaze to my coffee because I can't look at my twin. She's the kindest, sweetest, best person in the world, and I can't bring myself to meet her eyes while I try to explain why I want to keep this big secret from the man I love.

"I tried to seduce Sam when I was seventeen," I admit. "I went up to Notre Dame and went to a party at his house. I got drunk—stupid drunk—thinking it would make it easier. And he turned me down."

"Liz, I had no idea. Why would you keep that from me?"

"The same reason I didn't tell you about the first time Sam and I *did* hook up. Because it was mortifying. I didn't want to be that desperate girl, and it was like if I didn't talk about it, I could pretend it didn't happen."

"Pretend *what* didn't happen?"

My eyes burn, and I lift them to the ceiling to stop the tears from coming. "You know who I *did* sleep with that weekend? Do you know who was there to pick up the pieces when Sam turned me down?"

Her face shifts, as if something's registering for the first time. "Connor."

I nod slowly. It makes me feel guilty to regret my night with Connor. He was sweet and gentle, and as odd as it seems, that night was the beginning of a great friendship with him. But I do regret it. Because if we hadn't slept together that night, that door wouldn't have been opened and maybe we wouldn't have ended up in bed together last summer when I was lonely and Della had broken his heart.

"Sam hated me after he caught us in bed together. In his mind, I was as guilty for hurting Della as Connor was, and if he knew I had this whole online affair with someone and . . . *oops,* it's Connor! If he knew the real reason I came to the cabin after your wedding, I don't know if he could forgive me."

"So what's your plan? To carry on and hope he doesn't ever find out?"

"Not forever. Just until things aren't so fragile."

Hanna's quiet for a minute, her eyes tired and looking too wise. She went through a lot to get to her happily-ever-after with Nate. In a lot of ways, she's much more mature than I am. She's definitely had to make harder decisions than I have.

"I think you should do it sooner than later," she says. "I don't want you hurt. Please be careful."

Sam

I start my Christmas morning with a run. The sun's shining on the blanket of snow, and the air is crisp but not cold enough to keep me inside. I should have had her stay over last night. What would it be like to wake up with Liz in my arms every day? To bring her coffee in bed and make love to her before I leave for the bank? What would it be like to know she'd be there when I got home?

By the time I've logged five miles and am coming back around the block to my house, I'm straight up grinning. I didn't have her stay with me last night. I didn't get to wake up next to her on this Christmas morning, but next year—

"It's her second Christmas."

I jerk my head up to see Asia Franks sitting on the floor of my front porch. She's leaning against the door in a big black coat that swallows her up.

"You aren't supposed to be here. You got your money. Leave."

When she lifts her head, tears clots her thick, dark lashes. "I can't stop picturing her. This pudgy-faced two-year-old tearing at Christmas wrapping." She shrugs. "I don't know."

"Get away from me," I breathe. "Get away from my house. You have no right—"

"How can you act like I'm the evil one here?"

Because you took my child. But I don't say the words, because the woman in front of me isn't the calculating witch who blackmailed me weeks ago. This is a mother with a broken heart.

"They won't let me see her," she says, her voice small. "I just want to see her."

"What are you talking about?"

She stumbles as she pushes to her feet. God. She's drunk. Christmas morning and she's so drunk she can hardly stand straight. "You have to talk to that man. You walk around thinking I'm the devil and that man is the one lying to you."

"What man?"

"The man who bribed me to get out of your life. The man who told me I had to tell you I got an abortion, even if I promised to give her up for adoption."

My thoughts of Liz must be making me hallucinate. That's the only way to explain all this hope in my chest. It's the only explanation for the question I hear myself asking. "Are you saying you had the baby? You had *our* baby?"

"I sold my soul." Her face is wet with tears now, and my gut twists into knots. I don't know if I can believe her or if this is just another manipulation. "I sold my soul to a blond-haired devil and now I'm paying the price."

Liz

I don't know why he invited me.

The dinner table is overflowing with the dishes Sam's mother and sisters prepared, and the dining room is so full of people, smells of warm food, and at least half a dozen conversations that I don't feel like there's room for me to breathe, let alone think.

Watching Mr. Bradshaw with his wife and kids is fascinating. He's not the candidate today. He's the man. And it's so refreshing to see that the two aren't all that different that it makes me like him even more.

I love the way Sam's siblings poke at each other, joking and teasing.

I want to love this. I want us to be any other couple sharing a family holiday for the first time. But I feel like everything changed the minute I walked in the door. Connor was holding his baby and paled at the sight of me. Della sneered. And when Mr. Bradshaw spotted me, something flashed over his face, and I could tell he was hurt that I didn't stay away from Sam as he'd requested. But worst of all is Sam. He barely greeted me when I arrived, and he hasn't said a word the entire time. He keeps glaring at Connor, and he barked at him when Connor dared wish him a merry Christmas.

If Sam's rethinking having me here, I wish he would have called and asked me to stay home. That would have hurt, but it would have been preferable to being a pariah at another family's Christmas.

"Potatoes?" Sam asks from beside me. I jump at the sound of his voice, then paste on a smile and dish myself some out of the big ceramic dish.

Sam's younger brother, Ian, takes the seat next to me. "If you have some time after dinner, you should let me show you the Corvette I'm restoring in the barn." He drags his eyes over me meaningfully, obviously. "I'm pretty good with my hands, you know."

"Little man," Sam warns in a growl, never turning toward his brother or me, "if you don't take your eyes off my girlfriend, I'll do it for you."

Ian flushes and turns his attention to his food, and my cheeks burn too. Maybe he's in a bad mood, but he just called me his *girlfriend* again. Such a silly little word, and it means everything.

"He's fine," I mumble. I wish he would tell me what's gotten him in this mood. Unless it's me.

"Girlfriend?" Della says. "Huh. Interesting."

It's his mom's turn to give me her attention, it seems. "So with your sisters marrying and starting their families, are you looking to do the same, Liz?" she asks. It seems like she's the only one happy to have me here.

Across from us, Ryann starts humming "Fixer Upper" from that Disney movie. I cut my eyes to Sam, but he seems unfazed. I'm guessing he's not familiar with the song.

Della stabs her chicken so hard the fork screeches against the plate.

"Um . . ." I look to Sam for help, but he's scowling into space. *Real helpful, buddy.* "I don't know? I mean, I'm just starting a new career and . . ." *And this is Sam we're talking about here, right? Do you know how he feels about commitment?*

And yet here I am.

The best plan of action is to change the subject. "So, what are your hobbies?" I ask Ian. "Do you spend a lot of time restoring cars?"

Ryann snorts. "That's just want he wants you to

think. He spends more time at his computer running code."

"What kind of code?"

"Ian developed the code for the Something Real dating site," Connor says, grinning at his brother-in-law.

I choke on my wine. "That's *your* site?"

"Yeah," Ryann says. "He understands how hard it is for ugly guys to find a date, so he invested hundreds and hundreds of hours into developing a workaround."

"Just because you're too shallow to appreciate *true connections*," Ian says to his sister. "*I* am a romantic. I believe in love."

The rest of the meal passes in a haze as Ian chatters on about his pet project and the rest of the family chimes in about the various ways they helped. On the outside, I'm a quiet woman pushing food around her plate, but on the inside, I'm panicking.

"So, you're pretty young for such a venture," I manage when I finally find my voice. "Who are your investors?"

Ian grins. "Lucky me, I was born into a family of investors, so pretty much everyone you see here."

You need to tell him before he finds out from Ian, my brain screeches, but my heart knows this will be over when I admit what happened.

Maybe it's not Connor. Maybe it's . . . maybe it's Ian. How pathetic am I to sit here *hoping* I had inappropriate sex conversations with Sam's little brother?

"Didn't I see in the *Tattler* that you are a member of

Something Real?" Della asks me.

Mrs. Bradshaw is clearing the table. I barely ate a bite. I couldn't. "I gave it a shot," I say. I shoot a look to Sam, hoping against hope that he'll say something about how I don't need sites like that anymore because I'm his. Something. *Anything.*

But he's too busy glaring at nothing and doesn't say a word.

Next to me, Ian pulls his phone from his pocket and starts tapping at the screen. "Oh!" he says, scrolling down through something. "I found you, Liz. You haven't been active for a while."

My stomach lurches. "Excuse me." I push out of my chair and rush out of the room.

In the formal living room, I lean my head against the wall and try to slow my racing heart.

"Liz?"

I turn to see Sam has joined me, and for the first time all night, the anger has left his face. Does he already know? "I'm sorry," I whisper. I'm a coward. I can't risk breaking his heart, can't risk making him hate me until I'm one hundred percent positive that Connor is River. "I need to go." My voice is shaking as I head to the door, but I won't cry in front of him. I won't fall apart in front of this family.

"What's wrong?" He follows me out the door, and when we're alone in the glow of the porch light, he cups my face in his hand. "Tell me."

Please don't do that. Please, please don't show me kindness I don't deserve.

"I forgot I promised Hanna I'd do some baking for

her tonight," I lie. He knows it's a lie. I see it in his eyes. And because this is Sam and he's been lied to before, he drops his hand and steps back. He doesn't want to touch the woman who's lying to him.

I rush down the steps and to the sidewalk, doing all I can to keep myself from running as I head in the direction of the bakery.

He doesn't come after me. That's for the best. I'm like a shattered piece of glass—still whole but broken all over—and his touch, his voice, his concern, any of it would be enough to make me fall apart.

CHAPTER
TWENTY-THREE

Liz

As IRRATIONAL AS it is, when I get back to my empty house, I miss River more than I have since we stopped talking. Does that even make sense? I'm angry with Connor. Disgusted that he would do this to Della. But I miss my conversations with my faceless friend. I miss feeling like someone wanted me for me.

You make me believe there could be more. You make me want more.

And I know it's stupid and it doesn't make any sense, but my chest aches with grief. As if my heart still needs to mourn that Sam wasn't River. I wanted it to be him so badly that I'd convinced myself it was.

I open my laptop and log on to Something Real for the first time since the morning I left the cabin.

Tink24: *Are you there?*

Riverrat69: *I'm on my phone. Are you okay?*

I shake my head. No. I'm not okay. The man I trusted most in this world—the man I've defended a thousand times over to his wife—wanted to have an affair with me.

Hell, one might argue we were already having an affair. We crossed lines. I haven't allowed myself to think about it, but I do now. I had an affair with a married man. Maybe we didn't touch, but we talked about it. We described it. I'm as guilty as the woman Sam's father had an affair with.

Tink24: *I know you're married.*

I stare at the screen, waiting for his response. I don't know what I want him to say. That he isn't married? Do I want to find out he's someone else, someone other than Connor? A stranger using the Bradshaw cabin to lure in women and seduce them? How is that better?

I'm making myself crazy with analyzing my own motivations when his reply finally comes.

Riverrat69: *You figured out who I am.*

Tink24: *Yes.*

Riverrat69: *Because of the cabin.*

Tink24: *Yes.*

Riverrat69: *I should have never invited you there. That was careless. Reckless. I apologize.*

Tink24: *You're saying you didn't plan to cheat on your wife?*

Riverrat69: *Can we talk about this in person?*

Tink24: *No. You're married.*

Riverrat69: *You know how people talk about their significant other as their partner? Well, that's how I feel. I'm her partner. On the bad days, I feel like her assistant. The person there to make her life easier. I didn't particularly want a partner. I wanted a lover and a companion. So, yes, I'm married. But I don't have a lover. And you've been the closest thing I've had to a companion in a long time.*

I squeeze my eyes shut. I'm the other woman.

Tink24: *You have made me into something I never wanted to be. I can't forgive you for that.*

Riverrat69: *Lizzy . . .*

SOMETHING RECKLESS

My hand flies to my mouth and my whole body starts shaking. He knows it's me. He's been working next to me, talking to me, telling me about his baby and what a great mom Della is, and he's known all this time that I was Tink24.

I close my eyes and concentrate on my breathing, forcing my lungs to accept air. It's so much harder to breathe the air in a world where the people you trust the most let you down.

When I open my eyes, I see he's sent another message.

Riverrat69: *You knew it was me. You've known all this time, but you didn't quit. Doesn't that tell you something?*

Tink24: *I don't want to quit. I love my job.*

Now, more than ever. It feels important. I've spent my whole life never being taken seriously, and suddenly I have this job where people take my words very seriously. What I do matters, and if I leave the campaign, what are the chances I'd ever find another politician to take me on?

Riverrat69: *You wanted to be close to me as much as I wanted to be close to you.*

Tink24: *I won't play a role in destroying a marriage. This—whatever it was? It's over.*

Riverrat69: *I respect that. I apologize for hurting you. I never wanted that. I was blinded by our connection. I've never felt that with anyone.*

Tink24: *I thought you were someone else. I wanted you to be someone else.*

Riverrat69: *Sam?*

I draw in a ragged breath. My cheeks are wet. I'm crying, and I feel ugly inside. I haven't only been avoiding him because it was the right thing to do. I've been avoiding him because I didn't want to face what I've done.

Tink24: *I'm deleting my account. This will be the last time we talk this way.*

Riverrat69: *I'll miss seeing you. Take care of yourself.*

Tink24: *Are you saying I don't have a job anymore?*

Riverrat69: *You're welcome to stay, but as long as you're close, I'll want you.*

I jump when my doorbell rings. Wiping away my tears, I answer it.

Sam's looking across the street, hands tucked into the pockets of his jeans.

313

Slowly, I open the door, but when he turns to me, his eyes aren't angry. They're hot.

He stalks toward me and slams the door behind him, making the entire house rattle. I back against a wall. "What's wrong?"

"Nothing. Everything. My sister just had a baby, and her husband's a piece of shit. My dad's running for governor, and I don't know if I can trust anyone in my own damn family anymore. And . . . I have a girlfriend." Then, as if that explains anything, he closes the space between us and kisses me hard. His lips crush against mine, then his tongue, and I'm opening to him without a thought.

My hands wrap around his thick biceps and his go to my neck and move their way down, sweeping over my shoulders and down my arms until he's holding me with both of his hands at my waist, then further down, his fingers digging almost painfully into my hips.

He sweeps one hand between our bodies and cups me between my legs, rubbing me through my flannel sleep pants.

I don't know what's gotten into him. Don't know what he wants beyond greedy hands and hungry kisses. But I know I can't do this while my mind is still spinning about River, so I pull his hand away and sidestep his grasp.

He presses his hands against the wall and hangs his head as he catches his breath. "I'm not my father," he whispers. "I've spent my whole life trying to prove I'm my own man, but I've never believed it." He turns slowly and looks at me. "I'm sorry about tonight. I let family bullshit ruin Christmas with you. Forgive me."

***

Sam

"You don't owe me an apology," Liz says softly.

I won't let myself be spooked and ruin our chance together.

After I called someone to come pick up Asia, I went to my parents' with my head spinning. I was determined to put what Asia said out of my mind until after Christmas, but then I overheard my parents fighting. Mom kept her voice low, but I could hear her through the study door, could hear the hysteria that laced the edges of her words.

"You expect me to believe you aren't sleeping with her?"

"I haven't touched her."

"This is the worst possible time. Think of the campaign."

Maybe that was the hardest part for me to swallow. My mom, his *wife,* when confronted with the possibility of her husband cheating on her again, was more concerned about the effect of an affair on his political campaign than about the effect on their marriage.

And maybe two years ago he was more concerned about his political campaign than about his own son's child.

SOMETHING RECKLESS

Liz is staring at me, her brow wrinkled, her teeth sinking into her bottom lip.

"I'm in love with you." The words just slip out, as if I can't hold them in anymore.

"What?"

I answer with my mouth, pressing her against the wall as my hands go into her hair and I kiss her hard. I'm terrified of what's going to happen to my family. But the taste of Liz, the feel of her mouth under mine, it relaxes me.

My hand slides between her legs as I drop my mouth to her neck, nibbling and sucking until she drops her head to the side to give me better access.

"I'm in love with you." It's the truth, but I hate how vulnerable saying it makes me feel, as if that one sentence has the power to catapult me back to a time in my life when my heart wasn't my own. I needed her after our first night together. She had my heart in her hands and told me she wasn't interested.

I don't want to go back there, to that kind of vulnerability. Not for anything. Except for her. I might just go back for Liz. Because once a woman owns a man's heart, it never really returns to him.

She attempts a smile but it wobbles on the edges. She wants to believe me. "You can't be in love with me. I've screwed up so many times. And I'm so scared that once you realize—"

"You think I haven't screwed up? That I'm not scared?" I hold her face in my hands and look into her big, blue eyes. "I'm terrified every day I'm with you. I'm scared of what it means that I wake up every day and you're the first thing on my mind. I'm scared that I can't remember what it felt like to spend weeks at a time without seeing you. I'm scared of how badly I need you and of how completely you've stolen my heart. But mostly I'm terrified that I'm not good enough for you, and that even though you deserve better, I have no idea how to live in a world where I don't get to smell your hair or hold you in my arms."

She stares at me, lips parted, eyes wide.

"Say something," I whisper.

"I love you too."

The words lift a weight off my lungs, and for the first time in days I'm able to take a deep breath. "Then nothing else matters." I lower my head to kiss her.

She stops me with a finger to my lips. "We need to talk first," she says.

My phone rings, and I ignore it. I can't talk to him right now.

Liz and I stare at each other.

"I messed up," she says. "Being with you is a dream, and if I'd had any idea this was possible, I wouldn't have signed up for all those stupid dating sites."

"I don't care about that." My phone rings again, and this time I look at it. The last call was from Connor, but this time it's Della. "Sorry," I say to Liz before answering. "Hello?"

"You need to get back to the house right away," Della says. "It's an emergency."

CHAPTER
TWENTY-FOUR

Sam

"Thank you for coming," Connor says, closing the door behind me.

We're in my father's home office, and I'm pissed. I broke the speed limit the entire way here, sure I was going to pull up to the house and see an ambulance taking away my mom or something. But everyone's fine. *Connor* just wanted to talk. Screw that.

"What is this about?" I look at my phone to see if Liz has texted. I wonder if I could talk her into coming by my place tonight. I could cook for her again—something with that red sauce she loves so much, and wine. And after I could take her to bed and—

"Sit down." Connor nods to a seat, but I notice he

doesn't sit. He's already pacing the length of the room, his face drawn, and his eyes tired. "We need to do some damage control."

Those words snap me out of my dopy haze. "Leave Asia alone. You've done enough."

He frowns. "This isn't about Asia."

He found out about Dad's affair. Whatever it is Connor needs to tell me, I don't want to know. It's his job to take care of this stuff. I want to be left out of it. My father likes women. A lot. And my father has a little trouble keeping his dick in his pants. This wouldn't surprise me about the average politician, and given my father's history, it *shouldn't* surprise me about him. But it does. He's supposed to love my mother and no one else. Forever.

"It's about Lizzy," Connor says. "She's been using Something Real, Ian's dating site."

I shake my head, my brain struggling to switch gears. "Why do you care?"

He drops a stack of papers in front of me and my eyes scan the top page of messages between Tink24 and Riverrat69.

"She's Tink24," Connor says. "Ian just found this tonight."

He's highlighted certain sections, and I can't help myself. I start flipping pages and skimming as I go.

Riverrat69: *Tell me what turns you on.*

Tink24: *Kissing. Secret meetings in dark corners. Strong men who pursue what they want but aren't* *too proud to ask for permission before taking it. What about you?*

Riverrat69: *Blondes, beautiful women in short skirts, sassy-mouthed vixens.*

Tink24: *Oh, so I turn you on?*

Riverrat69: *Yes. You do. But you already knew that.*

Tink24: *I hoped. Anything else?*

Riverrat69: *So much. The curve of a woman's ass. Hearing her scream my name as I drive into her. The way she stops breathing just before she comes. Your turn.*

Tink24: *This conversation turns me on. And if the moment is right and I feel safe . . . being tied up.*

Riverrat69: *I would love to tie you up. I've fantasized about it more than once.*

My fists tighten instinctively, wrinkling the pages in my hands. My whole body is on fire with the anger pumping through me as I flip through the messages. Plenty of the exchanges are tame, but Connor has highlighted the worst of them.

"Why are you showing me this?" My voice sounds funny. Smaller. Younger. Vulnerable.

"Keep going."

So I do. I flip through the remaining conversations. I make myself look at the pictures she sent him. The curve of her hip in lacy black panties, her legs bare and stretched out over crisp white sheets, her cleavage. I want to tell myself this isn't Liz, but I know that's just denial. I know her body better than I know my own. I could have identified that hip, those legs anywhere. By the time I'm halfway through, I want to stop, know I should stop even, but I can't. Maybe I'm looking for something that will prove this wasn't her. Or maybe I just need to know the truth.

I freeze when I get to the highlighted section on the last page.

Tink24: *Do you still want to meet me?*

Riverrat69: *More than anything.*

Tink24: *When? Where?*

Riverrat69: *Can you get to Brown County tomorrow night?*

Tink24: *Yes. It will have to be late. I have an event.*

Riverrat69: *5429 Water Pointe Blvd. I'll wait up.*

Tink24: *I'll see you then.*

Riverrat69: *I've never actually ripped a woman's clothes off before, but I might have to with you. I* *don't think you'll make it past the foyer before I bury my face in your pussy.*

My stomach cramps as anger floods through me. It's worse than anger—it has a thicker blade and a sharper edge. Jealousy. Hurt. A merciless thrusting of a knife working its way up to my chest. I haven't just fallen off this ladder and straight into love with Liz. I've plummeted to the bottom only to be beaten with it.

I lift my gaze to Connor's and the apology is all over his face. "You piece of shit," I mutter. "My sister just gave you a baby." And that's why he wasn't there. He couldn't meet her at the cabin because Della was in labor.

And I was there instead. I was supposed to stay at the inn with the rest of the guests, but I'd made a last-minute decision that changed everything. I wasn't the man she came for.

Connor shakes his head slowly. "I'm not Riverrat."

"You can't lie your way out of this. You help Ian with the site. You have the administrative authority to allow pictures between your accounts. You go to the cabin *all the time.*"

"I'm not Riverrat," he repeats. His voice is soft. As if what he's saying is an apology, not a defense, and that doesn't make any sense.

"Then who is?"

Pain flashes across his face, and the floor falls out from under me. I know.

***

Liz

I wipe away my tears as I pack up my few belongings. I can't work here anymore. River made that much clear tonight. *Connor,* I mentally correct. Thinking of him as River makes it easier to pretend it didn't happen, and I won't do that anymore. I need to leave this job and I need to tell Sam everything.

If I'm lucky, maybe Mr. Bradshaw will still get me the internship with Governor Guy's campaign, but either way I can't be here.

It doesn't take me long to gather my things into a single small box, but as I turn to leave, I see the light on in Mr. Bradshaw's office. What's he doing here on Christmas night?

I put the box down and go to his door. My hands are shaking as I knock. It's not fair of me to leave him so soon and ask him to pull strings to get me a new job, but it would be foolish not to ask.

"Come in," Mr. Bradshaw calls.

Taking a deep breath, I push open the door. "Mr. Bradshaw?"

He startles a bit at the sound of my voice. He sweeps his gaze over me twice—the first time a quick assessment, the second time slower and almost . . .

I shake off the thought before it can fully form in my mind. I'm imagining things.

"I didn't expect to see you today," he says. There's something in his voice, as if he's holding back the words he really wants to say.

"I'm sorry to bother you."

He pushes away from his desk and stands to come around to my side. "You're never a bother, Liz. What brings you here?"

I relax. The oddness I sensed with him when I first knocked on the door seems to have fallen away. I must have caught him off guard.

"If I ask you a question, do you promise to tell me the truth?" I'm surprised at the words. I should be focusing on the job, not my personal life.

His shoulders tense and something flickers in his eyes. "I can't promise I'll answer, but I can promise I won't lie to you."

I nod, licking my winter-chapped lips. My mouth is dry. Every inch of me feels like it's been dried up, had the life sucked out of it by the cold. "Fair enough."

His eyes flick to the door standing open behind me. "Want to close that first?"

"Oh. Yeah, sure." I close the door then turn back to him. He's leaning against the edge of his desk, legs crossed at the ankle. He looks so much like Sam. Or Sam looks like him, I guess. I know their family is close, and I'm not sure if he'll feel as if he's betraying Sam if he tells me the truth. *Just ask.*

"Why don't you approve of me dating your son?" The second the words are out of my mouth, the second I hear them instead of think them, I realize how juvenile this sounds and my cheeks burn. I study the floor. I'm a grown woman. The only one who needs to approve of my relationship with Sam is Sam himself. No one else.

"Liz, look at me," he says. Slowly, I lift my head. He's looking at me oddly, his mouth twisted into a grimace, something like pain in his beautiful light brown eyes. "You know me. Better than most. Maybe better than anyone."

I frown. I haven't worked for him for that long, and Mr. Bradshaw keeps to himself, and when he does confide in someone, it's family. Trusted family surrounds him. I'm the exception. I don't actually know him *that* well.

"Did you really think I could watch you date my son and *enjoy* it?" He straightens and takes a step forward, closing the distance between us until he's standing almost uncomfortably close. "Do you think watching you two together has been easy for me?"

"I don't understand," I whisper, but it's a lie.

As his hand goes into my hair, I understand all too well. Even before his hand touches my face, the truth reveals itself to me and slips right from my lips. "River."

THE END

This is the end of *Something Reckless*, but it's not the end of Liz and Sam. *Something Real*, the second book in the Reckless and Real series, will be available

SOMETHING RECKLESS

in March of 2015.

ACKNOWLEDGMENTS

As always, I thank my family first. Brian, thank you for the time, encouragement, and patience you give to this crazy career of mine. For sending me to the "satellite office" to work when the kids won't leave me alone, for listening to my endless out-of-context plot concerns, and for proving day after day that happily-ever-after exists outside my head. You and the kids are my world.

My friends and family, who celebrate my successes as their own, cheer me on every step of the way, and pimp my books out to every literate adult they meet. I am humbled by your enthusiasm and grateful to have built a life surrounded by such amazing people. I hope you know how grateful I am to have you in my life.

To everyone who provided me feedback on and cheers for Liz and Sam's story along the way—especially Adrienne Hogan, Mira Lynn Kelley, Heather Carver, Karen Newman, and Samantha Leighton—you're all awesome. To Lexi's Midnight Readers, who were ready for this story back when it was only a kernel of an idea, thank you. You remind me daily why I love this job so much!

Thank you to the team that helped me package this book and promote it. Sarah Hansen at Okay Creations designed my beautiful cover, and if I have my way she will do many, many more for me. Rhonda Helms and Lauren McKellar, thank you for the insightful line edits, and Arran McNicol at Editing720 for proofreading. Thanks to my PA, Chris, who does her best to keep me organized, even when we're juggling fifteen tasks at once. A shout-out to Julie of AToMR for your work to promote my books, and to all of the bloggers and reviewers who help her do it. Amazing. Every one of you.

To my agent, Dan Mandel, and my foreign rights agent, Stefanie Diaz, for getting my books into the hands of readers all over the world. Thank you for being part of my team.

Thank you a hundred times over to my NWBs—Sawyer Bennett, Lauren Blakely, Violet Duke, Jessie Evans, Melody Grace, Monica Murphy, and Kendall Ryan. I'm sure you were ready to strangle me when I was trying to figure out how to approach this series and tell the story in the best way possible. Thank you for always giving it to me straight and handing me the brown paper bag when I'm panicking.

To all my writer friends on Twitter, Facebook, and my various writer loops, thank you for your support and inspiration. I must say, ours is the coolest water cooler in the entire workforce.

And last but certainly not least, thank you to my fans. To those who read the other New Hope books and wanted more, to those who've declared you'd gladly read my grocery lists, and to those who have been with me from the very beginning, thank you. I appreciate each and every one of you. I couldn't do this without you and wouldn't want to. Thank you for buying my books and telling your friends about them. Thank you for asking me to write more. You're the best!

~Lexi

OTHER TITLES BY LEXI RYAN

The New Hope Series
Unbreak Me
√*Stolen Wishes* (A *Wish I May* prequel novella)
Wish I May

Here and Now (A New Hope Series)
Lost in Me
Fall to You
All for This

Reckless and Real (A New Hope Series)
√*Something Wild* (A Reckless and Real prequel novella)
√*Something Reckless*
Something Real

Hot Contemporary Romance
Text Appeal
Accidental Sex Goddess

Decadence Creek Stories and Novellas
Just One Night
Just the Way You Are

CONTACT LEXI

I love hearing from readers, so find me on my Facebook page at facebook.com/lexiryanauthor, follow me on Twitter @writerlexiryan, shoot me an email at writerlexiryan@gmail.com, or find me on my website: www.lexiryan.com.

Made in the USA
Middletown, DE
22 April 2015